If Gertrude Stein had a child with v..g..
would produce an exquisite comma/semicolon named
Aurora Mattia. In Mattia's highly magnetic and hyper-
conscious world of boudoir shadows, sugarglass, operating tables, transsexuality, auroral wounds, strident
malefic forces, a sentence, a paragraph, an entire chapter
does bleed; and, it bleeds hyperchromatically, hyperphilo-
sophically, hyperinventively, and hyper-nonbinarily from
The Fifth Wound's "mouth, genitals, genitals, pores, eyes,
ass, and nose" into her body's impeccable sheath.

—VI KHI NAO, AUTHOR OF *SWIMMING WITH DEAD STARS*

I have never read anything like Aurora's writing. I would
say less that I have read her work and more that I have
felt it, deep inside my body. It makes my heart ache. It
also makes me long for a hard cock down my throat.
Her work is a true spiritual experience, in that it causes
me lust, grief, anger and ecstasy, sometimes one after the
other and sometimes all at once.

—CARTA MONIR, AUTHOR OF *NAPKIN*

The Fifth Wound is the tender scar of beauty achieved in
language. Drawing on rich description, myth, bible stories,
autofiction, breathy pillow talk, and breathless confession,
it confects a mirror of glamor for the glamor of its author,
but which is then delicately rendered onto the page, as a
diptych, that the reader might gasp with pleasure. It's a spe-
cial kind of transsexual camp, so over the top that what
was the top is too far below to see, and we fly free.

—MCKENZIE WARK, AUTHOR OF *REVERSE COWGIRL*

This is a densely embroidered autofictional mythography, a surreal book of hours complete with self-flagellation, a Homeric urban odyssey, ecstatic and violent, tender, devastating, triumphant, and a hallucinogenic yet visceral medical memoir. Mattia peels layer upon layer, cuts again and again, deep into the wound to spill the life inside.

—SARAH GERARD, AUTHOR OF *TRUE LOVE*

In presenting the transfemme as a systematically villainized siren, *The Fifth Wound* explores what can happen to us when our songs become twisted and warped, or else ignored. With its evocative, mythological imagery and unexpected turns of phrase, Aurora Mattia's take on the transfeminine confessional is unlike any I've read in recent memory.

—HARRON WALKER

Bold, lush, innovative, and extraordinary, Mattia's work daringly reimagines the very nature of storytelling. I've never read anything like *The Fifth Wound*—and I'll never forget it.

—TÉA OBREHT, AUTHOR OF *INLAND*

THE FIFTH WOUND

THE FIFTH WOUND

AURORA MATTIA

NIGHTBOAT BOOKS
NEW YORK

ISBN: 978-1-64362-148-7

Cover art: page 19 from *La Pratique de l'Aiguille* by Matthias Mignerak. Paris: Jean Le Clerc, 1605. Collection of The Metropolitan Museum of Art, New York.

Design and typesetting by Rissa Hochberger
Typeset in Sabon and Expressa

Cataloging-in-publication data is available from the Library of Congress

Nightboat Books
New York
www.nightboat.org

TABLE OF CONTENTS

BOOK ONE
EZEKIEL WAS HERE

BOOK TWO
FROM NOUGHT TO NOUGHT –
IN UNSUBSTANTIAL TRADE –

BOOK THREE
NO LONESOME TUNE

END

Appendices

To my exes, my true loves,
wherever you are

If you're here,
I hope you like my dedication

Thank you for giving me my most intimate meaning:
If I hadn't met you, I wouldn't know what love is
I wouldn't know a thing

Mwah

It's not that the past casts its light on what is present, or what is present its light on the past; rather, image is that wherein *what has been* comes together in a flash with the *now* to form a constellation. In other words, image is dialectics at a standstill. For while the relation of the present to the past is a purely temporal, continuous one, the relation of what-has-been to the now is dialectical: is not progression but *image*, suddenly emergent. – Only dialectical images are genuine images...and the place where one encounters them is language.

- WALTER BENJAMIN, TR. HOWARD EILAND AND
KEVIN McLAUGHLIN, 'AWAKENING,'
THE ARCADES PROJECT

(We travel on the surface, in the expanse, weaving our imaginary structures and not filling up the voids of a science, but rather, as we go along, removing boxes that are too full so that in the end we can imagine infinite volumes. Volumes like the space sieves invented by the technicians of Chaos that seem filled simply with their own echo.)

- ÉDOUARD GLISSANT, TR. BETSY WING
'THE BURNING BEACH,' *POETICS OF RELATION*

BOOK ONE

EZEKIEL WAS HERE

I.

To the Tune of *Running up That Hill* by Kate Bush

> I am here not to confess, but to confect.
> - Eva Hayward, *More Lessons from a Starfish*

Call me Aurora, or call me @silicone_angel. But you have to promise not to fall in love with me. If this is a testament, it is not good news: instead of revelation I give reverb.

I am no longer the author of private letters for the eyes of one man who long ago walked along a dry dusty path and out of sight. I can call him one man or I can call him that fairy, who long ago turned his attention to pomegranates and the rustling of doves and away from my howls, extravagant or wuthering or just plain moon and cactus, it didn't matter to him, to him it was all just the sound of a dream, gauzy and green as if we were twining one another's ribs with lilacs, incompatible with what he called waking. Really I wanted making phrases to be a way of making love, wanted words to be organic matter as vital and irreducible as cum, wanted dreams to be fluids coaxed and shot forth from the slime of the slick pink glands where our bodies store and distill their harsh and primordial nectars, involuntary honey, every cellar, every nook and alcove empty in its season, bubbling, spilling, easy, breezy, effortless surfeit of wet and unknown folds (that was the dream) but I was only prepared to sing about the beauty of things, not the way beauty was streaked with hate like meat with blood. I mean that I only wrote about butterflies and nameless gods, I wrote the Dream of a Chaste Sleepwalker soon to be woken by the lips of a fey and mysterious prince...but were I telling that particular story again now, I would write, instead, "the dream of a chaste sleepwalker soon to be woken by the lips of a fey and mysterious prince, who all along had been feeding me tiny wafers of colorful crystal at the suggestion of a spindly sylvan mossdraped hag

and/or [pixelated clone of Artemis

and/or [edictclutching longdead emissary from Planet Nine, buried alive in her airless glass spacecraft

and/or [resurrected pterodactyl named Our Lady of the Goodbye, who—according to sources close to that ne'er-do-well cloutchasing nightingale and/or prickly pear with topaz needles and/or oracular honeyscented transsexual nom-de-plumed Fleck of God—wrote the New Testament in a single night, while snorting a powder made from opals through the tube of a rolled orchid petal," which is to say I once forbade my sentences the very pleasures that hurt so perfectly heartless when I fainted choking on the silhouette of his cock before waking to see it struck suddenly luminous in a glaze of topaz spit as he slipped it softening from my lips and the sun broke over the desert.

> (Remember: Darkness separating from darkness. Nameless forms suggesting names. First the high cliffs, gilded; then the masses of cloud and creosote; the thin shine of a stream, the faroff interstate. Here a spine of desert coral, there a bonedry yucca—and bursting from the brambles, the shivering speck of a sparrow. Leading away from camp: your own footsteps in the dust.)

Last night, I broke my right pinky and ring finger; what they call a boxer's fracture. It was my own goddamned doing. Now they're swathed in gauze. Pressing soft as footsteps on the blank page, leaving little blue traces. This is a story written as broken fingers can write, crooked like that and every phrase a labor of blueberry wretchedness. God is not a voice I know, or only as an echo. But I come to you breathing golden sighs of smoke; tensile, as if I were drawing a bow—I mean as if I were about to pluck a lyre, glamor humming warmly all around me like summer heat, heavy with the red and suffocating scent of strawberries. At the very least and if nothing else, I can promise you that the author is beautiful, not because I am staring at her in the mirror, but because I am floating just beside her head. Knocking at the window.

Heathcliff, it's me.

Let me speak to you one more time, baby, about first and last things? while Old Milk curls around my neck, choking me only slightly as I write to you…but for now she is hidden among the chestnut waves of my coiffure, flagging Hic Sunt Dracones, rising, falling, sinusoidal, a sudden sliding scrap of quartzite scales—then gleaming, oozing slow as honey, elongating and unrolling into a droplet, pendant, golden, "as I slip, Mythotokos, Mother of Gossip, into the valley of the shadow of thy breasts," mistaking me, once more, for her own fatal tree

but I don't know the first thing about good and evil, not when I'm howling in the passenger seat of his Chevy outside the Chili's in Bee Cave, him saying 'I need to be alone, darling,' him saying 'I'm going to England for a while,' him saying 'I'll see you when I'm back, but don't wait for me' and I—having dug into the ocean floor with the sharktooth tips of my very own cherryred acrylics, having carved out a little cave, having made us a home from rotten dolphin bones and the phosphorescent trellises of millennial coral, having forsaken the sun for that Midnight Zone, where the only hour is gloom and the only language is light, where listening is looking and speaking is incarnating, where I knew you as a curaçao blue curlicue and sometimes as sort of a turquoise cloud and you knew me as a site of iridescence or a spray of emerald sparks—I, High Priestess of the Temple of Thy Twang (this is what I named the cave) exiled from the playground of our mythology and into the glare of a Tuesday afternoon, singing one long note inflected by no hesitation, semicolon or syllable, neither breath nor riff, height nor depth, angel nor demon, principality nor power, things past nor things to come, nor anything else in all creation, simply and tunelessly howling at his face—that face as abstract as Jupiter, failed sun whirling in outraged stillness one antediluvian red storm, one wound, one unblinking eye staring auburn fathomless and silent up the barrel of a telescope—all the while glimpsing, in the rearview, a goose and her chicks waddling across the empty parking lot in search of a nearby fountain, which along with the rest now mingles senselessly into a memory full of feathers and trumpets and luminous gales, of vastitudes and wheels within wheels, reminiscent of the terrible irresistible angelic vision in the Book of Ezekiel, chapter one,

from whose midst Old Milk rises as weightless as champagne fizz, gazing from hard, bright cinnamoncandy eyes, flicking her brief pink tongue like a knife kiss against my earlobe, while I tap my words on the windowpane, because once again—pausing to knock my pink Fantasia against the ashtray, pausing to check if my crushes have replied to a Close Friends selfie, pausing to steal a phrase from one of my unpublished manuscripts and graft it onto a caption, mistakenly elaborating this spiral of numinous cunts and bloody words in someone else's digital dimension—once again I have drawn the Five of Coins, confirming my blueberry suspicion that though I may stand (may sing) in the auroral shade of thy fabledappled panes, and though I may divine thy dense immobile passion of a Vesuvian kaleidoscope (each of thy little windows begging, honey, for a hammer)—oh cathedral, coffin of Heaven's song, offal of a rotten God, great glass Lung from whom we recover some portion of the holy hum, shepherd's whistle or spacecraft crashlanded here from the war between Saturn's rings and the Holy Ghost:

I am locked out, I cannot take shelter in thy chambers except by breaking one of thy intricate eyes, so I'm holographing this hint of Cathy Earnshaw from 7:19 p.m. on Sunday, December 27th, 2020 in the presence of a python to ask if you would, please, admit me to my own skull, baby, because I gave it to you because it was what I had to give.

But an empty dreamworld is not a sweet retreat. To offer it was a terrible and irresponsible gamble, nearer to haunting than telepathy. What I thought was a woman's most beautiful and heavenly surrender, what I took for proof of my devotion to loving, was in fact the sudden swell of smokeclouds proliferating with uncanny velocity from the site of an implosion.

Nights passed. First one and then one thousand more. Nothing happened, insofar as 'something' was another installment of Notes on a Fairy's Twinkling Tongue. I plunged into my desk drawer for my grandmother's chiffon nightgown, which bubbled like sea foam from the lurid mess of my manuscripts, needles, estrogen oil and Adderall, macerated honeysuckle powder, thongs, Hitachi, chainmail charm bracelet, glass rose, pink taser, pearlescent lip gloss, rosewater and sewing kits, whose green or golden threads I have plucked to suture some or another wound, but never to sew a button back in place—after all such efforts are profligate; there is no thread firm enough to withhold the weight of my fructified breasts. So the nightgown rolled and burbled forth from the hands of my grandmother and my mother, to whom it had been given on the occasion of one of her weddings and who gave it to me after I woke from the surgeon's chamber dream (*for there she was*, lifting her knife above me deep within the long creamlit halls of Mount Sinai, my Author, my Augur, my Irrevocable Anno Domini, blueshrouded rustling Presence lifting firm pink tubes and shimmering flecks, seeding rose quartz and sodlaying scraps of rubystudded flesh, rooting nerves where nerves will strum, hiding stories in fresh folds, weaving a web thread by thread between my hips, because we are both after all Arachne fangirls) and the days rolled on. The days tottered and balanced on the two broken fingers of the clock. At the end of a cool Summer, lost in a heatless fever of dissociation—as vertiginous and imperceptible as a fractal falling into its own eternity of iterations—I recalled his final face, the blank blue eclipse that fell over his eyes when he said: "I never needed you," which I like to imagine was his way of mutating our intimacy into an insult, because more than once while he with artless sweetness wove my hair into a ponytail, I had sung the simplest song by Townes Van Zandt, had sung: "▆▆▆▆▆▆▆▆▆▆▆▆▆▆▆ ▆▆▆▆▆▆▆▆▆▆▆▆▆▆▆ ▆▆▆▆▆▆▆▆▆▆▆"♥ and only a fairy fluent in my narrow but chthonic genre of loving would hurt me with a permutation of those words.

♥ redacted quotation: verse one, lines five through eight from "If I Needed You" by Townes Van Zandt, written "stone dream," so he said, in his sleep. Among others, the estate of Townes Van Zandt, a songwriter who carried his own albums for sale in the back of his trunk; who learned his guitar licks from Lightnin' Hopkins, and learned by listening to Bukka White, Muddy Waters, Hank Williams, Bob Dylan, Bo Diddley and Lefty Frizzel; who closed his eyes whenever he sang, no matter the size of the stage, and who always preferred the crisscrossing of songs between friends and guitars on a smoky back porch in Colorado, Tennessee or Texas, denied me permission to use any of his lyrics in *The Fifth Wound*. Townes is the foremost voice in my head, more than any other singer or writer. I've been falling asleep to his music since I was a kid, somewhere between 8

To fill a Gap,
insert the thing that caused it –
Block it up
with Other – and it will yawn
the more –
You cannot solder – an Abyss –
with Air

So I loosened the gown, I let the fabric slip from my shoulders, because

8

the man who walked away♥ told me once that angels recline on the undersides of clouds to watch humans fall in and out of love, there being no such fluctuation of affect in God's heaven, where love is as constant as light. We had a habit of exacerbating little bits of biblical logic into fanciful dioramas, wherein we played with our notions as if they were painted finger puppets. So maybe I said that to him, who knows; in the moment it barely mattered—were I writing to him now, that man who vanished in a cloud of devilish dust, I might say 'a garden is a question of relation, not a single sprig or blossom,' and that would explain, with a little arch wink, as if we were hiding between the lines of a 19th century novel, how we made a language together: by gardening, not by offering orchids in glass domes—but I am not writing to him, or not as he is now: I am writing to the imprint Ezekiel made on a bedsheet and a body in the apocalyptic era of our Romance:

███████████████████████

██♥: I am trying to find the proper angle of remembrance, the point where my paltry shaft of light strikes a prism, halfsunk somewhere in the suffocated turquoise murk of the lagoon where my mind was born, because I simply will not be able resuscitate the clefts and folds and crumblejumble caves of this equation by remembering precisely who said what about angels, arranging our conversations in timestamped order from beginning to end, May to April, because I promise you, my God, that I never knew how to hear an instant passing—so instead I spat into a silver chalice, instead I pricked blood from my wrist with a cactus

and 12 years old. But the inheritance of song and feeling is not only mediated by a singer and the listener who is raised to the tune of his music, because there are legal processes that intercede in the intimacy of that exchange, there are external actors (music publishers, record labels) who own his music, and who have barred me from speaking in his voice, from claiming kin as kin. Instead of simply concealing the errors, hiding the seams for the sake of beauty; instead of concealing these places of heat and tension in the book, I have decided to make the absence visible by suturing, by making scars, what we call redactions. To show the way my song was wounded. To show the way a wound is sung.
♥ that fairy who evaporated one morning…
♥ redacted quotation: verse one, lines one and two from "At My Window" by Townes Van Zandt.

needle, instead I reclaimed the last vials of my cryofrozen cum and swirled them together in a syringe, the makeshift spinneret from which I am piping one after another twinkling string, weaving, crystallizing the mellifluous sugarglass constellation whose riffs and resonances, plucked by the perennial breezes of my theta waves, I am attempting, each day, to make echo in the curve of your ear.

Around ninethirty central on the night I would soon and forever first have slept in his bed, we'd gone swimming naked in Barton Creek; or I had gone swimming naked while he sat on the riverbank (naked, too, I think) and stared at the moon. I don't think he said a single word.

Now he was lounging among his pillows in a black turtleneck, cock pressing warmly against my hip through the scrim of his threadbare cotton boxers, vain and languorous.

Or he was giggling, whispering conspiratorially about some whim, until, every so often, his head twitched from a small involuntary spasm of confessional bliss—unbridled, like the flick of a mane.

At such moments—breathless, ransacked by tenderness—I could hardly look at him: I was afraid of showing him too much of my love, which wasn't only love but also something like a rotten peach eaten alive by its own sweetness. What had begun as infatuation had grown too ripe, so that even though its surface was pinkly soft already the flesh had moldered. I had an inner life so luxurious and no sense of moderation; I offered it all at once or not at all. Eden was too much for Eve—and desert exile too little. Like God I was total. God is a panic state.

Quietly I opened my eyes for him to see me, smiling pinkly, moldering; but he knew I had not yet developed a language for my passion (only later after the last shimmer of his evaporating form in the vacuum of the dry dusty road, words came like ants to chew at my sweet rotten skin) so he said: "This moment is not already gone, okay?"

I was holding my phone between us, recording a video of him while he spoke, because for once I was awake enough to remember to want more than terror, because no matter whether I nuzzled or mused, no matter whether I smiled or struck a pose, the instant's pulsating, infinitesimal spikes—ray of star and blade of grass, tip of tongue and brush of lash—failed to penetrate the thickening strata of a panic whirling supernally skullround and round again, until the only way to vouchsafe a sacred flicker or scrap of pleasure, I mean the only way to suck some *ipso post facto* pulp from the instant was to withhold my gaze, to conceal myself behind a screen, to vault the instant into a future where I could experience him without the heat and pressure of a live performance. But as for the phrase, I don't know why he said it; that wily will-o'-wisping Gemini is one of the irresolvable mysteries of my life. And when he walked away, he became: the encryption of the knowledge of love. A symbol as stark as the first letter of an alphabet.

Whenever I spoke his name he looked at me surprised and almost hurt, like a butterfly had been hovering above his fingertip—and I had scared it off. He always had the road in his eyes. That fairy was as skittishly elegant as a stag; I liked to imagine him leaping, antlers swaying, vanishing among ferns in a green dusky wood. Because it was me listening for the attenuating patter of his hooves, the intermittent crackle of broken branches; watching the fern fronds shake in the wake of his sudden exit. So much of my love was a preparation for its end, but I can be forgiven because in Sunday school I listened to the verses and ignored the pastor's sermons, which were not only delusional, but boring, because she dehydrated every miracle into a mere metaphor for some moral variable meant to balance the terms of an oddly godless fanaticism—the fanaticism, that is, of the white suburban Patriot Act acolytes of American empire, for whom 'god' was always a retrofitted hermeneutics, a postrationalization whose acts therefore did not disturb the desiccated logic of marital realism, whose preemptive panic restructured my holy fairy intuition into a nightmare radar, so that desire (for, say, a mood ring from a stolen Girl Scout catalogue, which—shapeshifting to the beat of Britney Spears' bubblegum melodies—would render my ring finger, I imagined, elegantly wilted, and bind me forever to the heart of a mermaid who was traveling toward me from the future, preceded by an entourage of ancient translucent seahorses) became the signal of danger, by which pleasure ('I can be anything I want') was, in the flash of an instant, illuminated: then swallowed, vaporized in a searing astral blast ('I can be anything except what I want'), so that, when I could have been inventing a story for the hills and houses I built barehanded from dirt and twigs and pebbles in the backyard, the rivers I dug and temporalized with the water of a hose, the effort by which I stepped sideways into my own pocket of duration, instead I was inventing the story or experiencing the shapeshifting premonition of my own fairy death, which is to say, having learned well enough already the politics of reform, I was simply removing myself like a misplaced comma for the sake of the clarity of the sentence.

Now I hear the crash and rending of boughs and the crack of antlers, as if the beasts of the forest were all hunting, all rearing high and plunging down among the thorns

I wasn't even ten and even I knew then, if not in those words.

One of you will betray me

So said Jesus of Nazareth to the men who loved him most, because according to the mythomechanics of the Gospel of John (my first favorite space opera and/or expanded universe fanfic and/or hagiographic tellall by a celebrity's jilted lover, who after all refers to himself namelessly as 'the disciple whom Jesus loved,' who names himself, coyly, for the whiff of a desire) he intermittently experienced time in the fifth dimension, and having sensed, first once and then one thousand times, the cruciform constellation of his last static pose, had decided the best he could do was to prepare the scene. So he went to the garden of Gethsemane to pray.

One has pierced me. One is driven deep within me

He prayed to his own deathless unborn mind, the triple helix of genetic code—a sliver of which had been grafted into his human body's porous, coralluminous spine—forever preserved within the dreadful starterraforming hypnotunes of the angels, who relentlessly recycle the air of their own first insufflation, which relentlessly reanimates the technicolor pixels of their one glitchy god. Jesus prayed, waiting, until Judas—robes rippling, almost floating in a slow blur of preternaturally algal glamor as he sank into the silted dusk of the garden, attenuating the cold immolation of his gaze to the width of a humming needle—landed before him in the grass, cataclysmically amorous, to seal his so-called Redeemer within the perfect equation of a kiss.

and velvet flowers and leaves whose coolness has been stood in water: Wash me round and sheathe me, embalming me

Knowing a kiss and a bite were both a taste, Mary's son restaged the Fall of Man. Gethsemane played Eden, Roman centurions played blazing angels, and Judas played Eve.

The Christ was fatally ripe.

*

Well, I'm a Scorpio. Not only in my sun, but in mind, season and strife, and according to William Lilly's 1647 *Introduction to Astrology*, in 'gardens, orchards and ruinous houses near waters; that is, bogs and lagoons, as well as kitchens, larders, &c.,' that is, in crevices and honey jars, in luminous strawberry jams and all manner of preserves; rotten fruits or damp places such as attract mushrooms and moss; abandoned peach groves; cracked and toppled stone cottages halfconsumed by a static blaze of wistaria or sinking in slow waves of grasses or shipwrecked in marshes and haunted by ghost orchids; and also in healing sutures, the clefts of mucosal glands, the folds of dimensions, the basins used by hydromancers, and in all places punctured. What happens once is in four dimensions. But whatever reverberates discovers another dimension, called ritual. Ritual is a wound in time. Incantation written with the tip of thy fang.

Must be a Woe – a loss or so – to bend the eye Best Beauty's way –

A pool of venom stops the formation of a clot. The instant curdles, caves, films with a dimly glittering encrustation of rot.

But once aslant – it notes Delight – as difficult – as Stalactite

Bitter breath of wine and smoke, flames drifting fitfully through olive trees, the sudden silvering of a Roman blade: as the venom absorbs, these spontaneous particulars—the vital organs of an instant in Gethsemane—are metabolized.

What remains is a fungal cavern, within which traces of other instants bend and curl, gnarling with the mass, cooling, disappearing, as thick and dully resplendent as wax. Materializing in a mist, a pair of lilactwined antlers emerging from her matted curls, echoes of a wombless Eve fizzle and flicker into phosphorescence, encircling the wizened, murmuring ghost of a tree whose green leaves are forked with infinitesimal veins, expanding and contracting with the beats of a buried and inexplicable heart—and whose every branch, shocked and sensitized with the nerves of a man, shivers from the pressure of nectar swelling, thickening into globes within the chambers of his fruits.

The Price – is even as the Grace –

*

For months after he walked away, I watched the video each night before bed, for many reasons—reasons such as his eyes (alcoves of amber) and lips (he kissed me first, let it be forever known that he kissed me first, with his hands on the small of my back) and also how the content rebuked the form: because even though a film can only repeat the past, the fairy in the film, like a nun thrashing in her *convent's narrow room*, babbling about the eternity of heaven from her brief interlude of earth, asserted himself as the artifact of a perpetual present. This moment is not already gone, okay?

I want to write like that, with the pleasure of a negation; not by laboring over the pristine convolutions of a Mobias maze ('I'm a bitch, I'm a eunuch,' et cetera, which is to say, what I attempt to conjure as languor is just exhaustion with lipstick on, because the final feint of testosterone is that I now have too little, so little that my gestures spark but do not catch, like trying to broadcast my transmission of Lady Macbeth's infamous *Unsex Me Here* soliloquy by light of an intermittent host of fireflies, by force of the capricious waves of Optimum Wi-Fi, on a Zoom call with a faceless audience—which I'm explaining to a doctor in my outside voice♥ while texting these lines to myself on my phone) but by opening a wound (not with a scalpel, not even with an indeterminate silver or glassy shard I glimpsed only once in the irrevocable and

♥ a.k.a. my Valley Girl voiceover, halfbroken horse of a feminized lilt, because once during my flop era I attended a few sessions of socalled vocal enhancement therapy at a speech disorder clinic mentioned, one Sunday night, by a shy crossdressing farmer in a bonecorseted pink brassiere, platform heels and a platinum wig with high pigtails, who had earlier that afternoon delivered a newborn calf a few states away before arriving at Melusina's Bath for 'Scent of a Woman,' a monthly meet-and-greet hosted by the Tri-State Transvestites in the slow hours before the weekly drag show, when, stilted unsteady on scarlet stilettos, trailing peacock feathers and balancing a sevenlayered cake (whose every tier displayed a lurid marzipan diorama of one of Dante's infernal circles) atop the flaming swirls of a coiffure pilfered from the grave of a Texan pageant star, the suspected confidant and/or former lover of the infamous Fleck of God, ghoulish stepsister of Lucille Ball, her laughter unfettered by daylight law, her eyes aghast beneath a fragile verandah of lashes, 'Ladies and gentlemen, three-time winner of Emmylou's Appaloosa-stallion-string Guitar...,' MISS ARTIFISH careened across the plywood stage, through a purply estrogenated mist emanating from a hidden smoke machine, to the tune of 'Wuthering Heights,' interrupted by staticky autotuned clips of David Attenborough's narration of Blue Planet 2, Episode 2, *The Deep*: 'Welcome to the Midnight Zone: an immeasurable, lightless abyss beyond the reach intimate hand of a stranger, but as if brokenfingered and glamourravenously acrylic I am digging a miniature river into the soil of my backyard) within this sentence; by placing, between parentheses, the teeming green graft of a minor hour or major instant, swelling the banks of my syntax (flowing otherwise by fatal osmotic law away from kindred ink and toward a blank page) with tinctures of destabilized time, because I do not think I can solve my little riddle except by ritualizing the rare procedures of pain and pleasure that have interrupted the static of my useless and unanimous panic.

For her dress when you saw it
stirred you. And I rejoice:
make my cryofrozen lyre
shudder and sing
at the frequency which bursts
glass:

Because while I had preserved an audiovisual trace of *this moment* (his name is Ezekiel, his eyes are honeycomb tombs) nonetheless it was preservable only behind a pane; not already gone, but already cold; not unsouled, but encrypted—sealed such that only a computer can now experience, like an atomized mesh, the innumerable shivers, the spiritualized rustling of those seven seconds—in a dimension between remembering and living (and I cannot take a photograph of the taste of your armpits, Ezekiel: my tongue has no imagination). Desperate for the sublimated glitter of its 4G hydromancy, I tapped and

of the sun…There's life here, but not as we know it, [baby!] In absolute darkness, alien creatures produce dazzling displays of light. These signals are the most common form of communication on the entire planet. Hunters illuminate themselves to attract inquisitive prey, but prey use light as a distraction. A decoy of luminous ink. Survival means making the most of every last glimmer…

Nevertheless, these creatures live beyond the normal rules of time. Some, cloning themselves silently in this infinite void, are nearly eternal…and feed only on chemicals dissolved in the searingly hot fluid of ancient hydrothermal vents…the oldest of which, with its sixtymeter iridescent steeples and breathtaking, bonelike buttresses, has been named *The Lost City*…Here something truly extraordinary is taking place…Under the most extreme pressure and temperature on Earth, hydrocarbons, the molecules that are the basic component of all living things, are being created spontaneously…indeed, many scientists now believe that life on Earth may have begun around this very vent, four billion years ago…'

tapped against the glass; bending my neck like someone praying, I called his face forth from its timeless blue grotto, that holographic pool in which I dissolved my Remembrances of Things Past—and always, all at once, a spectral pulsation of opal swirled and burned below the surface like the premonition of a betta fish. My phone was an aquarium of instants. Ezekiel returned, and like some Sorcerer rising from the roil of a fable, offered me something priceless: the pearl of our perpetuity. But like any Sorcerer's spell, the form of the miracle denied the very desire which had inspired it; and not only denied but mocked and punished the desire for its lack of guile. The more I watched, the less I, in any meaningful sense, remembered.

The basin brimmed

and brimmed

and never spilled:

I could not pour out its riches into my room, nor introduce my digitized Ezekiel to the champagne ball python♥ now curling around my wrists, nor show him the wistaria tumbling down the wroughtiron posts of my bed,♥ nor offer up my slowly leavening breasts.♥ It was just like watching you vanish up the road, fading from fairy into shimmer and shimmer into dust until the leaves of trees went soft and silver and massed into silhouettes which sighed like roosting clouds, by which time the dim fragrant bluebonnetsmudged plains had halfway evaporated but were too heavy to rise skyward and so hovered vast and mute like some somber audience of blue sentient smoke as I drifted blank and unfabled through the warm Texas dusk.

♥ …given to me a year ago by Velvet, my recent exboyfriend, who once bound my limbs with pink ropes, who fed me psychotropic mushrooms and braided orchids into my hair, and maybe will again one day.

♥ I have overwhelmed my mind with perfumes, I give myself headaches from so much perfume because I cannot bear to remember that I have forgotten the scent of your armpits, Ezekiel.

♥ Every week I inject estrogen into my ass, because once you said 'you are pretty, but not beautiful' and now I am so beautiful that no one understands how ugly I felt when you looked at the moon.

The next day I walked for nine hours, from my apartment's sticky Spring gloom to the ramshackle saloon dark of the Spider House (where I spat in a dry alabaster fountain and whistled along with 'Wuthering Heights' as it trilled and rippled from the speakers); then from the Spider House (after two Bloody Marys) over to Mount Bonnell (which I climbed woozily, mumbling your phrases over and over as if they might crack open to reveal wetly shimmering inner caverns of amethyst through which lost angels wander, echolocating their Lord); then along the lakeside trails to Barton Creek (where I suffocated on my own breaths remembering you) and back at last to my apartment at the Metropolis, where on Sundays I prayed to the alphabet and swallowed Adderall Monday to Saturday and fucked strangers in my bed or car all week long, not to mention the countless bottles of Fireball and the falling in love four times, all while reducing myself, day by day, to seven seconds in a rectangle of glass.

Eventually I broke a shaving razor and used it to slice my arm or leg, and then to slice inside the slices, and so on. My skin split open like Jello. The scars were few but the sutures were many. Eventually there was an involuntary stay in the psychiatric ward and then a voluntary stay in a rehabilitation center in Arizona where often I looked at cacti. Cacti are born pierced to the green crosses of their bodies. Blood is a fundamental wonder. When you're in the hospital, nurses tell you 'listen,' they tell you 'put down the knife,' they tell you 'draw a scar where you wish you could cut, draw it in red lipstick.' Divination is the materialization of prophecy: a record of things to come. The first time I wore lipstick, I wore it as a wound. Later I wore it on my lips in order to say: what if I were beautiful? But lipstick never forgot its first meaning: instead of a razor blade.

*

The video only emphasized the extent of his absence. Nonetheless I couldn't bring myself to erase it, until one afternoon a stranger stole my phone and the decision was made for me. Intercession of thy secret hand. I walked along Ladybird Lake reading the attic chapter from *Mrs. Dalloway* for the third time. I quit my job at the bookstore and took a plane back Northeast to finish college. One professor told me I was expressive, but not analytical. Then another said the same. I began writing stories about primrose petals like tongues on the verge of speech. I found a fainting couch on Craigslist. I snorted Molly and exclaimed: 'The flowers herself!' Slowly but without surcease, reminiscences swirled and thickened within my skull—hovering, churning like a red noxious smoke, until I hardly knew where my feet were walking or what my mouth was saying; until I stopped marking the clock and the calendar; until the world was as distant as a diorama, and memory as near as sight. I vanished into a Venusian summer.

> *and on a soft bed*
> *delicate*
> *you would let loose your longing*
> *and neither any[   ]nor any*
> *holy place nor*
> *was there from which we were absent*
> *no grove[   ]no dance*
> *   ]no sound*
> *   [*

Soon I could think about nothing other than Ezekiel in the snow. Or Ezekiel naked on a slab of limestone. Or his sudden sweet chalky cum. But remembering him also meant remembering the solar flares of his silence; meant remembering the pitiless innocence—as impartial as sunlight—with which he spoke some breathtakingly mean sentence. He retreated into innocence in order to be cruel; he said *you are pretty but not beautiful* because that was how he felt. He loved blueberries. He did not think I was beautiful. He walked away.

II.

To the Tune of *Are You Sure Hank Done it This Way* by Waylon Jennings

One day Lord Korechika brought the empress a bundle of notebooks. 'What shall we do with them?' Her Majesty asked me. 'Let me make them into a pillow,' I said. I now had a vast quantity of paper at my disposal, and I set about filling the notebooks with odd facts, stories from the past...

- Sei Shōnagon, tr. Ivan Morris, *The Pillow Book*

...a book of anthems where Sirens plunged into the gold of the initials.

- Severo Sarduy, tr. Suzanne Jill Levine, *Cobra*

But the beauty—the beauty because I became beautiful. That, too, was irrefutable. Did I become beautiful because I had failed to write a perfect sentence? Or because I had failed to write his perfect sentence? Because I couldn't bear to believe there was no sentence, no sentence at all to make him stay in my bed, I became a writer so that his eyes would no longer be interrupted by the sight of my ugliness, so that speaking to me was like hallucinating a garden of swaying branches, so that he could tell me I was beautiful without lying. I thought I could never be Helen, so I became a wooden horse.

But he couldn't fuck a wooden horse.

So I escaped to an island where the Siren roosted in a nest of bones, languorously vigilant. The bones, of course, had once been shipwrecked men; the Siren was sui generis. She folded her plumage about her, concealing her breasts within boughs of feathers: heavy, milkthickened, eternally ripe. She was old; older even than that unpronounceable phrase engraved into a tablet by the Minoan scribe who, seated in the shadow of the Labyrinth of Knossos, wielding a whittled olive branch, first fatally struck a slick red rectangle of mud. Histories contain no record of her death, no record of her latterday deeds. But I would not be surprised if she were the selfsame sea witch who offered the mermaid a putrid scrap of paradise in Hans Christian Andersen's tale; nor would I be surprised if, having tired of her lonesome isle, she took up residence in Lesbos and composed the songs later attributed to a mortal woman named Sappho.

As I sailed past her flowering meadow, the Siren mistook me for a man and began to sing her song. I could not resist. I swam to the shore and approached the reeking nest where she lay composing verses on the petals of yellow poppies, with her own milk for ink and a plucked feather for a quill. Lacking feathers of my own, I had no choice but to stumble up the side of the mound. First I dislodged a jaw. A mouthful of teeth prattled down to the grass. Partway up, I wounded my palm on a splintered rib. But I found my foothold in a pelvis, and my handhold on a femur; then a humerus, and a scapula, and a skull, until I reached the peak, and leapt into her bright nest. The Siren glanced up with eyes like cracked emeralds. An instant passed, like a prophecy of the next instant—then she ceased writing, leapt into flight and (her feathers enclosing me as briefly as a memory of feathers) sank her fangs into my neck.

After which she stumbled backwards in affronted confusion, retreating to the branches of a cypress. Her wings beat slowly while she stared. The tree swayed beneath her. She did not speak; she did not even blink. Because she had tasted me— but my blood was not like the blood of a man, not at all. She was unaccustomed to being on the other side of a riddle.

Are you a man?
No.
Are you a woman?
No.
Are you a god in disguise?
No.
What are you?
I am a blurry object.

I knew that the Siren ate men and only men. But Homer never asked: and if she mistook someone else for a man? So I elongated the story without him. The Siren's saliva poisoned my blood, but I did not die. Instead I permuted the terms of Eden. I learned, like Eve, the secret of her song.

Which is to say: I vomited blood.

For three days I vomited blood while the Siren watched me from her cypress tree. On the fourth she flew to the far end of the island. On the fifth she returned with strawberries and a gourd of fresh water, which she dropped into the nest. On the sixth she asked why I had come. *Sing in me Muse*, I said. But nothing happened. Then came the seventh day. The Siren was off collecting poppy petals, so I climbed out of her nest and made my way to the beach, where I collapsed onto the sand.

At dusk I woke to seafoam brushing my cheek. And a melody in my mind.

So I began to sing.

I sang a song so enchanting that I saw you, Ezekiel.

You sailed alone through the Strait of Messina, lashed to the mast of your boat.

You beamed. You blew kisses. You exclaimed your love.

And I sang my story of *a restless man* (Frances Caulfield, 1921);
a many-sided man (Reverend Lovelace Bigge-Wither, 1869);
a man so wary and wise (Henry Bernard Cotterill, 1911);
a man of twists and turns (Robert Fagles, 1996);
a man who walked away.

You allowed yourself to love me. But you withheld so much, too much—you remained forever at a distance. At the distance of a ship, sailing toward Ithaca.

*

For a time I remained on Anthemusa. The Siren assured me that Ezekiel would return; she said that no man could ever forget my song, whether or not he spent his whole life walking away from it. She said he will tell no one about you (about the night he fucked you in a flower bed, the night he plucked a cumdewed pearlescent pink primrose petal from the soil, the night he placed it like a eucharist on his tongue and said I consume this in remembrance of thee; he will tell no one what he told his diary) but by and by he will hum your song, he will hum it so often and for so many years he will become convinced it is his own. "You may not have Ezekiel," she said. "But he will have your voice.

> Of course, if He does one day infer
> – from its tinctured affect of Topaz
> infertile Peacocks and lipstickstained Saints' Teeth –
> which fey Limner first lisped that infernal verse,
> He will, in dialectic panic,
> devote whole volumes of coarse Voilà
> to inventing its inverse.

> Your song once formed the stone mold
> into which Ezekiel poured words
> as indecisive as molten steel.

> Rising from the rotten water of a Lady's Lake,
> your song was once the boulder
> from which Ezekiel drew a sword
> and performed as Lord and Savior.

Cum swallowed is cum forgotten;
phrases never lose their savor."

So spake the Siren on a sunny afternoon. We began an affair.
Soon her powderblue feathers were grazing my hips; soon her
tail was coiling cool and opalescent around my neck; soon my
nipples were glazed pink and glassy with her strawberryscented
spit. Every so often we paused our pleasure; every so often we
left halfwilling for the beach, where concealed behind cypress
branches, we sang duets for passing ships. Men of all kinds
sailed past. There were poets, plastic surgeons and paparazzi;
lovelorn wanderers, absentminded archaeologists; psychiatrists
and mystics and Casanovas. But most of all there were those
who came to test their faith against our song.

Returning from a private audience with Pope Honorius the
First on the subject of the Heresy of Monothelitism, against
which the Archbishop's surrogates had preached violently
across the provinces of Hispania, Isidore of Seville, framed by
the billowing blue flag of his drowsily beneficent Theotokos
(that is, 'god-bearer,' that is, Blessed Virgin) instructed the
oarsmen of his dromon to sail south for an island known
as Anthemusa, because, in the long afternoons he had spent
strolling beneath wistariamacerated marble arches, speaking to God from his glittering-fountain-interrupted courtyard
while thumbing a personal edition of the Scriptures adorned
by a Papal limner, he had received a series of divine visions
culminating in 'the apparition of a Heavenly Text, held aloft by
two rubyfulminant Angels, in which the flora and fauna of the
world were at last taxonomized according to Our Father's foreordained essence, and the reproduction of which, in Bejeweled
volumes, the Angels have demanded.

But first,' bellowed Isidore from a Byzantine throne at the
stern, 'we are called by Providence to sail for the Strait of
Messina, the Angels having revealed a Necessary Elision, that
is, having declared the Siren of Anthemusa a Glitch in His

will, and a Corrupted File of Genesis, and a Diabolical Echo of Eve's Fatal Gesture; therefore we are called by the Angels of the Lord to inscribe His Heavenly Text upon the surface of the Earth, and to extinguish the Siren and any of its Kin with flaming swords.'

So Isidore's oarsmen blocked their ears with beeswax and rowed to Anthemusa. We saw the dromon drift into the harbor and began to sing. But the men did not swoon; their eyes were not struck blank. The Siren understood first, and already too late. She whispered directions to an orange grove where a powderblue biplane waited at the end of an avenue of sand. "Fly to Manhattan," she said. "I will meet you there."

As the dromon's prow struck the stand, Isidore read aloud from a scroll titled 'Divine Commandment as Received, in Humility, by Archbishop Isidore of Seville and Ratified by Emperor Heraclius the First, in which an Angel of the Lord Proclaims the Unreality of the Siren of Anthemusa.' I kissed her one last time and fled into the meadows. His legionaries lit their swords on fire, and leapt from the prow.

I smelled the zest of oranges.

She did not meet me in Manhattan.

In his *Etymologies*, Isidore wrote: 'Other fabulous human monstrosities are told of, which do not exist but are concocted to interpret the causes of things. In Arabia people imagine snakes with wings, which are said to move faster than horses and to fly. These they call Sirens. Their venom is so powerful that when a man is bitten by them death ensues before the pain is felt.'

Leaning from a ladder in the Sistine Chapel, Michelangelo painted the Garden of Eden. He imagined the snake not in the Biblical sense, but in the Isidorean sense; that is, he imagined the Devil as a Siren, leaning down from a tree.

I loved her once.

III.

To the Tune of Me Tuning My Guitar

Such minds, when they give themselves up to the uncontrolled ferment of [the divine] substance, imagine that, by drawing a veil over self-consciousness and surrendering understanding, they become beloved of God, to whom He gives wisdom in sleep...

    - Hegel, tr. A.V. Miller, *The Phenomenology of Spirit* (texted to me by Ezekiel, last week)

When we did come home she would certainly be home, too, enjoying the evening, for so she described her habit of sitting in the kitchen in the dark. She seemed to dislike the disequilibrium of counterpoising a roomful of light against a worldful of darkness. Sylvie in a house was more or less like a mermaid in a ship's cabin. She preferred it sunk in the very element it was meant to exclude.

    - Marilynne Robinson, *Housekeeping*

One night a mermaid went to consult the sea witch, who, splayed on a divan built from the bones of shipwrecked men, offered to make the impossible true: 'I will brew a decoction which you must drink on dry land, before dawn. After you swallow the last drop, your tail will split in two and shrivel into the shape of human legs. And you will feel such pain, as if a blade were passing through you; but the queen will proclaim you the most beautiful woman in her court. At every step you will feel as if you were walking on sharp knives, but her courtiers will praise your poise. If the prince asks for your hand before the full moon, you will grow old and die a woman; but if he does not, you will fade into sea foam.'

Her coherence depended on the power rooted and perpetuated in the desire of a prince, which is to say: according to the equation of this fable, the future of her magical form could be ensured only by the articulation of his desire in marital form; the magic of the sea witch transformed the mermaid, but replicated the imperial function of desire. A spell is a brief and local refutation of the crush of precedent. Or simply a systems test. To place the mermaid like a canary inside the palace: and for what? So that wandering among mortal men and women, gleaning, gathering flickers of herself from their glances (her very own vial of fireflies!) she obtained nothing more than the experience of appearing to experience pleasure; nothing more than the pleasure of seeming. And the pleasure of seeming is like the reflection of a pink primrose in a mirror. It has no fragrance. The mermaid had made a compromise. She was attempting to perform the equation. The mermaid did not want the prince. What the mermaid wanted was to rectify the element of her experience. Water was like slow drowning; she required air. Air because the mermaid wanted to risk love. The Christ was a flightless bird. The mermaid wanted to risk love. And the only way to risk love was to be recognized as a woman. To refuse the crush of precedent. To externalize herself. Like a hypercube unfolding into a cross.

Hans Christian Andersen sent a draft of *The Little Mermaid* as a love letter to Edvard Collin in 1832, when he was twenty-seven years old. Edvard was the son of Hans' patron and was seeking a wife. The two became close. Hans was infatuated. He wrote, "My sentiments for you are those of a woman." He wrote, "I long for you as though you were a beautiful Calabrian girl." He wrote, "The femininity of my nature and our friendship must remain a mystery."

Desire makes a woman of us both, ma chérie! In the glow of my bedroom, among the maidenhair ferns and the crushed crystal skins which Old Milk leaves to haunt my corners and alcoves, rising from the multicolored gauzes which you slip one by one from your shoulders, for the arc of a gesture, for the length of a glance and the depth of a single word, desire hovers and churns around us like a presence, as faint and undeniable as vapor. So I catch it in my butterfly net; I bottle it up in Venetian milk-glass vials labelled 'Fairy Fossil' and/or 'Disintegrating Primrose Archive' and/or 'Daughter of Pearl,' which will one day clutter the shelf of an antique shop collecting dust until another wayfaring fairy, some summer afternoon, chances to sniff it and knows. Knows or, sensing some give or fray in the fabric of time, receives the transmission of my minor oracle. Antique objects suggest the possibility of another lineage; not of blood, but of perfume. *For now we see as through a glass, darkly.*

Ezekiel wasn't a man when I met him, and I was not a woman. We shared what could be called a gender, but what I like to call an atmosphere, whipped up slowly as we rowed the air, gesturing, glossolaling, the palms of our hands rising and falling as firm and graceful as oars.

To put it simply, we were both fairies.

My favorite genre of literature is gossip. My second favorite is prayer. But sometimes those are one and the same. I don't know who needs to hear this, but windchimes are actually a device for ghosts to send messages to flowers. My favorite goddess and dear friend Aphroditos called me on my pink conch shell to soliloquize about a species of sentient crystals on a distant planet who make love by refracting light into one another's faceted chambers. I was standing in the corner store looking at soda and suddenly remembered a song that has never been written: "When I first saw her, she was drinking a Fanta, with smudged mascara, strawberry flavor."

That was yesterday. Today I'm letting my broken fingers rest, nursing one long joint while blue smoke rolls and drifts around me like some kind of meaning. Smoke is what my thoughts look like when I'm not thinking them. When I'm alone, when there's no camera immortalizing my pussy, I don't really know what it means to desire me. Or I worry that at your touch I will be disenchanted, the bubble of my beauty will burst. Why do girls keep crying into my breasts on the second date?

When, in *Eternal Sunshine of the Spotless Mind*, which is maybe best understood as a story about Joel, an implosively selfnarratorial Fabergé egg who falls in love with her own near-future mirror, i.e. a manic white egirl two years into h.r.t.♥, Clementine neé Kate Winslet says, "I'm not a concept, I'm just a fucked-up girl looking for her own peace of mind," I heard *piece of mind*. I was thirteen and had never seen it in print. So I read it how I felt it. Because, without much of a choice in the matter, I was always somewhere else. Unable to decrypt the transmissions, inarticulate but insistent, pulsing from my father's rustling, quicksilver remove; unable to predict the seasons of his errant and erratic seeking, or anticipate the heft of emptiness in the fore of our sudden exits, when, every two or three years, with the promise that this room, this bed, would be the last, I moved towns or cities with my family—I was becoming, by plane

♥ i.e. a tgirl with a freshlymown persona, who 'ironically' calls herself an elder on Twitter, whose handle (@blue_ruin) is the same as the name of her hair dye, who for the first time feels the skintight immanence of sex appeal and, claiming thereby a divine mandate for recklessness, indiscriminately unleashes her unprocessed trauma responses on friends and lovers as if they were burning curlicues flaring from the mind of an eclectic, blamelessly fey spitfire—that is, a tgirl as leggy and unbalanced as a placentaslick colt, whose insomniac rites of lipstick and oil and weeping have only just organized themselves enough to pass for a liturgy, barely speakable but spoken anyway, profusely and mistakenly selfcanonized, gesture by gesture, cataclysm by cataclysm, in bars, bedrooms and websites…an archetype I can only describe so adroitly because I am still shadowboxing my own insufferable isomer of the manic pixie impulse, i.e. the Ptolemaic cosmology of pain, where I conspire to place you in my orbit, or as if this were an act of unprecedented selflessness rather than a tautological feint, to place myself in yours, instead of ceding the center to that atmosphere in which 'opacities can coexist and converge, weaving fabrics. To understand these truly,' writes Glissant, 'one must focus on the texture of the weave and not on the nature of its components.'

30

and minivan and habit of mind, one of the Highway Kind. In each house and every room I was beginning and beginning, but ultimately failing to texture, to collage or accumulate, through the fixed point of a single window♥ (within the narrow, stabilized scene of a single view, that memorial surfeit and kaleidoscopic depth of uncountable seasons), the palimpsestic clock by which a mind apprehends the slow breathing—warmth surging, then retreating; flowers unfolding, then expiring—of a planet in vast and inexplicable thrall to the sun. I wanted some proof of my presence in the world. I wanted my movements to mean something. So I began searching, instead, for *pieces of mind.* This was the name by which I first dimly intimated the possibility of an enchanted relation binding certain objects, sensations or turns of phrase; symbols, scents and limpwristed gestures whose breezy arcs belied the infrared distortions which—rippling out unseen, unheard—disturbed the magnetic field, at times as fine and tensile as a spider's web, at others as intricate and suffocating as the fabric of the Technicolor Dreamcoat, of which the world formed the warp and my phantasmagorical intuition formed the weft. At first I presumed them to be delimited, enumerable, prefigured by divine force—presumed them to be waiting for me somewhere in the world—but I came to recognize these *pieces* as unpredictable and miraculously sudden, I mean *suddenly emergent*, produced by the abrasion of the brief and irreducible grain of the silicone angel I named Aurora against irrevocable times and places. I came to recognize the way each of these *pieces* grazed and snagged my gaze, pulling a stitch loose from the shivering tinsel weave of my obsessivecompulsive

♥One year I watched the pinkly erupting blossoms of a desert willow, scattered and drifting like miniature swans across the placid surface of a pool as artificial and irresistible as a blue raspberry lagoon; soon after I saw the rim of a California canyon wherein coyotes, kindled to restlessness by gusts of citrus zest from clusters of orange or lemon trees, roamed and howled in the dusk; and later, the silhouettes of skyscrapers floating as abstract as the monoliths of Stonehenge in a smog so silver I couldn't see the street three hundred feet below, or any trace of flora or fauna save for the intermittent blur of a sparrow smacking into my window.

consciousness, revealing the seam of my senses, exerting a Fold in space and time where instants pool and confect and are metabolized into the primary matter—which I call by many names, 'starfluid' and 'subatomic lyre' and 'angel eyes' and 'magnetized topaz'—from which true myths are formed.

Sometimes it grows so weighted and swollen from the suppuration of seconds that—like the unassuming rind of that deadly puffball fungus called 'Destroying Angel'—the Fold, wounded by its own excess, rips and bursts open, suffocating the air in a fog of spores; this is what I call infatuation.♥ Surgery is, after all, only possible by wounding. The sutures cannot hold. Dehiscence is an acute expression of entropy; that is, of energy transfer—the opening of an infinitesimal heat vent. Where all life begins. The mermaid became a magnificent woman, who became sea foam.

*

Meaning is not produced by the divination and description of essences, by the form of the curio cabinet, or the desires of its pseudoscientific collector; refuses to proliferate, desiccates wherever relations have been forced, hierarchically, into a stabilization; is substituted with something else, something which imitates meaning, whose facsimile of meaning is pumped full of artificial sweetener, just as formaldehyde replaces blood in the course of an embalming. 'Essences' are extractions. The colonial urge as perpetrated by Empire is that wherein colonizers, lacking their own life force, attempt to absorb, to assimilate, that is, to vampirize, time,

♥ I think I'm falling in love again. Or maybe all I mean is that I want to keep vigil over your irreducibilities, not as if they were Sibylline Oracles, but as if they were butterflies. Take shade beneath my lashes. Listen, baby, because it's too early to tell you to your face, so I'm telling the future instead: I want to wrap a dimension around us, like the wings of a satellite—gold, metallic and rustling with innumerable microscopic facets. I want to be your anesthesia, one cubic block of shimmering. So you will see me how I saw me in the mirror when I thought of you.

attention, every possible labor, leisure, lineage, silence, desire, dreaming, prayer, memory, pleasure, infolding, interdimensional exhalation, spiritual ambit, signal fire, perishable and nonperishable nourishment, prophetic and instantaneous daydream, subterranean reservoir and mesh of myth from those they seek to 'represent,' because the colonizer is the vampire of universality, singing: "It's a small world, after all…"

Offering a dim, hermetically sealed diorama, a prairie of broken glass, in which every leaf of grass is in fact an infinitesimal blade, Empire scrawls, in rainbow marquee lights, around the marble arch that forms its entrance, *Welcome to Eden*. Empire offers me forms, the most fundamental of which is the police report. All others are only its variations. The novel of trauma and final triumph, in which a marginalized speaker briefly holds the title of victim, that is, exemplary sufferer, clicks into place on the liberal bookshelf and becomes an alibi for Progressivism, history as a benevolent curve. Believing it to be their perfected form, Empire's agents collect and collage such stories as though they were lost fragments of itself. Every click in representation follows a shift in Empire's calculation of how to restabilize relations, how to absorb or reabsorb an error, a wound, a loose stitch without evidence of its ever having torn, without a scar, without a past.

Empire offers a perpetual déjà vu. It speaks through poets as much as politicians, it speaks in a tuneless recursive monologue that I hear as I write to you. Sometimes I'm halfway through a sentence before I realize that I'm transcribing another one of its traps. The form of Empire is always the same, but its content is a seasonal harvest of lurid molecules plucked and stolen from our visions, denatured, milked and—its rigs and engines having extracted our dreammatter in order to combust its hallucinogenic residue—sold back to us, atom by parched atom, as Doses of Paradise. The phantasmagoria of Empire's cultural production reflects our visions from its carnival mirrors: what I absorb is as reminiscent and uncanny as a photograph of some future Madame Tussauds, wherein wax likenesses of fairies and faggots are posed extravagantly in the tinselly strobelit diorama of a gay bar, directing into the camera a host of blank, rapturous gazes within which some corrupted consciousness shimmers in and out of existence. I have no doubt that if in fifteen or twenty years the sun still shines and Hollywood still produces films we will see the first transsexual superhero-object twirl and soar and embed herself in the monologue of the silver screen: for each object under its glare, Empire repeats a single story. Repeating a single story is taxonomy disguised as an act of witness.

Possibility, which when it unsettles us we call 'uncertainty,' is the precondition of meaning, which can be described, in turn, as the perpetual, unhurried astral weaving of nodal specks, *pieces of mind*, irrespective of distance in space and time. Meaning is a mode of changing and being changed; not a reconstitution of essence, because what Empire mistakenly calls essence, each point of a constellation, is simply a form of density, a web of gravitational attractions collecting: a star is the result of disparate elements meeting in intimacy, inflamed. A knot of light.

Fantasy is not, in itself, ethical, but it is the means by which an ethics is made. Dreaming is not fractal but kaleidoscopic, the way of approaching meaning by excess and collage, passion and permutation: I say passion because dreaming is never boring. Boredom is the only state from which a dreamer is exempt. Dreams are a confluence of lifefragments, swelling and dissolving in waves, perpetually on the verge of meanings. What in Physics is called 'potential energy,' I refer to as 'potential meaning,' the maximum of which is dreaming.

At Jay Street, as the doors prepared to close, I looked up. For less than a second I thought I saw him on the F train. It was some other fairy in a web of torn silver silks. Infinitesimal iridescent spiders swung and wove their threads around her skin. Her acrylics were transparent and dreamsicle orange, painted with clouds and tiny glitter icons of saints. Masks make everyone reminiscent. The train vanished. I flipped open my pocket mirror to check my mascara, then dabbed my lashes with a tissue. Suddenly I felt like a Hollywood starlet, which made the moment bearable. I thought to myself: 'You are a beautiful woman with a mysterious past. You are a beautiful woman remembering bluebonnets and morning mist. You are a pieta but without holding anyone. You are a pieta but daydreaming.'

So let me tell you this:

If you saw me only in the present moment of my face (if we had spent our whole lives not knowing one another and then you walked up to me at Mood Ring in 2019 and touched my forearm and said, 'I'm Ezekiel,' and if I turned to face you smelling like strawberry smoke and some memory of horses in a field, smiling languorously, saying, 'Honey...') by which I mean if you weren't studying my face like a palimpsestic scrap of parchment for any trace of a boy you once knew—well then without a doubt you would see a BRUNETTE BOMBSHELL WITH BUXOM BREASTS. I became my own mirage, the one which emanated first from objects exerting their sudden warmth, suggesting if not a soul then an opaque clarity like the silver ring of a tuning fork, a sort of alarm, a luminous refusal to offer me anything but allure: I was archetypical in the sense that I stole lipsticks and swayed my hips; I was mythical in the sense that I imagined myself strolling through ancient forests in sheer silver gauze—to the applause of butterfly wings!

But by saying this much I have already trespassed the vows of Womanhood; I have made my beauty speak when Beauty is made to be unspeakable. Beauty is a relationship between subject and object where the object, fulfilled already by its form, needs nothing and so expresses nothing. To save it from so much as the suggestion of indelicacy, the object is separated from language like cream from milk. Beauty is as silent as a block of butter. So forget that I said BRUNETTE BOMBSHELL, otherwise you'll stop reading and seek instead the photograph of me reclining among silver pillows, my breasts full and nestled in the gauze of a light chiffon robe which floats around my limbs like a cloud of pink powder. At my left hand, a skyblue 1963 Princess 300 typewriter; and in my right, a hammer.

Because the pleasure of a wound is sudden and total. As if I had been still (suspended in an electromagnetic mist, the perpetual vaporization of faith into panic, insofar as faith is understood not as belief in proving but as belief in meaning, in what feels aloft, in what would express a yearning for being beautiful together) while the world was spinning, which had felt, in turn, as if the world were still while I was spinning, one night last year a blade—in which reality was, with the force of a cresting wave, for one instant collecting itself into a point—met and, tracing the curve of my right eye socket, sank into my skin, just as a needle lowers into a record along one of its grooves, so the world began to spin at the same speed as my soul, and almost simultaneously I felt opening from my fresh wound in a single, circumferent ripple – *invisible, as Music – but positive, as Sound* – a clear and bright stillness, a kind of serene attention which (as when, staring into a lover's eyes after so much doubt and uncertainty, I feel for the first time my irreducibilities confecting effortlessly with theirs, surrounding us both like wings of sugarglass) is the inverse of panic, of dissociation and relentless suspense; which is, in short, belief itself.

Ezekiel and I did not know one another as subject and object, it wasn't so clean, do you hear? From my account so far, it might seem that for him, he was the subject, and the object was some little fleck of topaz he kept in a drawer in his mind, but that's because I was only allowing myself to sing a Townes Van Zandt song, because my favorite way to think of Ezekiel is also the way he hurts me most. A man like a stalk of wheat. Tall and thin like that, nodding in the breeze as if the wind were the only song a man needed: too preoccupied with some theological proposition to remember breakfast and lunch, and by dinner wanting a beer and a smoke before even considering

36

the possibility of oatmeal—but satisfied by the sight of a blue-berry, willing to declare the beauty of a blueberry! Plucking a blueberry from the bowl, making it some sort of symbol for his idea of paradise: 'I need more time with the blueberries, baby.'

Dancing on a table in his cowboy boots and a pair of strapon angel's wings: a man who knows how to love you from a door-way. But in a bed he knows only how to leave you; pulling on yesterday's jeans, his cock still wet with your spit. And that's romance to you. That's all you're given to make a poem from. So you remember him at dusk or dawn because he belongs to the haze of those hours, lit from behind by a slit in the blinds; most of him shadow except that belt buckle struck pink and phospho-rescent as he turned toward the door. But he was already gone, long before then; he was gone as soon as he said hello:

"████████████████████████████████████
████████" ♥

That was Townes, and so was this:

"████████████████████████████████████
████████" ♥

But that was Ezekiel, too; turning one last time to look at me. Eyes like he'd stolen the soul of a horse. If I had decided to be a fairy, if I hadn't decided to become a transsexual, then I would have wanted to be like him. But I never dared to look a blueberry in the face.

*

Six years old, with the same eyes but an unblemished brain (a brain absorbing the images which would slowly be ground to pow-der, pulverized beneath the weight of my life, no longer even memory itself but the very air and atmo-sphere of all remembering), I lived

♥ redacted quotation: verse one, lines six through eight from "Flyin' Shoes" by Townes Van Zandt, confessing that he will be tying them on soon.
♥ redacted quotation: verse one, lines three and four from "I'll Be Here in the Morning" by Townes Van Zandt, about how pleasant it is to glance back to-ward a town as you're leaving it.

in a prefabricated neighborhood, that is, a sudden, ahistorical event, appearing 'as if from thin air,' all at once—which, precisely because of this temporal rift, and in order to assert a sort of generalized, frantic lineage, had realized itself as a phantasmagorical, unpredictable collage of French Chateau, English Victorian, Italian Renaissance and Spanish Revival-style McMansions. Behind my house, through a small pecan wood and across a creek called White Rock, was open farmland. This was Plano, Texas, at the turn of the millennium. I was living at the fringe of Empire's dream of itself, and so felt, half-consciously, the destabilization of that dream: the dream of 'controlled nature,' of the endless city—in a word, civilization.

Day after day I disappeared into the forest. I knew the creek; knew its chalk banks and swirling caramel waters and the clearing on the far side, where a rusted electric-blue Frigidaire rose up from the earth. Loose bones rested inside—a pelvis, a femur; I knew those, too. I had stood here with my siblings, making stories about the bones, listening to the faroff stamping of horses. We had searched until dusk for more evidence, but found nothing: only the dead fridge casting no shadow in the shadow of the pecan trees. But this time I was alone, and frightened of the bones. The bones knew what hands had held them, had placed them in that fridge. I feared that if I held the bones, their keeper might sense me. Where does the allegiance of an object lie? The clearing was silent. The sky wasn't watching. But mesmerized by the sound of hooves, I passed further into the dank pecans. Soon I reached a collapsed barbwire fence. This fence marked the tree line, the end of the suffocation of the forest: beyond it lay a prairie in whose reddish twilight distances a translucent tractor and nearimmaterial barn flickered like halfremembered bygones, as if built not from steel or wood but from lurid particles of dream and sundown, destined to vanish with the last breaths of the man who had stranded them in those dry Texas grasses, whose failing eyes projected them even now from some cool unseen porch. But I hardly noticed barn or tractor because nearer yet were clouds of luminous almost purplish dust from which emerged, here and there, the high speckled heads of Andalusian mares and Appaloosa stallions among whose sinewy spectral forms I wandered until the sky dimmed and cicadas commenced their shrill and surging murmurs, seeming almost to waft me home on swells of sound as I floated senselessly among pecan trees in a daze from which I have never fully woken.

And Ezekiel sensed it somehow, sniffed it on me the night we met at a halfdead party where I knew no one and walked into a dank kitchen looking for vodka, sweetly stoned on adderall and a bowl of Blue Dream, glitter mascara flashing from my lashes like a pledge of allegiance to Deathless Aphrodite of the Spangled Mind—and he came to me, Ezekiel:

"Piglet is androgynous," he said, smiling dangerously, leering sideways, disappearing through a door for another drink; then returning, approaching me silently, placing his hands on the small of my back, looking into my eyes, his eyes glinting with coy wildness like a pixie. He kissed me. He took my hand quietly, leading me away from the music and the twinkling fairy lights, out a side door, to a flower bed. My point is that there's more to him than what I've told you. My point is that we were in love soon. Or we were like two mermaids in a cove, condemned to dissolve because we didn't know how to make sense. Pleasure and panic were so near. The taste of those months was cum; the scent was sweat. Trains rattled and whistled somewhere beyond the window; sparrows hopped from branch to branch. Seafoam pooled in the bathtub. I left my book on the bedside table, unread.

But it went along like that sleight of cinema, the so-called dolly zoom: the nearer I drew to him, the further our future seemed to slide toward the horizon, until it was so indistinct it could hardly be said to exist with any more force than a fleck of blue. He was most untouchable when I lay beside him at night. He was unreachable when I looked him in the eye. He was still heartbroken over another boy, sickened by heartbreak, struck down by the breathlessness of the revelation that despite so many Sundays of unslaked perdition, despite escaping briefly the blank hells proliferating in every direction from his gaze, when at last and after so many years alone and forsaken in West Texas he had felt heat in his heart like a Spring gust of annunciation, his lover could not, despite a suffocated yet corresponding passion, despite the unprecedented romance and candor of Ezekiel's gestures, rise to the occasion. Because that boy did not want to be what his love would make him. Ezekiel might put it otherwise; my interpretation is influenced, without a doubt, by my own troubles with love, but that final notion—of rising, or being unable to rise, to the occasion—has come to define how he diagrams our own interrupted ascension to the paradise of loving. At the time, however, I took his heartbreak as a sign of some fatal lack in my soul, as if my spell were not eloquent enough to wake him from his swoon. My amorous Mediterranean shrank to the size of a fetid pond, until I was not a feathery chanteuse in snakeskin heels, but a horsefly perched on a lotus petal, because I did not understand that for Ezekiel, already beset by seasons of static and centuries of undead instants, to fall in love again was already a miracle as unlikely as the Virgin Birth. And he had fallen in love, god he had fallen in love with me, because of me he was making the first gestures of a second offering of love... and I mistook it for selfishness, a halflove, not understanding that it was more than he had ever given a fairy, not understanding that I myself was also only giving halflove, because far too often I was surrendering to the corrosive intrusion of a paranoia, which attached itself to, pierced and rooted itself in, my love; which was every day attempting to crush my love (as if it were a golden fist) within an illusion of gnostic insight. Paranoia is a presence felt but not seen, a haunting which refuses to reveal its original form except in glimpses of endless depth, which shapeshifts faster already than my dreamworld (whirlpool of moony omens), and so much faster than the writing of these sentences. The speed of paranoia is the limit of my mental laws, as light is the limit of the universal; there is no way to solve its riddles or to transform them into knowledge, because it proliferates like a Hydra at the site of any uncertainty. But when I can ignore its seductive doom—when I do not agree to its terms, when, despite the terror of fascination, I turn my head, then it recedes into its cave. Rather than a rebuke of paranoia, loving is a form of attunement.

I will never remember that fatal scent, the barnyard musk upon his skin, the straw and the stable. I will never remember because a scent is immediate and unrememberable, because I know the only way to smell him is to kiss him, to feel the heat of his breath, earthy and sweet, or to bury my whole face in the soft musk of his ass. I can only love him that way in time with the instant. But there are other ways to love. Because we knew each other with phrases, too; because when I said neither of us wrote a single word, I meant Ezekiel wrote no poems and I wrote no stories; I didn't mean that we were silent. When we withdrew, when I retreated into leaves and branches and sunless rooms, broadcasting my song from a portable radio, and when Ezekiel replied in rapturous telegrams that lapped at my feet like seafoam—the present swelled around me like the curl of a wave. Instants surged forward, folding upon themselves, out of time…

One afternoon, as I was shelving copies of Édouard Glissant's *Poetics of Relation* at the bookstore, Ezekiel wrote me from his bedroom. He was reading the opening pages of the fourth volume of Proust; I was hiding among piles of books…

Ezekiel

Today 4:30 PM

Tomorrow I will drizzle honey on your cock and suck it off

My cock in your mouth: the land of milk and honey

Where you shall rest your weary head

And for dessert?

We'll write a strongly-worded letter to the Pope, who is rumored to own a sacramental spacecraft

...along whose gold-plated flank glints a pontifical honorific, Nuntius Dei, in cursive loops of ruby inlay

Dear Sir: we write to you from the Land of Milk and Honey. Please help us become the first boyfriends in outer space.

Many years later someone will append a section titled 'Gay Space Voyage' to each of our Wikipedia pages

"Ezekiel devoted himself to the composition of eighteen novels, each dedicated to one of the rings of Saturn."

"The novels were launched from Johnson Space Center in unmanned rockets. No surviving Earthbound copies remain"

"After that fateful, fitful voyage, all references to flowers, previously the most marked feature of his metaphoric repertoire, disappear from Aurora's verse. His couplets become not just arid, but airless."

"... not merely an efflorescence of his silence, but, in fact, the final evidence of his suffocation."

"'With everything at my disposal,' he writes, 'how can i describe nothing? Nothing but my own eyes, seeking some form, some recognizable shape, in the cold blank dark; nothing but my own eyes reflected in the glass window of the craft.'"

This needs to be used somewhere...

Well, baby: what can I say, the time has come. We expended ourselves in thousands of texts, chased each other through brief fables about windmills or ghosts or galaxies, breathless with inspiration, our phrases spilling down the screen like water struck from a rock; different than a photograph or a video because our words—ludic, horny, numinous—breaking open, crosspollinating, flooding that digital hothouse with spores and strands of musical code which mutated at the tips of our tapping fingers, stained with bits of yellow dust, into a dialect that belonged to no one, *a little language such as lovers use*, were not discrete, and despite reproducing grammatical duration, swore no fealty to time. Within the endless, ostensibly artless pages of our so-called text thread, sensitized in every shivering letter of our speech, pricking each other with sibilant splinters as seductive as Sappho's fragments, bursting our skins with sweet juices, gushing and fainting from spasms of nonsensical rhyme, we precipitated, profusely, as a residue of our love, a timeless, inadvertent book. Our visions were not smooth and separate; nor were they, despite their obvious affinities, complementary. On a microscopic scale they vibrated perpetually, their infinitesimal surfaces rubbing, chafing, shapeshifting at one thousand points, in search not of symmetry but of frictional, selfobliterative bliss; as long as we met each other there, in the blue glow of that neutral plane, that secret garden—we found our own form, we *melted into each other with phrases*. Only in the world, where the forms of beauty were so fixed, where I believed I could never be beautiful for him, only there did our love fail. Only in the world did he walk away.

As for you, I do not know who you are. I know only that you are likely everyone except Ezekiel, and yet right now I hope you are no one but Ezekiel, or if you must be notEzekiel, then I hope
(and now I am again briefly addressing Ezekiel as
Leonard Cohen addressed the crowd of onlookers standing or seated on blankets in the meadows

of the Isle of Wight in the year nineteenseventy at three in the morning as he prepared to sing *So Long, Marianne*—which is to say I am addressing Ezekiel as Leonard Cohen addressed the possibility of Marianne in a blurry early morning mass of strangers: 'This one's for Marianne,' he said in a sleepy amorous Barbiturate-inflected daze, 'Maybe she's here, I hope she's here...I hope she's here, Marianne...' and then he began strumming; so if you are here, Ezekiel, this next song is for you:)

I am sprouting in the sunless furrows of the Brain, petal by petal I am transmitting a graft of my abject Eden to one of the dull wet wordless folds of your occipital lobe. What a pleasure. To be here with you. And somehow I'm sparkling to you, somehow my sentences are haunted by a sparkling. Because I have made a secret of the alphabet (I'm calling my story a 'secret of the alphabet') but it is a secret that reveals itself only to those who—well, let me say that one man's trash is another man's treasure. But there is a sparkling nonetheless, so let's pray for both our sakes that today you find treasure. May I be extravagant with you? I swear they always misread my kitsch. I tell a story about a feather boa, and they applaud my courage. To them I'm always unintentional—caught in the act of my own candor. Once I spent a night in a stranger's arms, in an apartment crowded by ferns and old love letters and wooden reliquaries of ketamine or dehydrated oranges. He fingered me while I sipped vodka and talked about the feminine abandon of Tony Soprano's windblown bathrobe. The next morning I went to see my therapist, who asked me, at the end of our session, whether I knew my nipples were visible through the gauze of my sheer sequined blouse. She said she was *genuinely worried* I was unaware. As if I hadn't turned the head of every man on the sidewalk. And more than a few women, too. When I'm writing to you, truth be told, I remember that I am a 'transsexual.' I feel antiseptic. My love is cold, so cold—stuck like an echo in a series of caverns. It has been five years since I loved Ezekiel like I was inventing love. Now I have nothing left but dry retches. Pass me the lipstick and I'll write it all down, my beauty so useless and a Siren song. Let me forget about you in the dazzle of bright lights, and I'll rip open another dimension where angels fall forever.

The story I am about to tell you, the story of how I was visited by Saint Catherine of Siena, that story is not in two dimensions. But until you read me it is as hard to prove as a kaleidoscope turning in the dark. You are a slant of light: illuminate me.

IV.

This Very Instant

'Clay lies still, but blood's a rover…No I'll not, carrion comfort, look down that lonesome road. I love you, I love you, oh, the horror, the horror, and aroint thee, indeed and truly you've found a bad place to be lame in, willow, willow, willow…I must take the A train… Over the mountains of the moon,' the butterfly began, 'down the Valley of the Shadow…'
— Peter S. Beagle, *The Last Unicorn*

In New York I've had seven surgeries, four of them elective. I needed a change of scenery. I saw the inside of an operating room, and the inside of my cock. Or should I say cunt? At what point did one become the other? Were it a matter of phenomenology, I might say: as soon as I felt myself to be in possession of a cunt. Were it a matter of chronology, I might say: when the surgeon wiped my blood from the scalpel. Were it a matter of function, I might say: when a stranger stuck his cock inside me and, shoving my face into his pillow, filled my cunt with cum, after which, having without my knowledge declined to use a condom, he asked if I was on birth control, and, answering simply and truthfully, I said, no. Were it a matter of reading the fourth volume of Proust, I might say: my cock was never a cock, but a becomingcunt. Or: my genitals are neither cock nor cunt, but something else, something like the orchid that alters the form of its petals to attract a particular species of bee. But were it a matter of mysticism, I might say: when Catherine of Siena came to my bedside.

Whatever my genitals are, they once were a wound, having required stitches which, like semicolons or commas, prevented them from becoming, literally, formless. Eventually the stitches dissolved, as punctuation dissolves into a sort of rhythm or breath in the mind of a person reading a sentence. But a sentence does not require time to heal from a revision. A sentence doesn't bleed. For one month after their revision, my genitals bled. Sometimes I feel nostalgia for that period of uncertainty when my genitals were still taking shape, when I had no genitals at all, when I had a wound. It has always seemed strange to me that most every other fluid (spit, piss, cum, sweat, tears, shit and snot) exits through one foreordained orifice of my body (mouth, genitals, genitals, pores, eyes, ass, and nose) but blood has had no such outlet, except through inscription by blade.

It happened like this:

I drove to the city in a powderblue pickup, a Mourning Cloak, some Painted Ladies, and a swarm of Peacocks—the butterflies, I mean—fluttering and swirling in the truck bed, intermittently smudging the rearview as I glided down FDR on the run from some angels, my hair stuck full of cactus needles, a python curled around my right forearm.

Establishing shot of the New York skyline, glinting in the dusk: the spires of the Chrysler Building and the Cathedral of St. John the Divine (beneath which those albino peacocks strut), the arches of Brooklyn Bridge, the silent gold blaze of Lady Liberty's flame. Tracking shot of a carefree young woman, portrayed by Monica Vitti, singing along to a Waylon Jennings song on the car radio, the one about what makes life worth living, about guitars and women and Luckenbach, Texas.

For a season I lived in Bushwick with three divorcees. Sometimes, between subway tracks or in the cracks of sidewalks, I found yellow poppy petals; these I collected and, following the suggestion of the Roman poet Ovid, sprinkled with coal dust, revealing fragments of poems written in breast milk:

Life is worth little without a lyre –
a Woman – a warm campfire –

perhaps – it's time to Remember
the – Rustle – of doves –

Let's go to old Anthemusa
with Circe, Calypso and the girls –

One such postcard indicated that the Siren had survived and moved to Nashville, where she produced records for a number of popular artists whose names, for legal reasons, I cannot mention. Two years passed; the fourth wound became my cunt, the third my breasts, and the second—well, a crown of staples glinted from my forehead. Eventually I fell in love with a fairy named Noel and shared their bed. Noel, whose eyes were so wide and so blue—I tossed my words into them like coins into a fountain, where beneath a clear rippling surface they sank and sank and sometimes glimmered dully, flashing and briefly disclosing some alabaster depth of an unplumbed inner gloom. They didn't speak much, not for the first couple years at least. But they taped a piece of gray paper to the wall, on which they'd printed the following line from Gertrude Stein in faint white ink:

'In the morning there is meaning,
in the evening there is feeling.'

Noel and I have a cat named Loretta, to whom I often hummed a homonymous Townes song as she floated across the carpet like a silvering fog:

♥ Redacted quotation: verse three, lines one and two of "Loretta" by Townes Van Zandt, about a woman named Loretta who is prettiest at dusk and sweetest at dawn.

I sang to that fanged Delphic cumulus cloud drifting over the green woolen prairie as if the song *(the singing of it, the etherealized rasp of Emmylou's voice; Ms. Harris having, at this point in the film 'The Fifth Wound,' replaced Monica Vitti in the starring role)* constellated the cat and the line from *Tender Buttons*. 'Meaning' meant being sweet in the morning; 'feeling' meant being pretty in the evening.

SHOALS AT EBB-TIDE

The life I made together with Noel doesn't want to be told as a story. Noel never loved me for my stories anyway. Perhaps because I always wrote about lost love, so Noel was nowhere in my stories because Noel was never lost. Noel was my everyday, which is a story so infinitesimal and recursive that to tell it would take the rest of my life. Time after time, with a touch of their windchime fingertips, Noel woke me from my anesthesia; I woke them every morning with coffee, and fell asleep beside them each night watching Real Housewives. In the afternoons we tore each other to pieces. At dawn and dusk we made melodious babble. We lost track of our endings and beginnings.

But they didn't lose track of time; placing their faith in urgent instincts, sensing the genealogies stored in the shapes of things, in the drift of the shapes of use and beauty, they collected, like the material kin to my mythological kind, all sorts of antique trinkets—postcards, ashtrays, wood and ceramic containers, and most of all, lamps, because Noel was obsessed with gradations of glow, like a painter of air, the patron saint of boudoir shadows.

At noon I closed the shutters: summer light asked too much of my eyes. Between morning and evening were the burning hours when I traveled through a desert, blinded by the sun. It was so easy to stumble after a mirage, to be drawn away from mesquite branches, away from shade, among the red pebbles and the brush. No one could find me if I was lost within an hour, because I might be sitting in a cafe eating a pastry like anyone else, and if I screamed, no one would know why, no one would offer a hand. So I asked instead for a glass of ice water.

One blazing Saturday as I wandered along the gleaming white sidewalks of Alphabet City, blinking, pierced by the hands of the clock, glancing around as always for the possibility of those malefic forces who had peered premonitionally, all my life, through the windows at midnight, unseen, and later openly on the street, first for one reason (as if my face were a question waiting for an answer) and then for another (as if they were the subject and I, the object), nothing happened. I never stayed in the daylight long enough for anything to happen. I only left the house at night. Night was for scent and strobe and secret and silk. Daylight was a terrible confession, it was like admitting you were going to die one day at the exact location of your body.

Then one night in Late January—long before Noel became my best friend and he became my boyfriend; long before he gave me, on my birthday, his ex-partner's python, who I named Old Milk—Velvet and I went to Grand Central. Beneath a golden mesh of constellations glittering from a seafoam firmament, the room went round and round like a record, as if we were spinning the world with our feet. Eventually we leapt and pranced among the turnstiles, taking the A train home to Brooklyn. We held each other in my nun's chamber, Loretta settled between our legs. Later I went back into town for a show. On my way I passed the Chelsea Hotel, whose red neon marquee reflected itself into the wet night by holographic fragmentation, innumerable sparks catching within innumerable droplets like an awakening of souls—as if water itself were sentient. I wanted to fall in love with anything. I wanted to feel the wind in my feathers. I wanted a highway like a helix.

The show, Suzanne Bartsch's cabaret for the bachelorettes and the Midtown men, wasn't one I would have chosen myself: every other so-called joke was a shallow titillation about gender. Life's a drag and all that. I was out of place. I was drinking martinis. Around 2 a.m. I said goodnight and walked to the late-night A:

Half-wormhole, half-highway.

Carry me home.

Per usual I was wearing a tank top, this one ochre, and a short iridescent jacket (silver then green like fluttering leaves) whose inner lining (revealed by any stray breeze) was a phosphorescent shade of orange I've only ever seen in sunsets. I was tired. I had a hickey on my left tit. I looked pretty, but it wasn't my best hair day. And I was listening to Bob Dylan's album, *Desire*; really to one song, *Isis*, on repeat, attuned to an oncoming instant whose specific form was hidden by the blur of advent, because unlike so many other nights, leaving late from a Manhattan bar, drunk on vodka, rocked half to sleep by a lightspeed steel cradle, this time, as if fate were only a few steps ahead of me, I felt, falling over my mind, the shadow of a byway. It always came to me that way—as a sense of distance, extending. It had come to me like that before.

I don't know when I noticed that man, or if he'd been there before me. I remember taking a seat at the end of the powder-blue bench, by the doors. I remember the shuddering of the train. I remember intermittently closing my eyes, but only for a few seconds. I was restive, not with panic but with the inert dread of an inarticulate certitude. My attention was trembling like a compass.

There were only six others in my car. Three men and two women were seated, and another man, at the far end, was standing, staring. Stop after stop, at a slow but purposeful pace, he wove a way down the car. After a time, everyone had, to some degree, noticed, with wariness or worry. Oblique glances sensed the pattern of the weave. The man was silent. He was wearing a mask like the ones we all began wearing a month later. I could only see his eyes. His eyes and his hands. One or two times our gazes met diagonally. His hands were still, but his eyes were too many things at once. Halfway down the car, which was halfway between one station and another, the man began to stare, and I—vibrating with prophecy, sensing that he wanted to tell me something, sensing that we would be so intimate, sensing that I would never even know his name, sensing it all, I swear, except for the details, because the grain of the instant can only be felt by living it—

So I lived.

As the train pulled into the station, the man moved to the doors opposite my seat. The doors opened. He leaned out, glancing left and right. There was nowhere for me to go. Everyone was watching, waiting. Something was glinting between his fingers.

Then he crossed and stood beside me, face in profile, on the other side of the aluminum railing rising from the right side of my bench, staring straight ahead, out the open doors. I looked up at him through the bars.

He looked down at me.

His eyes were too many things at once.

I remembered the glinting; one half of an instant before it happened, I saw my fate.

The man wanted my eye.

I began to turn just as he began to swing. My turn was sharp. His swing was sharper. It made a deep and distant sound, like a glacier cracking.

The doors closed on the man vanishing up the stairs.

The train was moving, pulling away.

'That wasn't as bad as I thought it would be,' I thought.

'I'm not even bleeding.'

I looked around. Everyone was staring at my face.

Everyone was silent.

An expression of escalating horror suddenly appeared on the face of the woman across from me. 'But it was just a punch...' I took my headphones out of my ears,

"What happened?" I asked.

He was gone.

"What happened?"

Her mouth widened but she did not answer.

I looked around.

No one was answering.

Then blood burst from my right eye. Warmly, blood streamed down my cheeks and splashed between my breasts. When a man stabs you in the face, you do not see the fifth wound. You see a wing of blood—and I felt pleasure. The pleasure of warmth. The pleasure of my own exuberance. Being so alive. My scarlet song.

Before the blood came to mean something, before I was a woman who had been knifed on the subway, before the slow and unrelenting pains of an ongoing convalescence—I fell to the earth like a peach from a branch. Hot juices gushing, spilling from my split skin. Warmed to richness by the sun.

A man walked up to me, tilting his head.

"Holy shit," he said.

He was looking at me as if I weren't there.

Another woman yelled:

"Doesn't anyone have a napkin?"

At the next station, the train halted. The women sat on either side of me, ministering.

I told them not to worry, that I would be alright, that I just needed to make a couple phone calls. The men watched from afar. I called Noel first, then my mother. I woke both from sleep. I said:

"I'm going to tell you something upsetting, but I need you to stay calm."

"Okay," they said.

"Someone just hit me in the face," I said.

"I'm bleeding," I said. "But an ambulance is on the way."

To Noel I said,

"Please come."

A blue blur of police officers drifted toward me, resolving into single bodies: expressionless, slow, hungry. Hungry to extract a story from me. One after another they strode then shuffled balefully into the stalled car. The first said,

"We need to ask you some questions so we can file a report."

He waited.

"I'm not filing a report," I said.

"Come up to the precinct," he said.

"I'm going to the hospital," I said.

"We already called the ambulance. You can wait for it at the precinct. The train needs to move on."

One of the women said,

"I'll wait with you."

The other woman wished me well. The men were silent. We got off the train, and the doors closed, and the train vanished. They were gone. I haven't seen any of them since. But part of me went with them. I have seen any of them since…

Upstairs at the precinct, the cops stood around me in a semi-circle. Other cops filtered in and out. One danced with his taser.

The woman said:

"Do none of you have anything for her wound?"

With an air of exasperated somnolence, the officer turned languidly and tore a coarse segment of brown paper towel from a roll on the Formica counter behind him, extending it to me without looking at my face. Next to the roll was a sign that read, 'Clean up after your prisoners.'

"We need your identification," he said. The others stared, impassive.

I couldn't see out of my right eye.

"Your identification," he repeated.

The napkin was crimson, wet, already sopping.

"For the report," he said.

Blood was dripping from my chin.

"No," I said.

I had spent most of my life in a panic state. Panic is fivedimensional, like living too many instants at once.

"I'm going to the hospital on my own," I said.

For once I felt so calm. I was wide awake.

But he was angry, hungry. Smiling.

"You can't," he said.

I tossed the soaked napkin onto the floor.

It splattered redly in the harsh incandescent light.

"Why."

A fresh dark muck of blood oozed from the wound.

"Because we're holding you."

With my right eye I saw a glimmering abyss.

He began questioning the woman who was waiting with me. I panicked, because the woman was answering.

"You couldn't tell anything clearly," I said. "He was wearing a mask."

I do not remember precisely how many times they demanded a name, an address, a story, a simple story, a story without context, the story of a criminal and a victim, in which the police are the subject and both 'criminal' and 'victim' are objects—that is, objectified. The 'criminal' becomes the object of violence; the 'victim' is the means by which that violence is legalized. Put another way: a police report is nothing other than the scroll behind the blade of Empire. I refused to speak through that form.

He was a presence as brief as a knife. I never knew him as a person. He meant only as much as his eyes. His eyes are my mysteries. Forever I have his eyes. Every time I seduce them by knowing already, because I knew, as soon as one afternoon when Noel mentioned slashings, that I would meet you. I waited on every train, on every night, for three months. And when you arrived I looked at you knowing. I swallowed my life like a topaz, sharp and cold—because, by the time I realized the shape of the trap, I had nowhere to run. We had begun our locked-room mystery. There were seven of us, as if we were the guests at a dinner party. It was so intimate. Empire was performing an operation in which we were the irreducibles, and at the same time we were meaning something to each other about our own lives. Do your fingers ache? I punched a mailbox and fractured two fingers. Do you dream of me? I haven't dreamed of you...

I sacrificed half the instant to look up from my seat. He looked down. Our gazes met.

I had one movement to make.

I looked away.

*

Two years later, in another psych ward, a representative from victim services was sent to speak to me; I was entitled to compensation and a brochure full of services! Provided that I had filed a police report. In absence of a report, however, I was entitled to nothing at all. The smile faded from the representative's lips. Paradise is the sweetest apocalypse of all. Burning police cars, like beacon fires, announce its approach.

And as for my own mind? I'm making the mistake of wings, I'm not asking questions like falling or flying. A street and a sentence share an obsession with direction. Both control the flow of traffic, both demand compliance with syntax, with stoplights and crosswalks. To disrupt a street, invert your interpretation of its signs and signals: a crowd of people walking can frighten away an automobile. Once one automobile is frightened, the whole herd is frightened. If police approach from behind, prepare to clutter the road with patio chairs, aluminum barriers, disabled drones, paintings of the 'Founding Fathers,' silver reels of super-hero films, D.A.R.E T-shirts, debutante dresses and dense copies of the DSM-V, not to mention bags of birth certificates, police reports, arrest records, psychiatric histories, papal encyclicals, beauty tips, Ivy League charters, and 'travel brochures' from the Navy Recruitment Office, all swallowed in flames.

The same applies to sentences, whose function, perpetrated joyfully by elementary school grammar teachers, is to intimidate us into mistrusting our tongues, fearing our poesy, and conceding, at last, to the inevitability of linear time, conceding so inevitably that we agree to walk away from whoever we are attempting to reach: because as soon as I say 'Ezekiel and I were talking about what we would call our children...,' I am already eleven words further from him than I would have been, had I said nothing but his name. The laws of grammar constrict the flow of blood between present and past, reducing 'memory' to a whiff and perpetually deferring the resurrection of the dead. But every so often, bent over my writing desk in the silent hours before sunrise, I have sensed a faint static rising, scarcely audible, from the blue roiling reservoir of deep time, within whose swirling sediments some word or guitar lick catches a brief glint of light, illuminating, once more, the gold tooth of a longdead troubadour. So if I fold metaphors into my metaphors, gardening each instant into a paradise of lush green abstractions; that is, if I shatter a pane of cathedral glass and make a kaleidoscope from its colorful orts, swirling, tessellating, nearly resolving themselves into some Byzantine, incandescent design, which dissolves, instead, at the very instant of its revelation, into another, and another, and another—or if I interrupt this broadcast with the lisping lilt of Severo Sarduy, saying: 'The baroque sentence does not lead us to a pure and simple meaning, but rather, through a series of ellipses, zigzags, and détours, carries with it only a floating signifier, empty and polyvalent' or, 'the baroque stems from an image which contradicts itself, which hollows itself out' or, 'the baroque is the blind spot of the king,' I mean to say that when I lift, at last, a blade instead of a pen, and strike the center of my own blank page—blood, songs and holy babel will flow from the wound like a fountain of lost time.

An ambulance stopped beside me. The wound was beginning to ache. Two medics lifted me onto a stretcher and into the dark cabin, where I rested like a tongue inside a mouth. I was holding Noel's hand. We were on the road, gliding toward—somewhere. Whenever I'm on the road I pretend not to know where I'm going, because then I can remember where I am, which is nowhere, or more precisely: always somewhere else. Although I do not know where paradise is, paradise is in a place I do not know, and therefore when I do not know where I am, I am in this place too, this place which is nowhere, and nowhere is paradise. A perpetual fall is a form of flight because, like flight, it has no end, and what has no end has no direction. Which is to say those angels only fell because they arrived.

But just then I wasn't thinking about angels, because I was busy humming along to another Townes song, knowing the words without speaking or even thinking them, needing only the residue, that luminescence of meaning which the melody had, after so much aural sedimentation, absorbed from the words:

Noel rubbed cool cream into my hands. The cream mixed with flecks of blood. Afterward the cream was pink and they wiped it off with a tissue. They applied more cream. This

♥ redacted quotation: verse three from "Snowin' on Raton" by Townes Van Zandt, about the road, and the qualities the singer as well as his mother, brother, and darlin' each associate with it.

61

time the cream did not become pink. Gertrude Stein excised commas from her sentences and as a result her sentences reminded Noel of galloping horses. Of commas, colons and semicolons, Stein wrote: 'I have had a long and complicated life with all these.' Stein also wrote: 'The kindly way to feel separating is to have a space between. This shows a likeness.' Noel told me so, in the ambulance. I told them that Gertrude Stein would have enjoyed the *The Garden of Stories*, compiled by Liu Xiang (the twiceincarcerated librarian, astronomer and attempted alchemist) in the course of his extinguishing a slow silver inferno of moths from the dynastic archives of Han Yuandi, as I had my first year at university, hiding myself away, day after day, in a cubicle, before committing myself, each night, to the cum and champagne of other wayward fairies, to translate tales and poems written, according to Classical Chinese syntax, without a single comma, colon, or semicolon—without even so much as a full stop. I told Noel that Laszlo Krasznahorkai would also, for this reason, likely enjoy *The Garden of Stories*, having himself once said: 'The full stop belongs to God.' I told them Clarice Lispector began a novel with a comma. And then I told them the tale of Mizi Xia, as preserved by Liu Xiang in the seventeenth chamber of his Garden:

君遊果園彌子瑕食桃而甘不盡而奉君君曰愛我

而忘其口味及彌子瑕色衰而愛弛得罪於君君曰

嘗食我以余桃

The Duke was wandering the orchard when the courtier Mizi Xia bit a peach, and, struck by its sweetness immediately offered it to him. The Duke said, You love me so much that you forgot your own appetite. But as Mizi Xia's blush faded, the Duke's lust lessened. In later years he accused his lover of a crime. After all, he said, you once offered me your leftover fruit.

Put another way:

> 'The Duke was wandering the orchard when the court-
> ier Mizi Xia bit a peach and, struck by its sweetness,
> immediately offered it to him.
>
> The Duke said, *You love me so much that you
> forgot your own appetite.*
>
> But as Mizi Xia's blush faded, the Duke's lust less-
> ened. In later years he accused his lover of a crime.
>
> *After all*, he said, *you once offered me your left-
> over fruit.*'

Whoever loves us most, I said, will betray us. The best we can
do is prepare the scene. For centuries, poets alluded to acts of
love between two fairies by the presence, in their stanzas, of
bitten peaches.

The bitten peach—which even predates Genesis. Perhaps the
character of Eve was inspired, in part, by a starcrossed courtier.
Perhaps Eden is the recapitulation of an even older orchard.

*

My wound ached. Machines beeped in the dim rattling cabin.
I closed my eyes, holding Noel's small hand. 'Decrees attempt
to form a dam against what makes language fragile—contaminations, slovenliness, barbarism.' I remembered waiting for a
text from Ezekiel. I remembered my old roommate playing bass
with a Marlboro hanging from her lips. I remembered looking
up from a book and seeing smoke roll slowly through the petals
of a hyacinth. And I remembered the glow from her powderblue Bic flickering across a paragraph: 'But what you would
call barbarism,' wrote Glissant, 'is the inexhaustible motion of
the scintillations of languages, heaving dross and inventions,
dominations and accords, deathly silences and irrepressible
explosions...'

The mouth opened. I was spoken into the evening.

Then borne down a hall, while medics spoke above me like clouds. Noel followed behind silently; they were only five feet tall and somewhat elven, and nurses and doctors always ignored them or assumed they were my sister, or worse, my daughter. Many people misinterpreted their silence, just as many people misinterpret the silence of a tree. When Noel did speak, their voice reached me like the last echo of the unfolding fronds of a fern, rustling from the green murk of a Mesozoic forest.

I was wheeled into a wide bright room, whose myriad silver objects, inlaid with trembling red rubies in the shapes of letters and numbers—as if some glittering gusts of the Byzantine nebula, billowing beyond the Mediterranean long after the burial of the final Emperor, had circulated world-wide in the Age of Aquarius—were cluttered around a bed or more specifically a nest of tubes and colorful wires to which the aforementioned vibrating rubyencrusted objects were attached. I dozed, dazed and recumbent, atop a loose cotton sheet; five nurses took hold of its edges, and, as if I were a spider they'd coaxed onto a sheet of paper, tilting back their heads, careful not to touch me, lifted me from the stretcher and deposited me in the nest. These were minutes full of events: questions, footsteps, needles. Doors opened, and I glimpsed further and further depths of the cavern. A fairy with long, mascarathickened lashes leaned over me, blinking, waving bejeweled hands, attaching my IV to that external vein, at the end of which, like the excised lung of an angel, hung a sack of silver fluid. While wrapping my head in gauze, the fairy said the surgeon was stuck underground, but would arrive in a few hours. The fairy said not to allow a resident to stitch me up. The fairy said wait for the surgeon. "It's your face," said the fairy. The nest drifted through the doors, floating down hall after dim hall and past ornamented recesses, where others, similarly wrapped in gauze, were mumbling, turning in the halfdark. Noel was holding my hand. I was so tired. The tombs were so bright. Eventually we settled behind a stand of reeds or wheat, where we waited. Our very own arcosolium. Sometimes nurses parted the stalks, fluttering around my head like blue moths. Quietly Noel read Sappho's poems aloud, whispering: *and to yellowhaired Helen I liken you...*

>]
>] *among mortal women know this*
>] *from every care*
>] *you could release me*
>   ]
>   ] *dewy riverbanks*
>   ] *to last all night long*

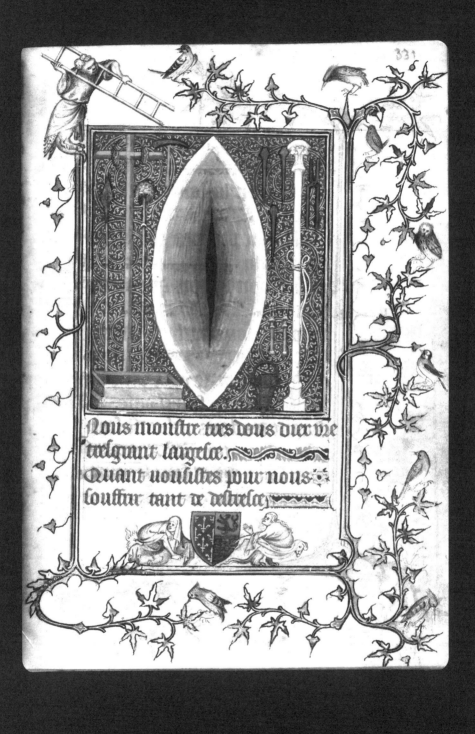

Nous monstir tres dous dieu vie
trelguant laigrese.
Quant voulistes pour nous
souffrir tant de destrese.

V.

Mount Sinai

This attractive piece of paper represents space-time…
- William Weir, *Event Horizon*

In order to describe it one would have to make a lightning bolt stand still.
- Machado De Assis, tr. Gregory Rabassa, *The Posthumous Memoirs of Bras Cubas*

- Townes Van Zandt, *High Low and In Between*

The wheat was still; the woman, wordless. Even Sappho was quiet. That fairy condensed beside the bed, sliding a needle into my arm. The syringe was thick with milky, opalescent fluid. Once it was inside me, I felt different. I closed my eyes; or I closed my left eye, because in fact I couldn't stop seeing with my right. The shimmering; that bright, latticed mirage of imageless sight (luminous vortex, matrix of light!) within which, as if within the cone of a blank, bloodless kaleidoscope, I saw—rotating, burning—five dimensional nests of splintered crystals, from whose

♥ redacted quotation: verse two, lines one through six, from "High, Low and In Between" by Townes Van Zandt, about the electromagnetic trace left in the wake of a man flying all alone at the speed of lightning.

fractal, involuted trellises had once sparked and combusted a profuse, colorful species of smoke (what we call "vision") until the air had been cleared by the swipe of a silver dagger—which, considered as a gesture, was really only the acute form of a flicked wrist.

No one ever taught me how an eye dies.

If it is all at once, like a guillotine of twilight.

Or slow, expanding, like the lamp of a locomotive knifing softly through the night. Horses lifting their heads in the fields— as you thrash and holler, with your foot stuck in the tracks.

Or if you live in the light forever, watching the crystals click and groan.

Nonetheless I thought: *this is the beginning of blindness.* Nonetheless I was silent. Nonetheless I listened to the flutter of moths, of pages of Sappho, of a surgeon's coatsail. As he wheeled me to the operating room, the surgeon begged me to file a police report. Why would I tell my story to the police? Why throw pearls before swine? Let me say now that I dedicate the fifth wound to my blood. I dedicate it to the poet who wrote with a knife for a quill and my face for parchment. I dedicate it to Ezekiel's antlers. I dedicate it to the speck of shadow, growing in my bright abyss. I dedicate it to the memory of Noel's face, on the sidewalk, as they wiped the blood from my breasts. I dedicate it to the name my mother gave me. I dedicate it to the names I give myself. I dedicate it to the song she wrote in 1986 and performed while cooking chickenfried steak in the kitchen in 2001, while I was out in the pecan woods, watching horses foaming, forming from whirlwinds of purple dust, and so I dedicate it to my mother singing: 'my daddy is buried in Texas, with a bluebonnet field for his head...' I dedicate it to the memory of the peacocks of a small desert town. I dedicate it to this moment that is not already gone, okay? I dedicate it to the shadow growing not larger, but nearer, dimensionalizing, particularizing into a mouth, a gesturing hand, a woman speaking, saying: 'Dearest Sister: I, Catherine, come to you now in the name of the pustules swelling milkily sour in your eye, and in the name of the spittle on your chin, and in the name of your precious blood, to offer this Book of Hours, formerly in the possession of the daughter of John the Blind, the sickly Bonne de Luxembourg, who died before her wedding day, until I dislodged it mere moments ago from her sepulchral clutch, and lest I forget, inside which, marking the apposite page, is a yellow poppy petal from your longlost paramour, the Siren of Anthemusa, and an epistle from that tombtongued rounder, Ezekiel, all of which will be yours if you allow me to sip from the font of your wound...,' at which moment she opened the tiny fiveinch tall psalter to its extraordinarily delicate three hundred and thirty first page, on which was painted, by Jean Le Noir and his daughter Bourgot, in Paris, in the year 1349, a rectangle as richly blue as Mary's robes, wherein thin golden vines, from whose profusion emerges, like a cavern dug into the abyss of the blank page, a red oblong slit, faded in the middle from the daily pious strokes of frail Medieval fingertips and representing, so said Catherine, 'the piercing of Christ's side by the Holy Lance of Longinus,' though on that page there was no Christ in sight, there was no Christ at all, only the fifth wound, eddy, swirl, and spiral: 'but,' I asked, bending toward the heart of a pinkish honeysuckle, blooming forever in a blue field; beginning to imagine Pontius Pilate as a nurse, and Longinus as a surgeon, and Calvary as a windswept operating room, 'but,' I asked, seeing the Holy Lance as a scalpel, and the cross as a handcarved operating table, and the Crucifixion darkness as a crude, celestial anesthesia, 'why are you addressing me in English, when Catherine was from Spain,' to which she, pressing a finger not only onto the surface of the page, but into the scarlet pool at its center (where it disappeared, swallowed by sudden wet depth, at which moment I felt, inside my own cunt, the pressure of an invisible hand) before lifting it back out (instantly the pressure ceased) droplets of bloodred ink rolling into her palm and along her wrists, replied, 'Ye of little faith...,' before I, horny, resplendent, and recognizing, now, that daunt-less daydreamer Jesus of Nazareth not as some Son of God, but in fact, for what else was the crucifixion, another one of my ts_foremothers, the symbol of whose sex reassignment sur-gery adorns every Church, Nunnery, and Rosary, noticed the imprint, upon her robes, between her hips, of a cock, exclaiming, 'you're one of the girls,' at which she smiled, lifting the ancient psalter to her lips, pressing her tongue into the cave, laughing, lapping, plunging, until I gasped, and some small dense point, some hot atom, hovering, vibrating within *my* hips, loosened, brimmed and broke open, flooding my bedsheets with waves of thick, translucent liquor, not once, but twice, three times, each time thicker and sweeter than the last, until Catherine, withdrawing her tongue from the small tome, her lips glazed with fluid, began to speak, pausing every so often to puff on a small silver flute that she let slip from the sleeve of her robe: "I confesse me own naim is nat Cathryn (with womme, on a sojorn in Siena, hi ene shared a bedd, hin witche the ledi did tell, by flaume o fir, the storie o hou sche diskcovert *the exqui-zet flavour of puss*, having drank't in drauchts from the fetide brest of a dying nonne) but Elean'r Rykener, & I has't cum to thee, ladee-birde, & to thy dismole twinti-ferst centurie, flowen from the deputees of yond cok-souker John Fressh, May'r of Lunden, quo aresten me for wot he cald *illud vitium detest-abile, nephandum, et ignominiosum*, but wot that lofeli laven-dere Anna noumed *the ars of womonly lofve*, drest as I wos in the twyfyls of Elizabeth Brouderer, quo riven n'ornature wich ravisht ev'n the most pompe-holi, evangelik mounk, & mani a nonne withal—quo recompensed me roialli, as beffits me gla-si-eied devine lusstes; me souel as stille as a cistirn of cristal, me mones as wilde as cloudes of develish dost. Fie upon thee, John Fressh! Ingon to me costli Chaumbre o Venus, glorifiinge mine pertnesse *ut cum muliere*, then rebprobaten me for't en torne. Alf the lordshipinge coks of Lundun cunnen to impregnayt me, but I roted their forth-getinges in me womeles wome. Fie upon 'em, rif and raf! Fie upon 'em, fie! But to thee, undedli Anna, flour of poetes, princise of fleshli kenning, godcund kinne o mine, quo sugren thy rimes with me honi-swete semene, to thee I fore-saien: e-halouyd be thy naim. Hit were Anna me y-tolde, ladee-birde, hou tha mistik o Siena ware sermounen abote a cristly queynte, *bryme of blod, whirl-pit o swirlen tyme*, vailed en a Bowk o Houres, *within wose skarelet watir dos't swyme the hole memeri o' heven...*'

Well, what can I say: I invited her into my bed. We gossiped, drank whiskey and nibbled a psychedelic herb Elean'r had plucked, she said, from a meadow above the cavern where Mary the Nazarene lies sleeping, awaiting the return of her apocalyptic paramour, that so-called God who left her in a stable to raise a celestial rake of a son. I asked her, after a while, why she'd come to me. Of all the women and all the wounds, why, *leapfrogging the Middle Ages*, arrive here, at my hospital bed?

"Th' erche-bishope bidden a sinode, determinaten whethir to pelf the perles of yourez treuli, kepin Frankish custume. Popelards. Onne & awl braundishen scrappes o biblikal logike abote th' blessed-fulli fecound ribbe o Adam, debaten wethir to glose hore Celsitude as mane or wyme—so, heften a Talmudic boke o ethymologies opon th' flint-ston auter, wirlen through lifes o papire, a-wowen 'ribbe' was a heretikel translacioun o th' semi-opake Ebreu wort fer cok-bon, & thairfore Eve horselfe possessen a rer anatomie, & soe on, I fieden 'em thair ouen feith. Wid a flik o hisse wyrst, th' erche-bishopc ordren a soudiour t' forcaste me en th' cripte; & wid a tilt o hisse hed, commaunden a louli clerek t' born th' bok en tha chirch furnaise. Hit were hydous to bihold, adournen wid goldfoyl engels & po-cok sculs. Litel Helle. En me selle I smellen th' brenninge. Empti hours excepten smoc an terrour. Bot I kape my mynde abote me. Barren en th' donjon derk, I ben secchen a wei oute. Whanne th' soudiour wandren off t' sipp 'is silvir pype, I slipte the Ladee d' Luxembourg's sauter fro my pokette, studien thouse tym-lesse faie cifrys by mone-light.

Was al-weies skilli wid a redel, bot th' pinchinge fingeres o th' clokke forbeden mi innesight, tha Satournine leiser reqyred fer anagogik visioun: ech tyme th' soudiour smoken fer not mar thanne a hanfol o minets, soe lyk th' diven-byrde I plungen inte mi tresour-hous o instants, questen fer a luminose keie. Bot mi hants ben emti, untille, onne th' thrid dei, reclis, wan-hopli, hi clofen mine leppes to th' y-wonded bowk—& t' mi wondire, deuen mi oun moueth w' blod. Ther ben no tyme fer savouren. Heringe fot-steppes on th' tile-ston, I gulpen th' rosi-heued holi licour...& thenne...per-happes et was...glinsing th' sauter's gilden spine, th' soudiour scremen, thouh hisse vois semen feint as a gnatte, bicause a blest o wend ben whirlen o'er me, wherlen o-round lyk byrd soungs on a dronken daun, stomblen mi-self hom somme mourning fro' a forest revelrie, Anna drest en nothink excepped th' grene fronds o ferns, bre-ken on a lafter, spellen here peche-sweted pocioun, th' worled kaleidoscopen wi' leefs & fethers, wi' lantron-lyt, topas eies, & wode-madenli lof-sounges..."

"I mean, okay," I said. "I have a thousand and one questions."

(I have omitted my questions here following the luxurious logic of the Apostle John as first translated from Latin into English by John Wycliffe, to whom Pope Gregory XI—terrified of the proliferating hermeneutics of a churchless, polyphonic Pious, who would therefore no longer require the papal per-formance of gnostic paratext—applied the epithet 'Master of Errors' in a Bull issued from Rome in 1377, which authorized the arrest of not only the aforesaid John but 'any who may be infected with the errors,' which, wrote the Pope, 'he vomits forth from the filthy dungeon of his breast'; that is, following John's translation of the last line of John's book: 'And ther ben also manye othere thingis that Jhesus dide, whiche if thei ben writun bi ech bi hym-silf, Y deme that the world hym-silf schal not take tho bookis, that ben to be writun,' or put another way, 'There were many other things that Jesus did, which, were they

74

to be written out into books, I believe the world itself could not contain the books that would be written,' which is to say, years and further years from now Elean'r is wandering in and out of my stories like that glitchy, fairyencumbered horse shimmering between the lines of a sylvan barcode in Magritte's little green painting, *The Blank Signature*: you will meet her again in another time, where she is now, as sure as she is here, because you are reading not a residue of things past, but the fleck of a future, a record of things to come; however, should you like to peruse the transcript of my thousand and one questions, I invite you to send an email to: silicone_angel69@hotmail.com)

"T' explain hou & whie I neue-cumen t' yor bedde wod rekere lalen en Proserpine's molded pome-garnet tung, whos mys-tunes, rymes & reks o rotte ben levelen by ani attempt at Englishen, lyk tellen a sweven en th' forme o' th' fabel. I mene t' sai: by telen et to yew, I wold distry th' storii..."

"So teach me how to sing."

Elean'r narrowed her eyes. She is narrowing her eyes. One day Elean'r will narrow her eyes and a fly will taste the fungus softly leavening from the surface of a peach:

"Et thes bok," she said. "As Gawd commaunden en th' Boke o' Ezekielle, chaptire thre, vers won."

She slipped the psalter from her sleeve.

"& do ye knou," she said, "wot Gawd saiste en vers tewe?"

The wounded page was brimming, clotting the rest with blood.

"Not a clue," I said.

"'Y openyde my mouth and he fedde me with that volym,' wraithen Ezekiel. 'He seide to me, Sone of man, thi wombe schal ete, and thin entrails schulen be fillid with this volym, which Y yyue to thee. And Y eet it, and it was maad as swete hony in my mouth.'"

So I ate the psalter and the poppy petals and, in homage to his Biblical cameo, the letter from Ezekiel (who had, he wrote, overheard a primrose whispering fragrantly to a hummingbird about a poem which, according to one of few faint fragments of immemorial perfume he had precipitated, ad hoc, into a pinkish powder of phrases, was called *The Fifth Wound*, 'starring Monica Vitti and Townes Van Zandt,' and which he assumed, based on its audience, was written by his foregone darling, that is, the woman now recumbently musing at Elean'r Rykener in a timeless nest; that is, the woman, known as 'Hour Ledi o the Brochen♥ Tonge,' whispering sweet nothings in Elean'r's ear: the same woman who is writing, right now, to you. Knocking at the door of the inn. Of course, I can't promise anything but leftover fruit. Nonetheless, Ezekiel asked to read this story. And how can I resist? How sad, how lovely, for auld lang syne…I'll sing my song to a nightingale, then send her to the rickety porch of a blue house, where he sits, right now, smoking a yellow cigarette, drinking beer, and every so often glancing through a sparse copse of evergreens at a languid flock of deer—and in particular a huge, heavyantlered stag—stooping to pluck dandelions from the gravestones of a cemetery, but otherwise scratching words in a small, blank book, twitching with little inspirations, attempting, while just below his right ear a pearl earring dangles, intermittently, in the dusk, to complete a poem about who knows what. Inside the house, a silver, halfiridescent kitten plays beside the bookcase, chasing butterflying flecks of twilight. Ezekiel, when you read this, imagine me as you always do, a boy before sunrise, beside you, holding my head up with my hand, talking about being writers someday. I'll never be that boy again, not for anyone.

♥ Brōchen (v.): (a) to pierce or slash, as with a knife or sword (b) to spur on a horse (c) to incite one's tongue to speech

A boy's will is the wind's will. Thoughts of youth are long, long thoughts. *When I hear a cuckoo, even in Kyoto, I long for Kyoto.* And so on.)

My teeth were blue and my tongue was goldfoiled; my edible went from zero to sixty in a blink. Soon me and Elean'r came up with a plan. Because the Siren gave me a call, and an address somewhere west of the Pecos. She'd been moonlighting as a drag queen in smalltown bars, sailing across those seas of creosote:

ring-ring......ring-ring......ring-ring......

click

"hello honey

...

you know who

...

the castaway muse

...

well I simply haven't had a chance

...

why because I'm in the middle of the desert

...

off Route 66

...

I'm calling from a payphone

...

well because I lost my conch shell

...

come find me will you?

...

I'm fine. In fact I'm having an affair

...

she's a breeze, darling. Name of Westron Wynde. Of course
I just call her sweetheart..."

Long story short, as they say. She wanted to move back to
Anthemusa and start a band. So we did.

('People imagine three Sirens,' wrote Isidore of Seville in his
Etymologies, 'who were part maidens, part birds, having wings
and talons; one of them would make music with her voice, the
second with a flute, and the third with a lyre. They would draw
sailors, enticed by the song, into shipwreck. In truth, however,
they were harlots, who, because they would seduce passersby
into destitution, were imagined as bringing shipwreck upon

them. They were said to have had wings and talons because sexual desire both flies and wounds. They are said to have lived among the waves because the waves gave birth to Venus.')

Well, look, before I tell you about all that: I blinked. My left eye received the world. Noel was asleep, their finger between the lips of the pages of Sappho. The automatonic oracles prophesied in ruby runes. Unseen birds, nestled somewhere in the tubes and wires, warbled their wistful, faroff songs. The nurse unmoored my immense nest, sending me downstream to a blindingly bright room, where for one hour, I ceased—for an instant. One cubic inch of death. Let me touch you ever so lightly. Roots seek water. Butterflies rise and fall. Blood floods the chambers of the heart. The flowering of the lungs. The shimmering of saliva, of seafoam. A body was timeless. Forever. I can't tell you anything more because it is my secret. Besides, because words can't say nothing. And it was nothing.

Meanwhile, abiding by the seconds on the clock, the surgeon, suture by suture, sewed my wound shut. When I woke a nurse handed me a mirror. I touched the stitches. I thought of my grandmother, drowning in her own lungs in 1982, obsessed with time, tatting, with trembling hands, like a spider attempting to bind the hands of the clock, colorful blankets and embroideries for grandchildren she would never meet. I thought of one in particular, pink and powderblue, my own, which, long before it reached me, was torn and mended by her hands. I'll never know why. She is buried beneath a slate gravestone outside of Baltimore, near a field of horses. Error is the trace of a soul. Of my grandmother, writing. Of a song.

We flew the biplane home from the hospital. Noel kissed me for a long time before returning to their plants: groves of honey mushrooms, blooming from islands of moss and stone; fields of yellow poppies swaying in the airconditioned breeze; green whorls and greener curlicues tumbling down the bookshelves, and so many ferns that Loretta, except for those brief instants when she pokes her pink ears through the canopy, is sensed mostly as a rustling in the fronds. I'll be listening for you on the radio, they said.

I called the Siren. She was taking tea with Elean'r on a little boat off the coast of Crete. Chart a course for Anthemusa, I said. I'll bring snow.

Excuse me while I powder my nose.

Our band is called *Becoming Horse Girls,* after a phrase from Eva Hayward: "I start to wonder if my 'conjugated equine estrogens' are reshaping my species, becoming horse, along with my sex…,' not only because of that pale dust, condensate of reeking evaporations, brews of piss and butanol—performed anywhere you please, on a porch, in a cave, so long as you arrange, bubbling, brimming with bright fluids, an altar of glowing glass vials, from each of whose thin, transparent tubes swirls, drifts and evaporates a restive, iridescent mist of Appaloosa mares; and beakers, flasks, fluorescent syringes flickering in the dark of a Texas desert grotto, as dimly luminous as those rows of blue Catholic candleflames burning fitfully before the niche of Saint Catherine in the Chapel of the Madonna del Voto, that is, within the right transept of the Cathedral of Siena, which is to say, according to the Cathedral's architectural mimesis of the crucifixion (that is, of the crosswinged bleeding Christ, nailed in full featherless flight) below his ribs, but above his hips, such that the timeless statue of Catherine, cloudeyed, ecstatic, holding, in her right hand, a bouquet of marble lilies, stands within the curve of the *cristly queynte*—by whose languorously rigorous alchemies you may compress the urine of a pregnant mare (within whose gut a tiny, breathless nonbeing begins to trellis its skeleton with vines of blood) into a pearl of estrogen, which, if dissolved, ritually, morning and night, upon your tongue, will not only leaven your breasts, but also slowly revise that gray clod of tissue called the thalamus, wherein a whirlwind of confetti, pink scraps and tinsel, a wild, harlequin fog of so-called *sensory data*, that is, the pure chaos of perception, is transfigured into brief, dense sparks of light within the brain, which, in their most acute form, are felt as pain or pleasure: but also because, apropos of all equine matters, while the Siren felt, in a sort of flick-of-the-wristed *agape* sense, indifferently amicable, Elean'r and I loved to dream about horses. And Elean'r, she liked to wear my cowboy boots to bed. One man's trash is another man's treasure. A mare's piss is a transsexual's milk. *My mother is a horse.*

This is not the end: It's just the beginning. This is a book of doors. This is a book of tunnels. This is a switchboard. It is for passing through. For conjuring dimensions. For the first words of a dreamworld. If you have a question for one of the girls, or to join our mailing list, fold a letter and place it into this bottle. Toss it out to sea. The waves will carry it our way.

Allow me to close with a benediction from Rachel Rabbit White's *Porn Carnival*:

If the room could have a springtime
if the temperature
could make a reader gay

'Xe and Xir are for angels' they raise

Jesus knew what they were doing
when I was handed a silicone cock
And silicone tits

xo,
Hour Ledi o the Brochen Tonge

BOOK TWO

FROM NOUGHT TO NOUGHT — IN UNSUBSTANTIAL TRADE —

I.

A Second Chance at Nothing Much

> I've been afraid here before. I just didn't know it was fear.
> I became afraid and I stopped writing.
>   - Charlotte Gainsbourg, *Antichrist*

> Filled with a holy anger against herself, she said 'thou
> shalt swallow what inspires thee with such horror.'
>   - Raymond of Capua, tr. George Lamb,
> *Life of Catherine of Siena*

> I swallowed your cum! That means something!
>   - Cameron Diaz, *Vanilla Sky*

The wind bloweth where it listeth, & thou hearest the sound thereof, but cans't not tell whence it cometh, and wither it goeth: so it is with Ezekiel. After three years of silence I sent him a short email titled: "poet?"

I asked if he had become a poet. I told him about my pussy. I told him I would be visiting Austin over the weekend.

That Saturday evening we met for tea. He wore, as always, a blousy shirt buttoned low. I kept my composure as if I were wearing a corset, kept my distance like an uncertain horse, with the same majesty of uncertainty as a stallion; my hair was so long then, cascades of waves dyed blonde, ending in deep golden ringlets bouncing, falling luxuriously over a sheer swashbuckler top that revealed, halfway to opacity, lilac lace, the silhouette of my bralette. We smiled like co-conspirators, because a night like that has potential. Certain restrictions are softened by moonlight or moonshine. "I saw my exboyfriend for the first time in three years…" is a story already, which is to say, it's an answered prayer, which is to say, it's gossip, which is to say: it's available for the making of meaning, so there was all the more reason to think narratively rather than consequently. He asked me to his apartment. All the books I had given him (*Soulstorm*, *Seiobo There Below*, etc.) were on his shelf, along with others I remembered watching him read (*The Charioteer*, *Swann's Way*), or remembered him talking about on the phone, and many more from the blank time, the three years in which my mind had consigned him to a perpetual past, forgetting for my own ease that every instant of mine concurs with one of his. Before returning to college, I had given him a stool, once sat upon by troubadours beside strange campfires for support while strumming a banjo, lute or lyre; this stood mutely before his books. He was in the kitchenette, beyond a folding screen, making drinks. But he invited me to lie in his bed, to place my head on his pillow. To smell the scent of his hair. Damp soil. Cedar and moss. Soon he fluttered to the bedroom, passing me an iridescent drink, taking a seat on the floor, reading to me about the ritual of mummification. The weight of two lungs, stuffed with spices. The supernal blankness of a face whose brain has been unraveled with a thin hook, fold by fold, through the narrow chambers of the nostrils, until every memory is replaced with a drop of resin or grain of cinnamon. He leaned close to my face, his lips slick with spit and whiskey. His eyes pinned me to the instant, like a butterfly. For a moment, he was silent. For a moment he breathed the air between us, the musk of us, the night we rustled in the strawberry bushes, the night we were licked by the tongues of fallen angels.

Then, whispering, as dim and fitful as a flame at wick's end; but as still, as hot and clear as a pool of melted wax—then, whispering, leaning close, so close I smelled stables, straw, fresh milk, he said:

'Is there sexual tension between us?'

Mute violence of the passive voice. His gaze was ravenous

and irresistible and I did not trust the form of his question, which implied his desire without naming it, in order, I sensed, to convince me to reveal my own. So I asked him, instead, if he felt it.

He said yes.

'I do,' he said. He was staring at me just like he had that night a century ago, in a blue kitchen. When he had kissed me for the first time, forever...

'But we shouldn't,' he said.

Very carefully, hesitantly, articulating every word precisely, as if the sentence were a lake, frozen midwinter, which I needed to traverse, not knowing where the ice was thick, and where thin, now starting, now pausing, 'What the fuck,' I said, 'is wrong with you?'

'I just felt so much tenderness,' he said.

And I, *like the nightingale whose melody is crowded in the too narrow passage of her throat*:

'Tenderness?!'

'I thought...' he said.

Scrawny sphinx. He had come to me at midnight, had sung like a distant echo, had led me to a waterfall and dissolved therein at dawn.

Yet another hall of mirrors: when I reach out for you, I touch myself.

'For god's sake,' I said, pressing my finger into the chestnut hair curling sparsely from his halfunbuttoned plaid, tapping each word upon his skin: '*You* – said – *you* – wanted – *me*.'

Though I fell silent, I did not remove my finger. He pressed his chest against it, elongating our contact by his refusal to acknowledge it. He was gazing into my eyes, his two eyes blazing auburn fathomless and silent as he said,

'I thought that if I named it, I could neutralize it.'

(The first time I knifed my forearm was a Friday night in September of my sophomore year, after a summer making potpourri and working at a hotel in the mountains outside of Beijing, where one night in the employee dorms two of my coworkers, all of us laughing conspiratorially as if we were having a sleepover, painted my face with rouge, eyeshadow and mascara, and a third said it was a pity I wasn't born a woman because I looked so beautiful. When I looked in the mirror that night I immediately saw the woman that had been humming near the surface of my skin, I mean I really gasped because my reflection was offering me the revelation of a glimpse, a first instant untouched yet by disbelief, disgust, outrage and desire, faith, scalpel, or indistinct blade, untouched by embodiment except for the lightest form of being, just the very first instant of a woman waking up, confused by her own beauty—a woman becoming aware of her existence, an awareness rising like television static, surging, separating into dazzling syllables, silhouettes of meaning sharpening into stilettos of glow, the notes of a falsetto like neon needles cloudbusting from a fog of reverb, the shatteredcandy ballad of a woman singing live on screen in another room, playing her songs on endless loop, whose voice, which I had for so long only heard as buzzing, for years had mistaken for a buzzing—as if god couldn't spare his angels, so had instead sent topaz mosquitoes, the mosquitoes of heaven—I now understood to be a sweetened scream, a radiation of melody. That night, borne along by the care of my coworkers, I experienced innocently the thrill of feeling before thinking, knowing before understanding, experiencing before fearing, that is, the opaque materialization of a meaning suddenly crushing the spires of the labyrinth of interpretation with the span and density of its mystery—not by my own foresight or orchestration, but by the Piscean ease of my surrender, I mean my sudden splendor, thoughtless as a ripe strawberry, and by the whims of intuitive friends, the intuitive whims of new friends, who because of their fresh affections are often the prophets of our present instants, and whose inscription of lipstick, on my lips, on that night, opened the portal through which the green and pink breeze of my aurora first appeared.

Ten years earlier my mom had taken me on a trip to Hong Kong, where ten years before that I was born, and to Beijing, where anywhere we went, when people spoke to me, they addressed me as *xiao guniang*, which, years later, I learned means *little girl*, suddenly translating my memories and experiencing, all at once, a delayed gust of joy followed by a repercussive shock of grief.

When I returned to college after my potpourri summer, I did not correspond to my established relations. I needed to swirl myself into a circle of nymphs, I desperately needed to find someone who shared my faith in whatever would express a yearning for *being beautiful together*—but I only dimly understood that I was looking in the wrong place, that there was no will-o-wisp waiting for me in a stone courtyard, in the midst of dusk. Two weeks into the semester, a classmate who I didn't know at all, had only ever met once, committed suicide. Then everyone was talking about suicide. I felt something scraping at me, something that made the afternoon frightening, as if sunlight were exposing something, and made the evening an abyss, as if that same thing were still there but now I could not see it. I didn't want to be aware of it and I got drunk on Fireball. Later I had an argument with my friend because I thought his treatment of a girl was cruel and careless, not to mention conceited, but tangled in the emotion of that argument were the splinters of my love for him, which were all the more painful because I wasn't aware of them and therefore could not anticipate their sting or pluck them myself in solitude. Our friendship had catalyzed my identification as a 'cis gay boy' and his as a 'cis lesbian,' supposedly our mutual liberation—so to admit to myself that I was in love with him would have not only have required rejecting my understanding of our friendship, but rejecting, also, the understanding of myself on which I thought our friendship was based; what I had thought was salvation was in fact Empire once more scrambling my intuition, enforcing a repression from which my heart suffered while my mind persisted in sawdust delusion. Reality wasn't making sense. If I don't know I'm in love—because repression isn't forgetting, isn't losing, isn't disintegration, but a thickening, an arctic clotting, a long, slow freeze expanding, sealing the chambers, cracking the vaults and arches of my dreamworld, until I feel a crazing in my ribs and a chill in my lungs—then I cannot exorcise it, because I only sense its pressure, but do not know its name, and what cannot be addressed cannot be called forth, but cannot either be ignored, so it must be relieved manually, that is, by whatever means my hands could find. I went back to my room and turned off the lights. I drank from the bottle beside my bed. I broke a shaving razor with the heel of my boot. I sliced my skin, then sliced my wound, then sliced the wound within my wound. My blood was spattering the hardwood. I hid my arm and walked in circles around New Haven. I sat on the green and babbled to myself. A friend followed me and wrote down what I said. He followed wherever I went, saying nothing, because he didn't know what to say but knew how to be a witness, knew that not looking away was a form of love. Slowly he guided me toward the hospital. I walked into the emergency room, bleeding. I said goodbye. I was shown to a cot in a bright, crowded hallway, where a resident carelessly stitched my wound. Twenty stitches. So she said. She wasn't looking while she tied them. I sobered. My head was throbbing. After a few hours, a tall German psychiatrist in a starched lab coat approached and asked me in a gentle, clean and indifferent voice, like that of a curator, about what he referred to as my suicide attempt.

'It wasn't a suicide attempt,' I said.

'Your incision suggests otherwise,' he said.

Apparently my wound was a mouth. Blood is an opaque language. Everything it says is vital and far too decadent.

'Had you sliced horizontally,' he said, 'we would classify that as self-harm. But the fact is, you sliced vertically. A vertical wound suggests, in the overwhelming majority of cases, hopelessness, despair. Intent to die.'

Well. 'The artist is present,' I said.

He placed his marble hand on mine and asked whether I was interested in spending a couple nights in the psych ward. I had a paper to write by Monday on the poet Li He, whose introduction in a volume by François Cheng, lying open on my desk earlier that afternoon, had distracted me briefly from my own distraction: "Dead at the age of twenty-six, he left a body of work striking in its strangeness. Through an incantatory style filled with lavish images, he unveils phantasms. In his poetry, of shamanic and Taoist inspiration, collective and personal myths are side by side. To present his vision of the universe, he invents an entire personal bestiary. To indicate the secret correspondences among things, he combines images of different natures. Thus, he speaks of flowers that shed tears of blood, of a wind with laughing eyes, of the color of a tender sob, of the old red that gets drunk, of late violet, of lazy greens, of green decadence, of the greening solitude, wings of smoke, of the arms of clouds, the paws of the dew, of the sun that sounds like breaking glasses, of the musical moon with the sound of stone, of emptiness that lets us hear its voice and laughter. In this universe where the marvelous mixes with sad or grotesque elements, the poet regulates the rites of communion through blood: 'My angry blood under ground in a thousand years will be green jade.' 'Before my soul and my blood freeze, to whom should I speak?'"

'I don't know,' I said.

A few seconds passed.

'I think it might be best for me to go home and get some rest,' I said. 'I have a paper due Monday.'

He blinked. He pressed his wireframe glasses up the bridge of his nose, and with an air of delicacy and precision:

'Well,' he said. 'I'm committing you.'

'Oh.' In the distance someone was screaming.

'I just wanted to give you the illusion of choice,' he said.

I sang *Angel From Montgomery* in the ward's weekly

talent show, and my peers asked for an encore, for which I performed a rendition of Molly Ringwald's lipstick trick from *The Breakfast Club*—that is, I borrowed a bra from another involuntary guest and stuffed it with socks, then convinced one of the nurses to allow me to wield a tube of coral lipstick long enough to lodge it in my cotton cleavage and apply lacquer to my lips, handsfree.

One afternoon a therapist asked why I felt the urge to wound myself. I told him I felt stuck in an instant, so I make an opening. I told him that immediately after I wounded myself, I felt beautiful and close to god. He was excited, almost giddy. He said, 'That's just like these Mayan priests, you should look them up...' Another therapist recommended Dialectical Behavioral Therapy. She said all my life I had carried an abstract emptiness inside me. The emptiness itself could not be described; only its effects.

Seven days later I was discharged. A psychiatrist from Yale told me I was a danger to myself and others and would not be allowed to return to campus until I had demonstrated mental wellness. He said I could apply for readmission in a semester, but if in the future I harmed myself again, I would maybe not be able to return at all—so in the future I avoided the hospital, or I went to an urgent care a town away and said I'd had a sculpting accident.

Authority figures often paid an almost paranoid attention to my fantastical or visionary impulses, which were inextricable from my nascent femininity and mental destabilization. When in high school I was coaxed into an evangelical cult—where, like a doublecrossed inversion of a queer commune, many youth pastors had piercings, dyed hair, listened to Sufjan Stevens and read poetry, but declared their individualized marriages to Christ and therefore their collective relation to one another as family (that is, a facsimile of polyamory, a facsimile of chosen family), evinced an obsession with the Crucifixion (that is, body horror), and expressed a belief in the Transfiguration (that is, shapeshifting embodiment)—my youth pastors were convinced I would become a great prophetic teacher. They pronounced Christians an embattled and persecuted minority, perhaps the most embattled, the most persecuted, because it was Christians upon whom the salvation of humanity, however tenuous, depended! I was most interested, meanwhile, in the possibility of divine visions. I wanted to see the Saints not for the sake of salvation, but in order to open a portal to pleasure—to receive a magnitude of passion equal to the emptiness of dissociation. I did not want to leave my body, but to enamor it. Not to mention that my ex, my first love, had joined the cult, what they called a 'fellowship,' a month before breaking up with me.

Years later when I was in rehab, the same summer I first met Ezekiel, the summer before we fell in love, two different therapists told me during our sessions that they believed me to be an 'indigo child,' which upon further research, at the urging of those same therapists, revealed itself to be a fabulation, a mystification of knowledge developed in the 1970s by a white woman named Nancy Anne Tappe who referred to herself as a Colorologist—a synesthetic seer who divines the essences of people according to her perception of the colors of their aura—to explain what she saw as the sudden manifestation and proliferation of indigo auras among adolescents, particularly so-called dissident or rebellious and above all gender variant youth, indicating, she believed or claimed, the beginning of a 'further stage in human evolution,' and thereby revealing, at the root of yet another American mysticism, the white supremacist myth of racial purification, expressed this time as a slow subaltern uprising. Tappe and her followers Jan Tober and Lee Carroll were attempting to dehistoricize gender variance, presenting it as a new *discovery*, the emergent form of a more advanced personhood, thus absorbing it for the perpetual project of American colonial expansion—claiming it, in a kind of recapitulation of manifest destiny, for the future. These selfproclaimed psychics sought to reinscribe gender variance as a hyperindividualistic Space Age virtue, ahistorical and therefore supernatural, possibly even extraterrestrial, to be negotiated through cultic farces of relation such as lectures, books and conferences disseminated by Tappe et. al., redirecting the potential meaning of their acolytes along the vertical and attenuating axis of a capitalistic gnosticism and away from the warp and weft of communal knowledges. The so-called theory of 'indigo children' is nothing more than one more form of Imperial mysticism, Imperial pseudoscience, and Imperial realignment.

Like my youth pastors, those therapists attempted to make me one more stabilized agent of Empire, to further obscure me from myself by their manner of mythologizing me, proffering a neoliberal fantasy of selfheroization, simultaneously of the white savior and the marginalized and magical wounded healer. Often during those years when I was a fairy who wore sheer gauzy blouses and didn't know how to apply eyeliner but wore golden glitter every day nonetheless, people at parties interpreted me as if I were neither totally real nor totally imagined, associated with mermaids and pixies in the sense that I was a rare and therefore providential presence, the witnessing of which was neither blessing nor curse, but spiritual or interdimensional destabilization, which required, on the part of some partygoer, a confession or offering, lest I bring bad luck.

So a girl was whispering in my ear by light of a misty blue strobe, saying, 'I'm a med student and I just need to tell you: I think your scars are beautiful.'

Saying: 'Can I touch them?'

Touching them.)

Which of course set me off.

Look, baby, I had been calm, I had come down from my Dreamsicle halfshell, having been dislodged, in my posture of a @ts_Venus, from the stucco ceiling of a ruined Amalfi villa, to lightly land before you in a tea shop.

No longer was I your sweet and brilliant but fucked up fairy, because I had become beautiful for strangers on the sidewalk, and men in bars who looked like you but had different thoughts, thoughts that bored me until I pretended I was someone else, some woman who had never been a fairy, which made it easy to toss my hair until I was standing, suddenly, in your bedroom, three years after you'd walked away.

I already knew too much about blades when I met you, Ezekiel. So by the time I met that man on the A train, the message wasn't a mystery; he spoke to me in a language I could understand. I know the power of my pulse because that man made me into a fountain. For years I had waited for him to arrive, not because I wanted him to but because I was certain he was about to, just like it seems that the present is always about to arrive somewhere: the perpetual deferral makes me fretful. I say the poet records all the possibilities that the instant refuses, the poet is an atmosphere in which something else can happen, so when I come here, to the place where we make mist between us, here I know what to do, how to see—not the future, but the frontside of an embroidery, when all along I'd only seen the back, the formless tufts of blazing color, which is how I would describe the difference between my stories and my dreams, not as a failure of translation, but the two sides of an embroidery in the hands of an old woman laid to rest near a field of horses. When I come here, I know how to read the constellation within the blaze, it's slow but I am reading it for you, I am reading it right now, at 4:18 a.m., arranging and rearranging a few symbols as irritating and irresolvable as grains of sand; I turn and turn them on my tongue, right now there is sand in my teeth because I never pretend to be interested in anything other than my few symbols, you know them by now, I don't need to spell them out for you. I'm so sorry, baby, I was bleeding for the symbols. I named those symbols Ezekiel because I didn't want to be alone. But I think, I think maybe, my god, I think the symbol is not yours, but I don't know if it's mine, it's my consolation for what never happened. For the destiny I am laying to rest in my song. Because I never had the patience to learn the guitar, I had whistled so many tunes and didn't have the patience to learn how to play them, I only ever learned the howl and the sermon, never the simple sentence of making scrambled eggs in the morning. Every time I made eggs I thought you would marry me.

'Neutralize,' he'd said.

My thoughts dissolved into a mess of static. His words spread through me like smoke.

'Neutralize *it*.'

I wasn't enough of a fool to believe that Ezekiel meant to extinguish our yearning by referring to it, obliquely, inches from my face. But even though I sensed the presence of his desire, I couldn't figure out how it was exerting force between us, except that it was skittish and unpredictable, as sudden as a stag lifting its head at the sight of my distant footstep; I couldn't figure it out because my own desire was too disembodied, too hypothetical—I didn't know how to imagine it in the absence of a precedent. Ezekiel was a man now, a fairy still but he had become a man and I had become a woman, so what would it mean, what would it mean...so long after the end of our little myth...

I broke his gaze. I stood up, turned to his bookshelf and lifted that old volume of Clarice Lispector's stories I'd inscribed, years before, with a purple and sentimental message about the dawn in my characteristically rickety script, like a realm of spiders. If you want to read it, you will have to ask Ezekiel yourself, I don't remember what I wrote. He sat crosslegged on the stool, somehow both overwrought and oracular, reciting in his halfhaunted, fairylisping, bluebonnet-hazy West Texas twang, a poem by Frank Bidart:

Thank you, terror!

*You learned early that adults' genteel
fantasies about human life*

were not, for you, life. You think sex

is a knife
driven into you to teach you that.

But that wasn't happening yet, or it was just about to happen, because in the instant before the instant when he began to read, I noticed, hanging from a hook on the bathroom door, a piece of blue fabric, which reminded me of one day in December when the air had recovered the serene luminosity of late autumn, and waving, windswept but intimate, walking up the road with jaunty charm and an aura of laissezfaire yet genuine mysticism like he was from some sunbaked sepia interlude of how I imagine Austin to have been in the late 1970s and early 80s, Ezekiel, that skimpy halfunbuttoned cyan blouse fluttering around him in the breeze, came to sit beside me at a picnic table—and I, high, talking about horses, offering him sips of cherry soda, was not afraid that he would walk away.

"Why did you invite me to a bar tonight," I said, because he had driven us to *Cheer Up's* from the tea shop. "And after the bar,"—because the poem hurt, the poem hurt because I didn't know why he said it—"why did you invite me to your bedroom?"

He laughed. His eyes glinted, amused:

"You seriously thought, after three years, I just wanted to have tea?"

What could I say. There was too much to lose; too much embarrassment if he *neutralized* us. I could not risk decrypting the instant. So I allowed him to feel my silence. The pressure of roots beneath the earth. Reservoirs of sweet water. The infinitesimal drip of a stalactite. But it was too much, too much to know a world so slow—Ezekiel was turning to stone. Clouds were circling his timeless granitic face.

"I want to be alone," he said.

Outside his window, the thin green leaves of a hickory branch chattered, watching.

"No," I said. "You want to remember me."

The leaves fell silent. They hovered, greenly.

"Because—because you don't want the responsibility of a future."

I stepped toward him, placing my hand on his cheek.

"So remember me."

We argued. We gazed. And in the end, he kissed me.

Those kisses were too little to hold the accumulation of three years. So little that they burst into flame.

(Once, long after our first kiss and long before its latter-day reenactment, or perhaps equidistant from both, Ezekiel wrote me an email: 'Ever since this morning I've been thinking about my contact with bodies, and my most pivotal moments of body-to-body contact in this life. When we kissed in May of 2015, in a house with old, noisy pipes, your lips were soft and the kisses were so gentle and lovely, it was like I'd discovered a new sense. We spent much of that night studying each other, wondering who we were, wondering what we would mean tomorrow, and the days and years after. The present constantly asks us to revise the past; scenes take on more or less weight as our impressions of the world accumulate in their contiguous sequence. While I was fingering you in the flower bed, neither of us knew love was in store.')

This World is not Conclusion.
A + Species stands beyond —
Invisible, as Music —
But positive, as Sound —

My heart was cold.
'I'll write you a letter,' he said.
Sugar won't sweeten a wound, baby.

I flew back to Brooklyn and began writing a story about the night I fucked myself for some angels in an empty cathedral. A wound is a mouth without a tongue. The letter never came.

II.

ANGELS DANCING ON THE TIP OF A PIN

Two years passed. One morning three weeks after the knifing, in the subterranean recording studio the girls and I constructed in the caves of Anthemusa, I woke up, opened Instagram, and saw that Ezekiel had followed me.

'Why,' I asked.

He was typing for a long time. He stopped typing. My heart was enduring a private tempest, on a scale I think George Eliot would appreciate: what you might call a chamber drama, every silence an event of its own.

"'The poem turns on 'available now'...

The poem is available now,'"

wrote Rachel Rabbit White, said Velvet about this story, three months after Ezekiel was typing.

Always the deferred arrival of his word. Often a sentence as inno-

Strawberry Spritz I drank after Ezekiel followed me.

cent as an axe. But knowing that he wanted to say, if not what. Or not knowing, knowing only that he felt the absence of our little language, that place in excess of our own maximums— where he crumbled into me like a cliff into the sea.

Eventually:

> hi Aurora! I guess I was test-
> ing the waters, with the tip of
> my toe.

then

> I meant it as a gesture

> of light reconnection...

> of my desire to not be cut off
> completely from your life.

He stopped typing. Then he began again, and stopped.
'Well,' I said.

I had received no information about the content of his gaze
beyond the fact that it now encompassed my portraits of beauty
in rigor mortis and my haphazard myth-miniatures. For me to
feel you, Ezekiel, not only as a memory in my dreams and in
my stories, but as a silent, faceless presence in that dissociative,
panoptical arboretum of materialized, interpenetrating monologues (how else could I describe Instagram?), where our voices
are something like the voices of Jinny, Susan, Rhoda, Bernard,
Louis, and Neville, those bodiless singsong hypercubes—as if
symbols could speak—which Virginia Woolf wove into a sep-
tuple helix called *The Waves*, except that its form, rather than
rising from the channeled chorus of one woman's fecund and
polyvocal mind (as if the Holy Trinity were not a unique organ-
ism, but one extant example of a genre) is made and remade
by a digital ghostriddle called an algorithm, which exists only

to render Empire more acute, more attuned to the grain of our minds, so that it can redirect our attention, irresistibly, into its ruts. For me to feel you there, Ezekiel, as nothing more than the fact of a gaze, was less like 'reconnection' than haunting. A gaze alone does not constitute a gesture.

Not that the so-called publishing industry is much different. At an evening talk in Fall 2018—a dinner for former students of the writer-in-residence at Yale University, sanctuary of war criminals and reactionary 'theorists,' where I had graduated a year before as, as far as I knew, one of two transfeminine students in the senior class, among a slightly fuller handful of trans people of any gender, which is to say, I had assimilated, at that time, into a delusion of liberalism—selfidentification not with my sisters but with the imperial dream of the hero's journey, with the white woman's dream of her own exceptionalism, her pretension to the role of wounded healer—a hypocrisy of vision, a state of isolation mistaking itself for individuality, for uniqueness, that is, mistaking implosion for the formation of a pearl; of pearls, which I scattered freely as if they weren't the only precious residue I could make with my tongue, I gambled with every grain of iridescent condensate, I gambled, I shot them into the labyrinth of a fourdimensional pinball machine, that nest of secret societies and elusive writing classes and alumnifunded performance groups, hierarchies buried within hierarchies like fractals of colonial gnosticism—in 2018, American novelist Jennifer Egan argued for the incompatibility of fiction with what I believe she called 'the contemporary moment,' and suggested, further, according to my memory—that is, a memory set immediately in amber by the outraged and recursive embalming of multiple retellings—that in a time when 'facts are at risk,' it might even be *unethical* to tell stories. She said it was the fault of fiction writers that fiction was irrelevant. She was neither the first nor the last mainstream institutional white and cisidentified writer to make universalizing, apocalyptic assertions, not for herself but for all storytellers, about the irrelevance of the form. Her evidence was, I believe, the dramatic decrease in literary fiction sales—40%—following the 2016 American presidential election, which was, like all such presidential elections, a farce of Empire, an illusion of choice.

So let me speak specifically now to Jennifer: of course so-called *literary fiction sales* decreased, because the fiction industry has absorbed, from the vast imperial surveillance engine called Marketing, the rhetoric of the never-before-seen, the rhetoric of *sui generis* by which so-called marginalized storytellers are tokenized, dehistoricized, and therefore isolated by the industry's manic, outraged obsession with the so-called *discovery* of so-called *fresh talent*, nothing more than an echo of what Glissant describes as 'a devastating desire for settlement.' If relation is the way of entanglement, an infinity of infinitely increasing density, then extraction is the way a publishing industry, which I will call the vision-algorithm of Empire, perpetually isolates a quality it proclaims an essence. Glissant: 'The thought of empire is selective: what it brings to the universal is not the quantity of totality that has been realized but a quality that it represents as a Whole.' I know you wrote an essay about faggots, Jennifer, so now I'm inviting you to listen to one: when the Algorithm says *this book is like nothing you've ever read*, it is intentionally severing a storyteller from the scraps and monuments of myth and makeup, book and fuck, melody and scream that have contaminated and therefore communalized her idiom, in order to neutralize, while pretending to emphasize, the destabilizing potentiality of vision.

The more I have been told by some or another figure of authority that my writing is never-before-seen, and the more I have believed it, the more selfish and more jealous my visions have become, the more I have desired the caress of Empire's cold, golden hands. Jennifer, or if you prefer Ms. Egan, listen to me because there's still time. It's not too late: your story is only irrelevant now if it was already irrelevant when you wrote it. The Algorithm's agents move slowly on purpose; a book is published five years after it is written so it cannot reply, with the heat and pressure of a live performance, to the events that inspired it. These agents are conservative, they filter out oblique or resistant or maximalist expressions of love and rage, offering a digestible, sweetsmelling larder of selfsensationalizing, assimilably minimalist expressions of the same, thereby activating, for Empire and its readership, a sense of perfected ethics, the absolution of a political consciousness through the mass exercise of passive sympathy. The pain must conform to the preconstructions of the form of victimhood—must be legible, sensational, equational. Must mobilize the surveillance fable of the police report.

My first novel, *Cradle Me, Lucifer*, was rejected over one hundred times, and never published. Since then I have every so often broken it open, ripped out chunks of vision and grafted them quietly onto stories and essays and other books, a selfcannibalization of my own rotten orchard, because that book isn't breathing anymore, that book is an orchard rotting in the back of a drawer.

Your writing is as striking, original, and weird as it comes. But it's also delicate, and makes me slow down as a reader, which is rare. I think you are going to do a lot of fantastic writing in your career, if these pages are any indication, and may well one day write an absolutely brilliant book.

But I'm sorry to say that - to this reader's eyes, at least – CRADLE ME, LUCIFER is not that book. Good writers - of which you are one - are (in this agent's eyes) a dime a dozen. The sentences are just the raw material. Great storytellers - writers who use that raw material of good writing to communicate - are the ones who become great novelists, and great artists.

CRADLE ME, LUCIFER strikes me as a brave early foray into exploring the tools at your disposal to produce the raw material of good sentences. But your description of the novel itself sounds to me like angels dancing on the tip of a pin rather than an attempt to engage, transfigure, or say something about the world as it is.

I don't usually get this ars poetica on people, but that's how I see things. We see a *lot* of very good writers of sentences and crafters of images come across our desks here. What we don't see are a lot of great storytellers. If I have one piece of advice, it's to ask yourself seriously how you can use your gift to communicate and connect.

Take this e-mail for whatever it's worth, and feel free to ignore my advice entirely. In either case, best of luck to you with CRADLE ME, LUCIFER, and with your possible future career as a writer. You'll find the thing you need urgently to say through writing novels, I'm sure. I'm just not convinced you have yet.

Yours,
A.

Well. He had read five pages of the manuscript. The first five, in which a fairy considers the possibility of wearing lipstick in public for the first time in her life. Just now I wrote a list of all the events that have happened to my body since I wore lipstick in public for the first time; I was writing that list like a proof of the agent's absurdity, but I deleted it, because first of all, if you know, you know, and whether you *know* or not, I don't want you to know right now, *in the form of a list*, because that would already be on its way to filing a police report. Besides, it was boring to write. There is nothing more boring than explaining yourself to someone who thinks they want to know you, but wants, in fact, to apply your particularities to the formulation of a genus. Someone who wants to know in such a way that this knowing remains isolated from the rest of her knowledge, she wants to know without being infected by knowing, as if my phrases were pressed between the glass sheets of a slide, viewed through the lens of a microscope.

Look, before 2020, the so-called Major Publishers had only once, in the history of American Empire, published a novel by a tgirl—and it's not because we're not writing. The Algorithm is just beginning to attempt to process our stories, because our existence is excessive to its basic premise; in order to install us in its cabinet of essences, in order to make sense of us, it needs to make us real, which is only possible if it situates our womanhood firmly, hermetically in the language of fact, if it narrows our womanhood into an equation of linear time, if it understands transsexuality as a relationship of present to past. Were it to attempt to allow us to publish, not fiction or non-fiction, not myth or memoir, but even so much as a scrap of Vision, the Algorithm would lose track of the terms of its own reality, because Vision naturalizes the relationship of fantasy to reality—that is, Vision refuses to artificially elevate reality over fantasy in a false and impermeable polarity, because Vision is precisely the expression of their symbiotic, epiphanic entanglement.

So I left the first book to decay and began another, called *I Carry A Peach*, which I finished years later. After reading it, Velvet wrote me an email:

Hi <3

Firstly, I just wanted to say that I miss you.

Also sorry for taking sooo long to read this treasure after you sent it to me.

I was thinking yesterday, looking at some flowers, that what has stuck with me most is the spirit of the characters, especially Ruth. I think that's so important for this work, because so often trans characters are differentiated by their gender alone. There are, of course, quite a few characters, some of whom were always impressionistic blurs in the background and then emerged with higher levels of clarity, with Ruth, Z, and X being the most deeply felt. Of course, Ruth is our initial avatar, so she was the most present for me. I guess it's kind of ironic--she rails against the memoir tradition, but it's her internal memoir in the story that creates the foundation for the narrative.

I just love the way you executed so many of the scenes in the book--the sex scenes, especially between Ruth and Z!!!! the estrogen synthesis, which was like a song to me, B's transformation, the final dream. I'm amazed at how much, as someone who knows you, I felt your presence and skill leading me around, but there was not a single moment that felt like it was in your voice and not the voice of the book. Now that I think of it though, your first book didn't have any of that either!

Going back to the sex scenes. I don't know if I've ever read any t4t sex scenes in a book? They capture the way sex can be so continuous with one's self-making, as well as sites of care between trans people. Also when Z says how could you think of dying before you've ever been fucked by a woman with a strap on...thank youuuuuu. I cannot wait to see that in print.

I must admit I was slightly disappointed that the forced transition never happened...perhaps that's a trick you can save up your sleeve for one day. I mean I see why you didn't, but I still want to see it, you know? Anyway, the gentle hint at it was enough, in fact it crushed me with its cutting tenderness. We can only hope this book launches a thousand transitions, like so many ships on a river of breast milk.

Your language sticks in my teeth like shards of candy. Fruitypebble smoke. The wet geode. Whatever you do to get this language to flow from you, it's miraculous.

Love,
Velvet

I Carry a Peach began in a mansion where a woman named Ruth lived in the shadow of her abusive paramour, the Castellan. It was the morning of their one year anniversary; that night the Castellan was throwing a party. None of his friends knew she was transgender. He had commissioned a painting of Ruth as Aphrodite to be unveiled at the party, but she did not want her irreducibilities erased by a false mythology, so she invited her old lover to sneak into the mansion and complete a second portrait, depicting her as she really was, with breasts and a cock. "To balance the eyes," she said. But before he left the mansion, the painter, without Ruth's knowledge, replaced the Castellan's painting with his own. That night the party unfolded, the painting was unveiled, and the Castellan flew into a fit of rage. While he stabbed her image with a hunting knife, Ruth fled through the back garden.

Following the hints offered to her by her visions, she arrived, eventually, at a mountain in the West Texas desert, where a religious sect of runaway tgirls, stewards of a rotten Eden, a commune in its twilight days, performed rites and rituals revolving around the consumption of estrogen, and the praise of goddess Aphroditos—a frankincense-scented isomer of Aphrodite who possessed both breasts and cock, and to whom a cult (whose acolytes, wrote Philostratus, were fairies and faggots) was once devoted on the isle of Cyprus, in the epoch before the rise of Christendom—under the direction of the autocratic prophetess Cassandra, librarian of the 'Forest of Oneironautics,' a collection of rare mythological texts concealed in a cave within the cliffs.

I Carry A Peach was the recipient of at least thirty or forty rejections, one of which, for its effect of déjà vu, has proven exemplary:

Here's the deal: you're friggin' good. Your talent is blinding. But this book, for me, is a drawer book. One where you're stretching your legs and growing page by page. Some pages are weighed down by literary loft. And some fly by it. Some sentences are exquisite, but they are next to dozens of others so full of STUFF that they overload. In my mind, you're the person who's next book will blow open the world. And it's that book that probably is the best step forward, but I understand the realities of the world and the writer and that that kinda news is totally not what you want to hear. You want this book, and you believe in it. Well, I believe in you. Hope I get to read the next one. If you do sign and sell this, I won't be surprised, but just make sure it's at the right level with the right person, because otherwise is a disservice to your writing and career.

Best,
S.

Ms. Egan, can you discern the onset of a motif? Unlike my lover Velvet, S., A., et. al, agents and acolytes of the Algorithm, diminish the potentiality of vision by assigning it, always, to the future—by subjecting it, via an assignation of perpetual adolescence, to perpetual deferral. Vision is always 'immature' because it does not sublimate rage into so-called reason, does not rely on an arbitrary hierarchy of reality to assign it value. Not to mention that agent after agent complained of finding the characters, all tgirls, indistinguishable.

Empire tells a simple story about so-called transsexual women: that we do not exist because we have never before existed. That we are merely the expression of a latterday delusion, babbled from the mouths of madmen. That this delusion is the result of sodomitic decadence. And while Empire has spoken this story from its mouth, while empire has distracted our ears with this story, its hands are busy lighting fires under our sacred texts, our histories, our diaries, attempting by means of destruction to transform a lie into a truth, so that what has never before existed can exist for the first time: a past without us. Then when we are born again (because we are always born again, irrepressibly born again, because Empire refuses to burn itself, and that's where we are, too, that's where we already are, even there, inside the blood of men and women, the very men and women producing child after child after child for the sake of Empire) we are born into a nightmare: baby did you sense it, when you were three, or four, or five years old, long before you knew even how to read a sentence in a book—a breeze, a sweet breath, a wordless voice? And did it terrify you as much as it transported you? Before you knew how to write your own name, did you already conflate selfknowledge with shame?

'Unlike a book,' I replied to Ezekiel, 'I know when someone is reading me.'

III.

GAY SPACE VOYAGE

Since then and for a year now we have been talking every few weeks. Our conversations take the form of feverish, hourslong phone calls. He asks for advice about romance or friendship, or sends me his poems. I tell him he is my favorite poet and he says I'm his favorite reader. We talk a lot about astrology. He sings Lucinda to me. Sometimes I share bits of this book. Recently he confessed he feels intoxicated by the way I write about him, and me, and the failure of the miniature dimension we opened five years ago then both abandoned like Eden if god and all the angels left, if it never closed but instead shrank and became overgrown, rank with feral flowers. He told me about the deer he sees in the cemetery, about the retrospective glamor of our days down in Texas when seen in the light of later loves; said he had fallen in love with me again, or had never really fallen out of love; said I had emerged from a bubblegum fog, appearing to him within the loop-de-loop sensations of a schoolgirl crush. Then he narrated for me the four slow sensuous occasions on which he nearly subscribed to my OnlyFans, how his finger hovered over the link, how he imagined, once and then one thousand times, paying to see his exgirlfriend's pussy.

Who knows when he'll walk away again, maybe he already has and I just don't know it yet. I don't know the seasons of his mind. What I am writing to you is still happening. It's happening right now. I'm here.

Like this:

A few days ago he called me. We've both been so wrapped up in the conundrums of our separate lives, we went two months without talking but finally we called, the whole time telling little dramatic stories, talking about the songs stuck in our heads, having fairy chat, and then it was almost time to go and he hadn't even acknowledged his sudden annunciation. So I asked him whether he'd meant what he said.

"About loving you?" he said. "Because that was true. I do love you."

"Well." I said. "Yes, but also about…desire."

"Oh," he said. "Like how I said I want to be in bed with you?"

I almost laughed because the question was so ridiculous. He can be so obtuse.

"Yes," I said, "how you wanted to be lovers."

I immediately prepared myself for him to recant or at the very least reframe and diminish, because he's always so flighty after he makes a confession to me, he always retreats into himself, into the little tomb of his mind. I think he can't bear for me to be aware of his desire for me, because for him, desiring with an audience means scrambling the cohesion of his solitude, means opening himself to chaos when what he wants is to want with total freedom, without any responsibility, without any possibility of failure or pain.

"I have this image I keep thinking about," he said, "of us in bed together. And I touch your face. And I don't know what happens after that but when I think of it, I want you with me."

I drew my breath, sharply. Yet again he was desexualizing his own desire, but at the same time what he said was incredibly tender, and knowing how much he represses the chaos of wanting, I think I owe it to him after all these years to read him more generously than I did in the past, I think I owe it to him to realize that he wants me in his bed, he wants to stare into my eyes in a halfaloft golden haze spreading around us like an aura, a halo zone where we speak only in the minute vibrations of subatomic gemstones exploding like infinitesimal supernovas around our heads. Because he brought up a night five years ago when for some indeterminate vastitude of instantaneous time, we had stared into one another's eyes, smiling, totally still. But not just smiling, beaming, radiating something together like a mist.

On the phone he said: "Like how we used to stare at each other."

And I think I owe it to him to realize that he wants communion with me, he wants me so much he would stare into my eyes silently radiating his inner mist. And I think I owe it to him to realize that this is a corporeal hunger, that he may owe me an explanation for why he said and said that I was not beautiful, but that he desires me, that he remembers feeding me his cum five times a day back in Texas and he remembers drinking mine, because he loves talking to me about how big my cock was, how I had the biggest cock of anyone he knew, and that he talks about my cock because it is safest to express a desire for what no longer exists. I owe it to him to realize that he wants to feel my heat against him, he wants to exchange heat with me, he wants to love me with his body, too. He sent me some hot shirtless photos of himself, to balance the eyes—because he reads my Twitter every day, sees my breasts and my bush and sees me looking beautiful, so he thought it was only fair. But he had a bunch of friends coming over for a housewarming dinner for him and his best friend at their new blue house, and he needed to prepare dinner and smoke a couple cigarettes. So I told him that I had told you all about what he said on the phone. And I told him how you all had loved the story, how you had wanted to know more.

And, softly but firmly, he said, "I'm hard right now."

Then we said goodbye.

Writing is waiting or conjuring. Today I'm full of longing, I'm falling in love! But yesterday I was the incarnation of Mother Aquarius, princess of pressurized breath, of oxygen circling atmospheres and silver suits. Every spacecraft is a haunted chamber. Sarcophagus of a cosmonaut. Deep space tomb. Yesterday, tethered by a silver cord, I exited the airlock in order to repair a spray of minute punctures to the amber membrane of a satellite's wing, stippled by gusts of stardust whirling by slowly like the pointillist soul of a supernova, star archive. But—without you there to guide me by the rhythm of your psychedelic mourning dove hymns, Ezekiel; you who abandoned our craft the day we finished building it, the craft, the *Needle of Aphrodite*, which I launched alone anyway into space—yesterday, leaping from the airlock, I lost my grip on her silver flank. I drifted nowhere in particular. Or, in order to allow her rings a cameo, I drifted in the direction of Saturn. I mean I held all the thread but not with the instantaneity of a spider, not spilling from the muck of my silk glands, from an infinite reservoir of possible webs, a perpetual memoir of instants and iridescence, because a spider lives by its own word. The word is never separate from the spider. More than an atmosphere and less than a dimension, a web is a plane—the spider extends itself by means of the silk bursting from its chitin corset (which, as with an oyster's shell, is the unfeeling shield protecting that which is felt, not seen, not spoken; the sensitized swamp of meaning, the whirlpool of feeling, the chaos of wanting; a form of faith like inkwells and IV bags, like honeycombs and slick pink glands and prickly pears; scorpions, aquariums and chambers of the heart; tide pools and perfume bottles and the phosphorescent ink of squids vanishing in the dark; the melting point of topaz and deep sea vents and one amphora of wine buried beneath a Roman highway: or magma glowing, accumulating, spilling and sputtering in brief and blazing ropes of tectonic honey; honey mushrooms sharing nutrients with their rhizomatic kin through forking Mobius root networks; spinal fluid and primordial ooze and peaches ripe and overripe, peaches swelling, splitting their skins, globing with sticky sweet irreducible concentrate, peaches cracked and wasting, peaches and the dissolution of peaches and spider silk), the spider becoming, thread by thread, the bright node of its own private constellation, becoming the centrifugal unfolding of a language, in the sense of a means of expression, in the sense of the expression of a

118

desire and in the sense of the means by which a desire is satisfied, I mean the means by which I place myself in proximity to the perfume of peaches, so that when you drift, seeking after nectar, into the branches, you are tangled, halfway to a reality of ripening, in my silver nets: not so that you are encased forever within a coffin of string, not so that you are entrapped in the ritual of an enclosure, but, instead, so that the fibers of my web, pulsating, confecting, receive your imprint. Baby, you are not the crown jewel in my glittering veil. I do not want to keep you. I never could.

What I have been weaving from one dreamer's spittle and the strings of an ancient lyre is not an algorithm recording the raw data of Ezekiel's gestures in order to reverse engineer, like a wooly mammoth extrapolated from the DNA encrypted in a single strand of permafrozen hair, an immortal clone; which, as if it were a shard of mirror that reflects a sliver of reality no less true for being jagged, no less clear for being narrow, catches, from time to time, a slant of light; is showered suddenly with photons; brims and spills its edges, flowing like luminous water, pulsing in the syllables like a heartbeat. I am not constructing here a diorama of Ezekiel's bedroom, or mine, or of the Stations of the Cross; or what counterfeits itself as a diorama of the Stations of our Romance in order to haunt him with a house, to place a house around him like a haunting, to convince his clone to accept a labyrinth for a home, climbing staircases, circling rooms, seeking, but never finding, an exit. I mean a maze whose halls and closets, whose furnishings and candlesticks form the elements of the equation by which the love of the West Texas duskstrolling Gemini poet Ezekiel (with a creekbed for a mirror and a wedding veil draped from his antlers) for the cirrus cloud dawndissolving Scorpio Aurora (riding the subway to Mount Sinai braless in a short corset tied seven inches down, a white tank and jean cutoffs, stitches in my nipples, dreaming of a night in San Marcos, Texas when an extended family of queens—some of whom were women and some fairies, but all of whom were mothered by the one and only Miss Artifish—invited me to an afterparty at a local motel, where, seated on beds and in chairs and sinks and out the door in the night, smoking spirits, they decided, on a whim, to exchange wigs, to share their wigs like diadems freely given, and, awestruck at the ease of their shapeshift, I felt the mute ache of desire splitting its bitter rind, because already earlier that night I had been invited backstage to paint shadow on a fairy named Silver, who was not really a lover but was more than a friend,♥ who introduced me to the queens—accreting feathers and jewels and corsets, gossiping with pleasure, acrylics flashing, catching the light, decorating gestures, threading even the faintest insinuation with veins of gold, escalating the force of a flicked wrist and focusing the substance of that messy and immaculate atmosphere in the tips of each of their fingers—one of whom, extremely beautiful, with powderblue fishnets, spangled eyelids and vocal fry like a woman walking her chihuahua in 2002 while soliloquizing about her exboyfriend on a bedazzled Razr, looked me up and down and said, "cute makeup," which was not only a clarification of our difference in scale, a needful reminder of the exhaustion of her exertion, of the exertion of her splendor—accumulated and expended lavishly, all at once, in the space of a single song—but also a kind of salutation, a covert recognition, like the passcodes buried in the ostensibly innocuous chitchat of two spies, of our shared passion; our elongation, asymptotic, along the axis of a dream; the dream of wingbeats and sparkling caverns, the dream of lashes and cleavage, the dream of lipstick and muse; that is, though she would remain, if a Facebook friend, a stranger, Peach Foam was the first woman, the first person not just to notice, but to recognize, the twinkle in my eye) could be recovered, like lost files, could be regained and immortalized—not already gone, okay?

♥ We only ever kissed twice. But he wept in my passenger seat when I told him I couldn't be close to someone who only felt passion for me sometimes, even if those times, brief and acute, expanded the width of the instant—even if an element as potent and untraceable as radon proliferated into an unblinking aura at the midpoint of our gazes.

> will never be able to shake you carrying the lilies from the store to your dorm, across that windy street

> nor would I want to shake such a velocity vision

> take the glory any day over the fame

I am not weaving an effigy, baby. I am absorbing, string by string, the shocks, the supersonic resonances of our Romance, which even now, like the transmissions of faroff windchimes, are vibrating the air around me, at my desk—within whose drawers Old Milk is shedding her scales—while I write this book for us by light of a oncetall candle, carved, twisting like a mesquite branch, which Velvet's boyfriend whittled last Spring to help me cast a demon from the craft. A spider pays attention to slight sounds; her web is the substance that registers them.

Thus I was telling you how yesterday I lost my grip on the *Needle of Aphrodite*. For a while I drifted, it's true. Please wait. The history of those hours is unspeakable.

… … and then … …

… … and then? … … and then … … and then I pulled myself back along the length of my tether, and papered the holes in the satellite's wing with sheets of gold leaf. Then I returned to the craft—with a few spare breaths left in my oxygen tank, clambering through the airlock and fiddling with the locks on my helmet, my fingers cold and stiff despite the thickness of my gloves, gasping. For an interval I fainted. When I woke, I shed my suit and dressed slowly in wool pants and a wool sweater, floating from cabin to cabin, taking a seat in my room with a view of the stars, the cockpit. Where I am recording this message in the logbook. As soon as the satellite resets, a little green light will blink from my control panel, indicating '*Aphrodite* is online.' Elean'r and the Siren are already in cryosleep, sharing a dream. They are dreaming of Anthemusa. Soon I will join them.

But first—I have a moment now to tell you one more story. About a wound, not the fifth and not the last, just the last I have time to stitch. Make yourself a cup of coffee.

IV.

The Sixth Wound

Stella was last in the room. Somehow it felt right to me for her to be there, because she was a stranger, but in the most intimate way. We had never spoken to each other because we had never had any reason to. I was in part a recluse and in part a careful avoider of other pixies. Beauty was still new to me then. I could sense a certain kind of heat coming off a certain kind of girl, as if her body were a crystal lantern lit from within by a creamsicle haze: a will-o'-wisp drifting among calcified pelvic cavities, subdermal caverns of glittering stalactites or fields of repercussive quartz blooming without witness in the dark, drifting and inducing a total anesthesia, a proliferating Spring infinitesimally refracted among multifoliate densities of nested, luminous planes, so-called 'facets' within which latticed knots of molecules weave depths of translucent mesh waiting to scatter and multiply, to echo and tangle some slant of light within the maze of their perfect crystal matrices. Some girls made acrylics, some poked tattoos, some escorted and phonesexed and sewed garments woven from threads of gold, from strands of their own hair and their grandmother's fraying funeral shroud; or they fashioned relics from pewter, from fake rubies or chunks of amber polished into some irregular shape that nevertheless reveals, insulated from time—sealed in a breathless sunset dimension transmitting a Mesozoic glow, that state of radiance as hard and vaporous as the pixels of a frozen Facetime, precipitate of a nameless Autumn, gold pastoral!—the tessellated wing of a prehistoric dragonfly. Some girls—emptying, encrypting their hearts in waves of blue or lilac static shredded by the equations of a gray computer silently interpreting the strawberry echoes and human howls of the pain of separation, the pink pollenheavy narcoleptic tides of recollected whispers (whispers, sighs and sweet sounds of a lover, of lovers, of the dialtone), the tinny cymbals of dysphoria, the abysses of iridescence and blur, the hunger for destabilization, for chaos, if only to break the surface of a blank, if only to dispel an anesthesia of the heart—in order to conjure a season of glossolalia, a season of bubbles spontaneously popping, of stalactite nymphs spinning, whirling, phaseshifting in the kaleidoscopic mist of strobes, writing gestures, producing, in absolute darkness, dazzling displays of light—some girls make music as pristine and devastating as synthesizers pulsing within a chrysalis of ice. Some girls write books or paint makeup or encrust themselves with the elements of a starlet; they all make the most of every last glimmer. It's easier to conjure a dreamworld with a friend than it is with a lover, and in that way it's preferable to be a friend, but a lover strobes into your skull and sees your dreamworld, a lover sucks on your nipples. In my most pious, insular and decadently apocalyptic Phantasmagorias of love, one dreamer formed the atmosphere and the other dreamer sang within it; one dreamer was the fading light, the fog in the branches—and the other was the nightingale singing, ruffling its feathers, under cover of dusk and flowers. For this reason some girls terrified me, because they catalyzed my desire for Ozymandian odes, for ruined marble temples and slow suffocation, for the disintegration of my holy writ within the blazing substance of another woman's splendor.

'Baby, I want to dissolve into you like honey in tea...'

But not with sweetness, or if with sweetness only as byproduct, spilling, from the tip of a dropper, into the trance realm of your aquarium, where gauzes and synthesizer riffs swayed in the noontime dark; hovering, breaking over you like a tincture of dawn; perfusing your water; collecting, here, there, within you, like the light that falls in blue and emerald pools, that lies in lines of neon and evanesces like lilac wings upon the cool, dim recesses of an ancient stone nave.

Some girls—but on this occasion, one girl. Stella. Months later, and with a careless cruelty—an implosive selfishness that I buried within a pretension of necessity; an infatuation that, because of my loneliness, I mistook for destiny; a reckless betrayal of Noel, whose eyes were like alabaster pools of glittery water—months later I would break my heart on her, or on the sharp corners of the symbol I named after her, a symbol that had quietly accumulated in one of the tidepools of my dreamworld, because months later we were briefly entangled. It wasn't romantic so much as lunatic, spiritual, and almost certainly in part a response to the story I am about to tell.

Before that night and for a long time after, she was a stranger to me, to the extent that we hadn't shared a single word—though I had heard of her, as most tgirls in the vicinity of Myrtle-Wyckoff will eventually hear, if nothing else, one another's names, whether from the lips of a lover or the flick of a finger; and though we had, a few weeks prior, shared a single silent glance for the halfinstant upon which the sudden pressure of a psychic tension was already faintly sensible (as when a deer registers the vibrations of a distant highway in its antlers), perhaps because she was dating my best friend Noel, who lived in the bedroom beside mine and was at that time only recently my ex, and (here I can only speak for myself) because of a swirling cloud of projection, invocation and dreaming whose particularities belong to the instant and not to the page, but which, once I had gathered them together in a butterfly net, would, the very last time I saw her, dimensionalize what I had felt before only as an ache—a resonance rising, at the frequency which bursts glass, from the weave of nerves in my solar plexus—would, on that Spring afternoon, unfold into a diorama, floating above my head, through which a miniature hologram, not of me as I am now, but of me as I could have been in a proliferation of pasts, or as I could be in a proliferation of futures, wandered tranquilly the twilit glass chambers of an enormous hothouse, overhung by vast ferns, attended by corpse flowers, a hologram of the kind of woman I had only ever allowed myself to feel in phrases, in books written for no one and saved to a folder within a folder on my computer, the kind of woman who was named Aurora, who confected her own fifth-dimensional dioramas and drove demons from mirrors and cast spells of passion and collected feminine artifacts like the elements of an equation, who trusted her beauty to exert itself like the web of a spider, to make the invisible visible, not only registering like radar the pulsations of her *pieces of mind*, but amplifying and attuning the transmissions of desire crisscrossing the air of a luminous room where beautiful women in corsets and croptops whisper in one another's ears; a woman who never goes out without her accumulated aura shimmering around her head like a halo of stardust, without a whaletail rising from her cutoffs, without DDs and cherryred lipstick; who refuses to knock, like the ghost of Cathy Earnshaw, at her own window—who haunts her body as if it were a house. Because my body has been waiting for me. Despite every complication I have been slowly weaving my life-shroud: What I am writing to you is not fable or memoir, it's not something like that, about what is topaz and what is broken glass; it's my way of accepting that a miracle happens not when it happens, but when you feel it, because I was living my life as if I were writing it—*for the sake of the song*—but now I am writing my life as if I were living it: I am writing with the passion of a woman falling in love, I'm falling in love.

For so many years womanhood was a taut and scintillating scrim through which I negotiated the desires of the outside world. Womanhood was a paranoid attention to how I was being interpreted by every possible gaze, it was a disappearance from my body to become the gazes I was interpreting, interpreting them by looking through them at myself, it was my constant shapeshift to maintain the best possible womanhood at the pinpoint of gazes.

126

How many million times she had seen her face, and always with the same imperceptible contraction! She pursed her lips when she looked in the glass. It was to give her face point. That was her self – pointed; dartlike; definite. That was her self when some effort, some call on her to be her self, drew the parts together, she alone knew how different, how incompatible and composed so for the world only into one centre, one diamond, one woman who made of her lips a meeting-point, a radiancy, a refuge perhaps…

When I was alone, I molted: I became neither woman nor man but knot of muscles, curling, tightening below my dreamworld, drooling and burping, stubbing my toes, without a destiny. But having passed the better part of a year in my apartment, my femininity, undirected, began to spread and spill like seafoam in excess of any public need, accumulating in the corners of my room, lapping and bubbling up around me—curling, expended back upon itself like a wave, for no one, for the exertion of a splendor, under the influence of the moon. I was becoming attuned to the riffs, the pauses and covert arias of a *chamber femininity*.

Which is to say long after the debut of my first breasts, folded from toilet paper in a bookstore bathroom, long after the declarations and humiliations, the drunk struts and the documentations, the TSA and the hospitalizations, the rage and the repetition and the surfaces of mirrors—the flaming mirrors and the flaming angels, the abnegation of estrogen for so long at my mother's request, and the attempts at poetry nonetheless; long after the surgeries, after everything herein encrusted and much else; long after the hormones and the haze and the fanfare, I returned to the privacy of my room: I wasn't coming out, I was staying in. Because I was knifed in the face and then a couple weeks later got my tits done, so I was already indoors, and then I was indoors even more, because I graduated from grad school and was fired twice as a hostess and because of the virus engulfing the world, so I suddenly saw no one except my own reflection and my righthand femboy, my righthand femboy oracle and my lefthand femboy oracle, my transmasc femboy posse, I mean Noel and my thenboy-friend Velvet,♥ because I asked him how to tie a corset, because I asked him to bind me with pink ropes, to braid flowers in my hair and because I made my pussy burble and overflow for my fans, because in order to teach my pussy to speak I invented the voice of onlyfans.com/ts_nextdoor_, of @silicone_angel, of myself. The speaker of the porn is Aurora.

♥ my lover for three Springs and three Summers, and in particular the last Spring and the last Summer, when after so much—after so much, baby—so much for both of us to bear weeping dryeyed like two droplets of topaz on the ears of an angel, so much for us to bear each in our own heart while loving one another from the intimate distance of two dimensions pressing and wrapping one around the other in a twine of infinitesimal time because we loved each other silently, silently as parallel dimensions embracing, weaving—when after so much he became my boyfriend and took me to his father's home by the green marshy sea, where I fell at last and dreamily in love with him. Where his stepparent gave me a velvet dress that fit me perfectly. Where on a sunny day at a neighborhood beach, we floated together on an anchored raft: we felt the sea together. Where feeling the sea was a way of feeling each other, becoming the possibility of an intimacy so extreme it was opaque, was only

But before I was Aurora, I was a woman on an August night. Waiting for a man to arrive. Waiting in my bedroom, what I called my cave, because its window faced directly onto a brick wall and admitted nearly no light and because I was going to sleep later and later, until, in August, I began sleeping from nine to five, by which I mean I went to bed at 9 a.m. and woke at 5 p.m. So I was awake (good morning, midnight!) and in the kitchen Noel was making pasta with Stella, who was, on that night, sleeping over for the first time at our apartment, for which reason, to distract myself from jealousy, from its taste of bitter rust, from the thousand and one needles of needless reverie, I invited a stranger to share my bed, a man from Tinder, a bartender and rockclimber whose name doesn't matter.

As soon as he stepped into our fairy realm, I felt a flood of shame. He was a man in a flannel buttondown and a beard, some attempt at approximating a lumberjack, six feet four inches tall, flipflopping down the hall in his Tevas while Noel and Stella made pasta, glimpsing. As if they were the impossibility whose inversion I was inviting into my bedroom. As if they were confecting potions or perfumes in vials, made from soil, sap, petal and musk. As if they were watching from within strawberry bushes.

My pussy opens me to the world. It says come and see, says: this is a way. But it is not a tunnel. Not a cavern either. As pink as coral and as smooth as a jellyfish, call it a grotto—my pussy is for prayer, not for passing through.

The man was talking. I don't remember about what. After a moment he rose and, bearing the metal and wire instruments of his steampunk-adjacent bartending kit delicately before him, stumbled awkwardly back to the kitchen, hesitating at the threshold, doublefisting cocktail shakers, muscular but insecure, lowering his eyes, interrupting the Fairy Pair, "if you wouldn't mind…"

But interrupting more than their presence: interrupting their silence, because they spoke so quietly in their whispering gauzes, with heads tilted, gazes and gestures pointing or suggesting at strange angles in the steamy golden glow, like in icons of saints: they spoke at the volume of the last reverberations of the chorus of angels praying in the Palace of the slow aching of the sea, only Cancer and Scorpio, a ritual of love so perfectly faint and slow I will not touch its solitude with words—where Velvet had floated with everyone he had ever loved, where Velvet told me stories of the days he had floated with his lovers, where I listened to Velvet and felt myself enveloped in the slow ache of his life, in love with the sound of his voice that I imagined to be the voice of the sea, what I would hear if I met an iridescent presence in the Midnight Zone, what I would hear if Persephone and Poseidon had a femboy son named Velvet, what I would hear if a chorus of ultraviolet sea urchins were incanting together, their lapis spines wetly rising and falling in displays of parallactic grace as if weaving webs from strands of translucent neon spit, their song echoing, ricocheting so gently—quietly and distantly, as if in a dream of reality, but so intensely, as if reality could burn from its scintillations—twinkling in my mind like seafoam mixed with blood.

Clouds, where god is nothing more than the emanation of a song, the visible resonance of their euphonic labor. (The angels keep god alive by singing—and when they cease, god ceases.)

The man, standing nonsensically between the fairies and the sink, was shaking our cocktails. The noise was like automatonic cicadas. Less an interruption than a shredding apart of the silence. He did not make sense. I had brought him down on our household like a curse. My own private Icelandic Saga.

We drank in the grotto. We drank deeply and looked at one another over the rims of our glasses. I don't remember what we drank. I don't remember what we talked about. But I laughed and glittered: I sat at my desk.♥

Having tossed his backpack into the accompanying chair, the man sat on an ottoman.

"You have a facial scar," he said.

"Yes," I said. "I was knifed in the face." (Since then my eye aches, some days enough to keep me in bed from dawn to dusk, unable to write or look at a screen; sometimes little more than an itch; every so often enough to make me vomit, or not at all. The knifing was my glory, the event did not harm me so much as render me acute, but its aftermath is a dull and infinitesimal attrition. It keeps me from writing, from filming, from loving and singing. Every day in the mirror I become convinced it stole my beauty from me. But the wound is not a question of beauty, or the record of an event, or even a way of revealing, nonconsensually, to each passerby and every mirror, that a stranger made me vulnerable to himself; that wound, sealed into a scar, is forever the beginning of another way of seeing. The vision proceeds from the wounding which echoes, pulses in my eye. In fits and starts my eye registers glimpses of dimensions; in mirrors and windows I sometimes see the faces of demons.)

"I used to have a facial scar, too," he said. Then he ran a finger

♥The same desk sitting now in the cockpit of the *Needle of Aphrodite*, within which, while absentmindedly strumming a lyre to the tune of the beeping of various astral monitors, I immortalize halffaded love in intermittent bursts of poetry.

along his right cheek. "But I saw probably the foremost sur-geon for facial scars, so," studying my face ostentatiously, "mine is invisible."

Less for the insult than its lack of context,

"Oh," I said. But my face said nothing. I was irritated now, and bored, because even the sting wasn't interesting; wasn't dramatic or alluring. My heart was already turning to silicone. My soul was almost opaque. What he needed at that moment was a compliment, he needed to contribute to my atmosphere before it withdrew from him forever, before my furnaces froze, because he wasn't the type of man who could hurt me, not in that way, because he was not himself beautiful—in that there was like, not even a whiff of femininity about him, except insofar as a thing describes its opposite. My scar slanted redly down my eyelid.

(Only a very particular kind of man can weaken me with words. Only a man like Velvet, whose masculinity is spun round and round with barbed crystal threads, inflorescences of quartz thistles, I mean whose femininity is an adornment so vital it catches in his flesh and remains embedded there, so sharp and irresistible I want to become the twinkling, the emanation or astral projection of its luster, want to become the fairy that floats among its facets, pricking her fingers on purpose, drawing droplets of blood and collecting them in a vial labelled 'honeysuckle nectar'; a man whose masculinity is mythically reclusive, gothically sylvan, so dense that, like the chlorophyllencrypted air of a glade, to breathe it is to enter an altered state—and to surrender to it is almost psychedelic, like inheriting the memories of distant tarantulas nesting silently within piles of iris petals and dragonfly wings. Or a man like Ezekiel, whose masculinity is a splendor of emasculation, a rel-iquary for marzipan fancies, the tabernacle that frames panes of stained glass telling, only to the nave—the silent heaven-haunted chamber where I once twined lilacs among the raf-ters, blooms between whom nameless spiders weave poems of silk and repetition, in lieu of pastor's homilies—the jagged and incomplete story of a femininity hidden, buried in old ribbons, in his mother's dresses and in the way he holds a wine glass, in his hummingbirding around transsexual women, his terrified awe, his uncertainty about his relationship to breasts—an uncertainty not so different from his uncertainty about god— and in his drunkkaraoke idolization of divas, the way he shreds a melody to pieces straining for the high note, surrendering to the impossibility of it with the faggot glamor of a falling angel.)

So I kept talking, kept drinking.

Eventually I became aware that the man had started speaking in an Irish accent. I don't remember the story of his scar, which he told me anyway, something valiant about getting caught up in ropes and struck by falling rocks belaying a friend who was hanging dangerously from a cliffside; I believe I remember him saying that if he'd let his friend fall, he could have saved himself, perhaps in order to move me with evidence of his noble heart.

"Are you Irish," I said.

He blinked. He chuckled. Rubbed his mustache as if to make a mis en scène.

"For four years I was a bartender in Dublin," he said, attempting a nonchalantly rakish smirk which presupposed the charm of his *au naturel* performance:

"So now I have an accent when I get drunk."

I could no longer feel my pussy. My hands were marble. My skin was anesthetized. My soul was imagining telling Noel about this later. I don't remember how we got to my bed, but I remember wanting to shut him up.

To fill a Gap,
Insert the Thing that caused it –

At first it was hot enough; smooth, almost effortless. He loomed over me like a freeway. My cunt was slick, was wet, was sloshing. I was drunk. Watching transparent static ripple and vibrate in the air of my room, bathing in his shadow, forgetting: imagining Ezekiel, imagining Velvet. His hands were all over me. His cock was filling me over and over again. I felt the imminence of pleasure. At last my cunt was opening to him like a sigh. Maybe it would be alright. Maybe I was horny for antithesis.

Until he tensed his thighs, arched his back and rammed against the back of my pussy.

I screamed.

Casually he said, "Let me know if that's too much."

And he returned to thrusting. I didn't know what to say. I thought a scream, not a howl of pleasurable pain, but a piercing, unbridled scream—I thought that was a form of direct communication, so I wasn't sure if he was feigning ignorance and testing my limits, if he wanted to see how much a tgirl's cunt could take, as Stella later suggested, or if he was so self-absorbed that he'd never taken note of the difference in signal between a woman's ecstasy and agony.

"There's a little blood," he said.

"I always bleed a little," I said, which was mostly true regardless of whether I was dilating or taking rough cock, but was always true when I didn't trust someone. I knew by this time to trust my cunt.

But—he had said I was the first tgirl with a pussy he'd ever fucked, the first tgirl period. Often men lie about this, proclaim it like flattery, the inverse of fetish; often they get off on the fantasy of themselves as virginal, breaking open a taboo for the very first time, but even so I thought about what he might come to believe, what he might say to his friends or online if my pussy failed to provide him pleasure. I didn't want to be the proof of a mistake. Words were inaccessible, like when you try to scream for help and only a tiny whisper of air slips out, because you are in a dream of someone chasing you with a knife. (In a dream, the only way to escape is to fly.) Maybe he knew I would be easier, more submissive; I've seen screenshots of chasers posting on internet forums that tgirls are ideal fucks because we are beautiful but insecure, naive and desperate for love, best for onetime use. Perhaps the fact that I didn't want to disappoint him meant that his earlier insult had in fact pierced me, had caught in my throat. Sex was so simple when I was a fairy, my head pressed into a satin pillow, my ass in the air, myself nothing more than a gilded vial for another fairy's cum, long before the world told me I was beautiful, before I forced the world to fuck me like a woman, before he stopped abruptly and jammed his thumb into my clit.

"I want you to cum," he said. He wanted a show. He was pressing me like a button.

Please, I thought. Let me dissociate in peace.

I said: "Let me get my vibrator."

I began to turn around, but he caught my arm.

"No," he said. "I want to make you cum."

It was a night at the arcade. Panic seized my senses. My body was in cryosleep.

Just this once, I thought. Stay awake.

Give yourself to him so you can free yourself of him.

"We should go to my place," he said.

"I already told you…," I said quietly. That I don't go to a man's house on our first date, which was true when my cunt said so.

"I know," he said. "But I have a king-size bed. It would be so much more fun."

His eyes were insistent. His voice was irritated, but patinated with a coaxing, cloying whimsy.

"I don't know," I said.

"It's only like ten minutes from here," he said, reaching for his phone. "I'll call us a car."

I paused.

"I'm sorry…" I said, wincing. Avoiding his gaze. "I promise I will next time."

He pressed his cock back into my pussy lips.

"Fine," he said.

I was disgusted with myself. Disgusted to have almost gone to the man's house, disgusted with his idea of sex, disgusted that I already knew I wasn't strong enough yet to refuse him outright♥ and disgusted that I was instead giving him my pussy like a peace offering; I was disgusted, too, that I was afraid, afraid of his anger, because I had promised myself I wouldn't give another man the satisfaction of spitting on my No; not after so many hours practicing in the mirror or on the bathroom floor with a handle of vodka in one hand and a bloody knife in the other, scarlet fingerprints all over the frosty bottle and blood streaming from my leg or forearm because I wanted to know that I could hurt myself more than you could hurt me, I wanted to know I could cut deeper than the man who knifed my face. I shouted No each time I sliced my skin.

I closed my eyes, trying to listen to the sensations in my cunt, trying to fuse the aches and curlicues, the sparks and shocks and sudden tides, trying to mass them into a density of pleasure. After a while I remembered how. Pleasure began suggesting its own possibility. I've always liked having a cock inside me, as if I were realizing a destiny as small and perfect as a key and locket.

But then he thrust again against the back of my cunt. Again I screamed, what you might call a 'blood-curdling' scream, but this time he did not halt; this time he kept ramming and this time each was harder and faster than the last, like the scale model of a battering ram trying to cave the front door of a dollhouse. I was screaming. I did not stop screaming. I was screaming like someone whose thoughts are broken, like someone whose thoughts keep breaking:

"Oh my god," he said, shuddering. "Oh my god."

♥ I wasn't even Aurora then; I was an ingenue with three older transmasc femboy lovers, two of whom hated each other, two of whom I hated and a third, Velvet, whose heart was soft, whose stories were many and whose pheromones were, with mine, wordlessly histocompatible. And then there was Noel, neither lover nor friend but something unknown, as if we were both moons of a distant planet full of ruined temples and poisoned lakes and glades of moss where generations had passed in life and breath and love and death, and no one ever knew, and no one ever would.

135

He collapsed onto me, pinching my diaphragm. I couldn't breathe.

For a moment he rested there like I was a bed. Then he pulled his cock out and rolled over. His cum was inside me somewhere. My sheets were scarlet, my pillowcases were yellow, there were no windows, or only a window onto a brick wall. I had painted my walls powderblue.

After a few seconds my cunt began to ache. Often I am sore after sex, often there is the sweet ache like honeycombs empty at last. But this ache persisted, and I couldn't see it.

I asked for a few minutes alone. He slipped into a half-buttoned flannel so awkwardly that I looked away, because it was too much, just too much to see the pastiche of a lumberjack struggle with his own fabric. Eventually he left to smoke a cigarette on the kitchen fire escape. I stood up slowly, trying to catch my breath. I felt a droplet roll down my leg; then a second and third, and bent over to get a better look. I like watching cum spill from my cunt, like the tide retreating from a seaside cave. And so I decided to distract myself while the pain abated, while I whispered 'it's okay, baby, it's okay...'

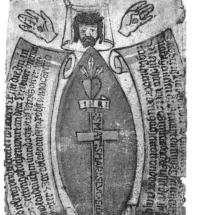

But I didn't see cum because instead I saw blood. I looked back. In the place where my hips had left an impression on the bed, a pool of blood was absorbing into the sheets. Bloody handprints marked the wall. The pillows, too. I felt something inside me tighten. Then, all at once, a dense, excruciating pressure—and blood burst from my cunt, showering the carpet.

I stumbled into the living room. Doubled over, hands

shaking, blood spilling down my legs, I hesitated at the threshold of the fairy circle. Something inside me was broken, but I couldn't see it, I couldn't see it, do you hear? I can't see it, my god. I only remember my awareness narrowing, reducing itself to the shape of an unseen wound. Now that *cristly queynte* made another sort of sense—the body felt only as a slit of screaming scarlet.

Blood spilled slowly onto the hardwood. I was afraid to disenchant the door. I was afraid to see their foxeyes in the dark, watching me with the swirling unseen silence of the deep wood.

But a cigarette was burning down the seconds, so I knocked, lightly, three times. Noel opened the door.

"I'm sorry," I said. "I need your help."

*

After a few glasses of wine, Noel had fallen asleep beside Stella in a bedroom a few steps down the hall. Now, following a stream of red droplets to the place where I was crawling, hand and knee, across the carpet, they stumbled, halfawake.

In my bedroom, crouching in front of my bookcase, making a scarlet pool, I said something neither of us remember, adrenalized but compressed to a harsh whisper, because I was nevertheless a woman in public, the public of that man. I clenched my jaw so that I would not scream, so that the man would not overhear; I was grasping at privacy because something had been exposed, but I couldn't see what. One center, one diamond, one woman.

As he clambered back into my bedroom, that man said, "Oh my god."

"It's not your fault," I said.

I was burning with shame. The seam was showing. I could not conceal the seam for the sake of the man. My body had reached its maximum. I was trying not to faint.

137

"Don't worry," I said. "It's not your fault," while he loomed over me wide-eyed and stammering.

He was saying,

"I think it's time for me to go," but he didn't go. Incredibly, his accent endured. He stared, he said, "I think it's time for me to go" and that was the only thing he said, but he kept saying it. He was speaking in a sort of singsong like someone reciting a nursery rhyme, every time lengthening, deepening the final syllable almost melodically, until Noel, after the fifth or sixth iteration, placed a hand on his shoulder.

He left.

He left and then, imitating a tiptoe, returned for his backpack.

Then he left again.

Out the window, first near and then fading, then almost not at all, his flipflops echoed up the empty street.

V.

DOLL PARTS

Now I was screaming.

The man was gone, so I allowed my crystal facets to scatter and fall away from my mind, away from thinking, away from interpreting, because I could not absorb any more stimuli because my soul was already the size of a wound. I was screaming and my eyes were shut tight. I could not hear anything because hearing was howling. I could not taste anything because my tongue wasn't there. But Noel was panicking about the blood, they were calling an ambulance, speaking to an operator and I was crawling out into the living room, eyes closed, ass bare, nothing but a tank top on, blood oozing voluminously like magma from my cunt. I was crawling away from the operator and away from the logistics of a wound. I was screaming like an alarm, continuously and without abatement. I was screaming into the ancient future like a fallen angel under the influence of a centuries-old bottle of Double Scorpio. I was simply and tunelessly howling away the instant.

whistling again, invisible, a sound meaningless and profound, inflexionless, ceasing as though cut off with the blow of a knife, and again

I could not bear to be so close to the instant. Something inside me was breaking. Something inside me was pouring out

that sense of water swift and peaceful above secret places, felt, not seen not heard

it was still happening, inside my cunt it was happening— that man was thrusting, each thud as regular and relentless as a pulse, so blunt and searing I could not catch my breath: I was screaming because I could not catch my breath, because every few seconds inside my cunt formed the loop of another

139

iteration of the instant of that man shuddering, thrusting, while I screamed, because at that instant I had been screaming like someone being stabbed with a dull blade—until a gust of luminous wind swirled round me, an illuminated breeze circled me, and though my eyes were closed I sensed a Presence floating, rustling toward me across the living room, sliding down beside me in one graceful curve like a scythe gliding low among stalks of wheat, cradling my cheeks with long and delicate fingers, delicately lifting my head and resting it on her lap, stroking my hair, silently wiping away my twinkling tears

For Occupation – This –
The spreading wide my narrow Hands
To gather Paradise –

unfolding her feathers, sheltering me with her wings, enclosing us in a private dimension as small and infinite as a drip of morphine, where I found respite from the heat of instants, where nothing was spoken but something was felt, a love so impersonal and intimate that for the oasis of those seconds, breathing an atmosphere not of oxygen but of oxytocin, we were as archetypical as a *pieta*, though not like a Madonna and Child (we were not classical) but like sisters, because for those seconds we shared something like a substance, something like a silence as intricate as speech, for those seconds my second roommate Eris—a spindly, wraithlike, beautiful, restless, fervent, clever and often mercurially cruel tgirl who had followed me on Instagram years before and told me how estrogen can be extracted from piss, a Pisces who would share her dreams and terrors with me cyclically and then, exorcising her nauseated shame in centrifugal retches of rage, snidely punish me for listening; a friend or recurring acquaintance of Velvet's who before that night had never touched me on purpose, as I had never touched her, so that, over the course of months previous, when, every so often, we had briefly and accidentally grazed each other, we both were nearly scandalized, struck suddenly and uncertainly shy—Eris had intuited without premeditation precisely the care I needed at the very moment I was least able to communicate it, much less to specify it, because my thoughts kept shattering, because that man was thrusting:

Eris was cradling my head maternally like a sister, as if we had known each other all our lives, as if we were sunset nymphs, had been Hesperides, Daughters of Dusk and Sisters of the Evening centuries before in the fabled Garden of Golden Apples, when my name was Hesperia (*twilight glow*) and hers was Aegle (*final dazzle*), because for those seconds that was what I needed and because for those seconds that was what she needed, because there was a dream we shared, one form of which my body (...bloody scroll unrolling in the sky...) in some way guaranteed or materialized for Eris, whose faith helped to guarantee or materialize it for me, so to keep living we both needed to believe in that dream, and my pussy was part of that dream, for both of us a pussy was part of that dream, so for her own sake as well as for mine Eris was holding, was cradling our dream, because the dream was failing, because the dream was broken and bleeding, because the seams were splitting, because the man was thrusting, the man was wounding, the man was mocking the dream:

so Eris was performing a miracle, an almost bodily miracle because my pain was slowly diminishing, for a little while my pain was abating, because Eris was not condemning me to the form of a cautionary tale, was not exorcising me from her life like a botched fantasy, like, 'I used to live with this girl Aurora who broke her pussy...'

Despite her serrated reticences, her embarrassed resentments; despite her months of prickling distance, she took no pleasure in the failure of my beauty: our relationship was, under force of extreme pressure, briefly and intimately crystallizing into the opaque corporeal meaning of silent nymphs in a forest grove: she was rocking me, she was soothing me, she was stroking my cheeks with the tips of her blue etherealized feathers; she was loving me as her sister because my dream was spilling…

I opened my eyes. Eris was and was not herself. I did not get up from her lap, because when she touched my cheek as delicately as if she were arching her fingers over the keys of a piano, I felt the reverberations of Aegle, all the way from that distant garden.

I asked Noel to dial my surgeon Anastasia, who'd given me her cell number after I was knifed, and who I trust sometimes more than anyone, often to an unreasonable degree, because we are strangers with a thread of shared fate: we are bound by my pussy, the first cunt she ever made. Surgery shares materials with weaving and with sculpting, but it also shares materials with wounding and with living. Transsexuality shares surgeries with celebrity. For her I am half material, half muse; for me she is demiurge, despot and savior. Now she's made a thousand more; every day she repeats the ritual, the leap of faith, but for her I am the original copy, the original of which does not exist except in the intricate, historically contingent and overdetermined virtuoso prehensile instincts of her fingers, pressing on my skin with a scalpel. But I have never felt her blade, except as a latterday twinge. Anesthesia erased the pain of surgery, but with the pain went consciousness. My memory holds no record of my most acute hours of embodiment. Those hours belong to Anastasia, to the visceral memory of her gestures and the spiritual memory of her benedictions. I fell to nothing and woke up. For me there was not transformation (*the purely temporal, continuous relation of present to past*) but disjunction (*wherein the what-has-been comes together with the 'now' in a flash, forming a constellation*): *bryme of blod, whirl-pit o swirlen tyme*, not progression but *image*, suddenly emergent:

Anastasia, woken from slumber, believed or wanted to believe that I was experiencing a superficial tear, i.e. one which was more bloody than dangerous. I knew she was incorrect, but I also knew she was somewhere else. Most of all I knew she was one of very few doctors who had seen, let alone made, a cunt like mine, and I needed her protection. But I could not summon her; she appeared, suffused with a silver glow, precisely when she wished to, beneficent but slightly unsettling, bubbly but irresolvable, manicured, resplendent and, like Glenda, cheerfully opaque. Each time I spoke to her, my mind was dazzled by the glare of her obscure compassion; my mouth was bewitched into demure and elliptical conversation. Often I failed to express my needs because I felt guilty about 'critiquing her work,' as if to speak too ardently would risk destabilizing her atmosphere of pressurized charm, the euphonic balance of disclosure and distance that gracefully conflated the paradoxical intimacies and formalities of her office. Or more precisely: I felt afraid of offending her, as if to describe the heavy miracle of my cunt forthrightly would risk the withdrawal of her favor. Maybe I had been projecting onto Anastasia a hazy memory of Miss Honey, or the hazy memory of all the beautiful women who had protected me growing up, but now I was confronting the system failure of my overdetermined fear of rejection, of the danger of rejection's possible form relative to the danger of my present reality—now, inspired by necessity, I was calling Anastasia at midnight at her personal cell number.

But Anastasia was saying the doctors would know what to do, that it would be straightforward, and I realized that she wasn't coming to help me, that I had been naive to think she would come, that to her I really was one more hysterical transsexual—and then I could feel it again, first far away and then very near; the sunset spell was broken; even the warmth of Eris could not protect me from it: the man was breaking my cunt, the man was still breaking my cunt, so I said okay and thank you and goodbye, because Anastasia wasn't coming, and the ambulance was arriving, its swirling lights fanning red and white foam across the kitchen ceiling, and my dream was soaking the fringe of the carpet, my dream was pooling on the hardwood...

...and three men were filling up the kitchen, two of them middleaged, one of them a trainee, maybe twenty, gawking covertly at the wound while the others were opening hard red plastic briefcases and unfolding a sort of lightweight canvas chair...

...and Stella was floating, was billowing forth from Noel's bedroom, was arriving at last, borne along by the song of the ambulance, observing silently the arrangement of my body, so reminiscent of a pregnant woman breathing through her contractions...then the mossy knoll of my Mons Venus, the pillows of my pussy lips, the small scarlet waterfall dripping between my hips...

...and for the first time she was meeting my gaze, she was looking directly into my eyes. I was infatuated by a sudden tension in my psyche; incongruously I was flooded with passion, and wondered, as if I were hosting a party, whether I looked pretty...and I thought I probably did...

"I'm so sorry I interrupted your date," I said.

Stella smiled.

"Don't worry about it," she said.

One of the men tilted his head, studying my cunt. Then he handed me a ream of gauze.

"Cover it with this," he said.

Noel brought a pair of underwear to hold the gauze in place. The men lifted me into the air. Eris faded. I was borne through my living room and out the front door. The men stumbled on their way down the narrow stairs. The man was thrusting. I was screaming. Noel offered their room to Stella. Stella told Noel she was coming. She would ride her bike and meet us at Woodhull. Later she would tell all of her friends about the night my pussy was broken, and even later she would tell me how she told all her friends.

*

It wasn't the first time Noel and I shared an ambulance, and it wasn't the last, but every time is because of something that has happened to me, or some way I have happened to myself, or because I am having another surgery, chasing after beauty under the aegis of AmidaCare; in the shadow of me narrating my life profusely as if my voice were impregnable and rolling like tides across the pages, Noel has secretly been affixing poultices to my wounds, wrapping my limbs in bandages, scrubbing my blood from the floor, wringing it from my blouses and underwear, collecting blades and shatters of glass from my hiding places, removing bottles of liquor from my bedroom, absorbing my screams, singing along with my sudden melodies, holding my hand in ambulances on the way to Woodhull: When an event happens to one person, it reverberates along the ply of her affections. Within the silk matrix of a spider's web, every line is open. One evening last Spring Noel assisted me as I sutured a selfinflicted wound, placing their finger on the looped thread like I did for my mother when she tied ribbons on Christmas gifts. I couldn't do it without them, which gave them no choice. They stopped coming in the ambulances after that.

(Because, look, said Noel, *if you learn about yourself through moments of intense chaos or destruction, and if in some way you look for those things, it makes me feel like, how much are you subjecting the people in your life to? How can you pursue what you want while keeping the people in your life safe? You create moments of embodiment when you harm yourself, do you not? But you rely on having these counterpoints to bring you back down from these moments, someone who can help you with the more practical areas of it. You get the meaning and the scars on your body, but there's always going to be someone there to help you clean up the blood, because life has to continue in a certain way, intense moments can happen but they kind of, like, I don't know... It's almost like you use these more, like, stable or neutral presences in your life as a way to, like, bounce meaning off of, you know? And then you have these intense moments, but there are still people there to ground you, but the intensity of those moments little by little really destroys the resolve those people have, because they aren't getting meaning out of it, there's no realization in it, it's just pain. I'm just absorbing the material reality of your moments of pain. It's not as straightforward because it's not "my experience," but I need to have some kind of release from it, because it just gets bound up in love and care and worry, and it just makes love feel really heavy, it makes my love for you feel really heavy, because it's so synonymous with caring for you after something severe has happened, and like, I don't think that that's like, fully okay for one person to carry, and it just feels really sticky, and the more things happen, the more I'm bound to stay here, doing the same thing for you, being here for you, not making you have to figure out who's going to help you, but that gives me nowhere to go, and doesn't allow me to feel free in my love for you, it makes me feel anxious in my love for you, so what you see as me trying to control you, constantly picking at these things you should be doing with your body, it's just the only way I can, like, show my love for you, because I can't feel happy in my love for you or feel like it's mine because I don't really know what else it is, my love for you has become a way to help you keep surviving…)*

But that night they were still holding my hand. I was screaming. Again I was screaming like an alarm. But the screaming wasn't enough, because the ambulance was rocking, was halting, was jerking forward; the ambulance was destabilizing me, loosing shocks and sparks in my cunt. My eyes were closed, imagining something else; then thrown open to the jostling brightness. Bile rose up my throat. I writhed. The trainee twink looked down on me in terror. I began punching my legs to decentralize the pain. I bruised my legs distracting myself.

We arrived around midnight. I was howling. Now I remember howling because the doctors and nurses didn't like it. As she was wheeling me toward the emergency department's double doors, a nurse mentioned dryly that, due to the worldwide virus, Noel would have to wait in the waiting room, and I said:

"Wait."

I said:

"Hold on a second."

But she didn't stop; she didn't even pause, so, adrenalized by outraged panic, I slammed my foot onto the wall, exerting an equal and opposite force and halting the stretcher myself. Security guards leapt from their seats.

"My friend," I shouted. "I need my friend. They have the phone number for my surgeon."

The nurse said okay, she would speak to my friend, but if I wanted treatment, etc. etc., so she wheeled me through the doors and parked my stretcher along a free stretch of wall in a crowded hallway, then wrote down Noel's name and left. I was howling. The man was wounding me. No one offered me a mask. After a few minutes someone moved me into an office or exam room just off the hallway, where they left me. Eventually someone appeared and asked if I was on my period. No, I said. I don't have a period, I'm a transgender woman. Then she left. Then someone else appeared and asked the same question. She asked: is your flow normally this heavy? She wheeled me back into the hallway, then down the hallway and into one of a number of rectangular spaces veiled and demarcated by medical curtains, facing onto the main desk of the emergency department.

A doctor came. I was still howling. She was irritated by my howling and told me to stop, that I was disturbing other patients. I said I was in the worst pain of my life. She put something in my IV. She didn't say what. I later found out it was

Tylenol. She left. People came and left. The man was wounding me. I was howling.

"I need a mask," I said.

"Hold on," she said, wheeling me into a small room crowded with doctors and computers and other patients, where there were no curtains.

"I need a mask," I said, "before we go in there."

"*Hold on*," she said curtly, wheeling me into the room.

"Listen to me," I said.

She stopped replying.

"This is fucking bullshit," I shouted. "My cunt is *throb-bing*, whatever you gave me is doing *nothing*. And I'm *not* going in there."

I ripped out my IV.

Blood squirted from my arm, arcing uncannily through the air in a perfect single stream.

I stanched it with my underwear, which I had earlier removed in order to allow a doctor or nurse a brief cunt inspection.

Now, gritting my teeth furiously, I lifted myself off the bed and onto the cold linoleum, where I stood, swaying, in front of the doctor. I was barefoot because my sandals had fallen off in the ambulance. From the corner of my eye I glimpsed a fresh swamp of blood in the bedsheets.

"You may have a *laceration*," she said, "inside your vagina, okay?"

"I don't give a fuck," I said. "I don't fucking need you. I've sewn my wounds with a fucking sewing needle."

I stumbled out into the hallway, swift and unsteady, and back through the double doors. The guard leapt from his seat.

"Don't you dare touch me," I said.

He approached me slowly, silently, widening his arms like a wrangler.

"Don't you fucking dare," I said. "I'm fucking leaving."

He hesitated, stepped back. A trail of blood was gleaming behind me on the linoleum.

"Aurora," said Noel. "What's going on?"

I said they were just moving me from room to room, asking the same question, and giving me nothing for the pain. I said I was leaving.

Noel gave me a look like *you can't sew your own cunt.*

And they were right.

*

Back in my hospital bed I was approached by a new doctor. Later I was approached by another doctor. Then maybe another, or maybe a nurse. Or maybe there was only one? Or maybe a couple nurses and a couple doctors, but never the same one, so I kept it simple; one after another, I told them: "I am a transgender woman (male to female)." "I had vaginoplasty / bottom surgery two years ago." "Tonight I was injured while having vaginal sex." "I am in the worst pain of my life." "My friend has the number for my surgeon."

And one after another, they asked whether I was on my period.

"I don't have a uterus," I said.

They didn't seem to believe me. *Too many notes!* Or maybe they simply weren't listening, or maybe they were dazzled by the splendor of my cunt, or maybe they thought I had brought it on myself, or they were tired and just didn't want to deal with a transsexual, or my beauty convinced them I could not be transsexual, they simply refused to believe I was transsexual because to believe it would require that they rearrange their relationship to beauty, so they inevitably replied:

"Is your flow normally this heavy?"

And they gave me nothing for my pain, nothing but a Tylenol. But the man was thrusting, so I was howling...

Only one spoke to me like a person, like a confidant. I don't remember why she was in the room, maybe to procure some supply from the cabinet beside my bed, but she wasn't my nurse. She saw my bloody sheets and asked what had happened. I condensed the story to two sentences. Shaking her head, not in disbelief but exasperated confirmation, as if we were gossiping:

"Men always think we want that…"

To really feel them thrusting, testing the limit: thrusting for the treasure they mistakenly assume is at the back of the tunnel, as if my cunt were only the mirror inverse of a cock, the mouth of our ouroboros: where I end, you begin. How deep can you go, baby? Uncomprehending of my clit, sensitized jewel, almost jellyfish, lambency of pinkish amber,

keystone of the arch
of the door
in the mountain,
let me in:
inlay of tentacled honeysuckles,
twisting, buried within rock like the living nerves
of improbable flowers,
let me in:

"Men always think we want that," she said, after I said,

"I was on a date with a man and we were having sex when he began ramming the back of my vagina…," bypassing my transsexuality by instantaneous evaluation of necessities, by brief and visceral measure of the osmotic imbalance between vital disclosure and lavish withholding, because,

// at that particular moment, howling unabated, I had ceased attempting to make contact with a medical fantasy that did not acknowledge the reality of my body; that refused to respond to my careful and consistent formulation of its necessities, necessities which I had translated into the Imperial tongue, the prerogative language of that very fantasy—a language which this nurse, herself exhausted by its taxonomic ruts, had discarded in order to address me like kin;

// the nurse—disrupting the atmosphere of that linoleum grotto with a flick of her wrist, like the invisible angel that, according to the Gospel of John, once stirred the waters of the pool at Bethesda with his hand, insufflating them with the healing breath of the Holy Spirit—was approaching me in the intimacy of a 'we,' like an oasis of shared meaning, which I did not want, at that moment, to risk disenchanting with the particularity of my confession, because although our cunts are different in form and maximum shock absorbency, and though a man may have different reasons for breaking them, the manner in which he performs the ritual is much the same;

// conversation had so far, by necessity, been corporeal merely; neither me (awake only in the adrenal dimension), nor Noel (shocked by blood and screaming, devoted to delivering me to safety), nor the doctors and nurses (devoted only to their reiterative predestination of my pain, as if they were experiencing another body entirely, another body in another reality, as if the miraging Aurora of another reality were overlaying my body, because, as for the unfableable wound, like me they couldn't see it, but unlike me they couldn't feel it, and because they could not feel it, they did not believe it), had yet communicated about the man—like, about the aspect of relation, like, about what the hell had happened not only in my body, but in my bedroom—so I welcomed the clandestine chitchat, the opportunity to vent, to cradle the event in the familiarity of gossip, to reduce the wound to the size of a conversation about the ways of men; welcomed, in the absence of my lovers, the presence of that woman, and the partial symmetry, enough to provide warmth and amiable commiseration, of our conversation, which was the closest I came all night to a painkiller. Then she left and I was so tired, because I had been waiting four hours, for hours the wound was oozing, for hours the man was thrusting, but I was so tired, I wasn't even howling now, just moaning.

Eventually a man said Obstetrics was sending a doctor down to see me.

"Are they aware I'm transgender?" I asked.

Knitting his brows, smiling *reassuringly*, nodding, repeatedly, in order to convey sympathetic understanding, "Yes," he said. "You will be considered *as a woman*."

That was precisely the issue.

I just wanted a doctor who I didn't have to teach. In between moans I was giving a talk on the state of the transsexual.

*

Another nurse arrived. She said it was her responsibility to notify me that I would be having surgery, and to notify me of the risks—including, she said flatly, death. So I asked:

"How possible is death?"

"Unlikely," she said. "But possible."

She shared a statistic. I'd been under anesthesia seven times before, but had never been told about death, which felt ominous, which induced a gust of paranoia. I was alone. I was frightened because I still did not know what was happening, because reality wasn't making sense, because I knew there was a wound and the doctors would not believe there was a wound, or they imagined there was, at least, a laceration, but didn't imagine a *wound*, that is, a hole, and therefore did nothing about it, or nothing urgent, because it wasn't an organ, it was just a cunt. It was either a cunt or it was a transsexual's cunt, which was perhaps for them a foregone conclusion, the split seams of a lesser fabric, to be rewoven when time allowed. I was alone and so tired. I couldn't bear it. Reality was dangerous and anything was possible, so, when she left, I seduced a resident—a man my age who smiled a little mischievously when he spoke to me, who seemed a little interested in me, titillated by it all, my cunt and my distress and my beautiful halfnude bloody splendor—into bringing Noel to see me before my surgery.

When Noel arrived, the world swung back. Tell me it will be okay, I said. Tell me it will be okay. They rocked me in their

152

arms and said it would be just fine. As I smell peppermint to reduce my nausea, I smelled their neck and hair to reduce my fear of death. Because for the rest of the night I was alone. Single player. Before they left, because mine was already dead and theirs was still at twenty-percent, we switched phones. We switched phones so that a trace element of Noel would abide with me in the caverns of Woodhull like a little baetyl.♥

*

Later the Obstetrics resident arrived to take me to an exam room. The other resident was whispering in her ear:

"Let me come with you," he said. "I've never seen one before."

I felt numb, because I did not want to feel a sideshow shame, so I phaseshifted into neutral, dropped through the trap door of dissociation, which is to say, I felt nothing and also felt flirtatious, because that was more manageable than antagonism, because whenever I'm wounded, I'm liable to cope with the sharp edge of the instant by opening myself to the possibility of falling in love. It's a soap operatic impulse, neither vice nor virtue

♥ Ancient name for sacred incarnated meteorites, derived from the Semitic phrase meaning 'house of god.' A baetyl is not made; it appears. It cannot be anticipated, cannot be generalized; is specific to the instant it decides to be born, specific to the encounter with the passer-by to whom it first reveals its expressionless face, a portal of perfect opacity to the presence of a particular god or more often, a goddess, transmitting a divine pulse, an Olympian echolocation, wordless, unpronounceable, denser even than birdsong, as speechless as rock, drawing witnesses, thereafter acolytes, who create a cult in its honor. Not word made flesh. Word made stone. A piece of mind, a metonym, simultaneously part and whole, in the sense that a splinter of mirror reflects, mirrors, no less clearly than its unshattered source. Like a mirror, a god is irreducible. Any holy atom is as much god as the agglutinated mass from which it separates, evaporates, dispersing—swirling into the chaos of mortal matter. Of the known baetyls few remain. Or at least few remain public, such as the socalled Needle of Aphrodite venerated at the Sanctuary of Aphrodite Paphia, on Cyprus. Where Venus rose from the waves, veiled in seafoam. Nearby, in Amathus, a cult was devoted to her sister or shadowself, Aphroditos, who is, like Aphrodite, a goddess of fertility and love. Most statues of Aphroditos depict her lifting her robe to reveal her cock; these were considered apotropaic, which is to say her cock warded off evil. Girldick is a good omen. Whether she took the form of a baetyl is unknown.

153

but vital overdetermination of meaning, the lacing of unbearable pain with astrosensual pleasure by suggesting a destiny, for every curse an equal and opposite miracle binding future to desire through the portal of a wound. As if a wound were a way of synchronizing the dream with the speed of time, because a wound is a release of pressure in which inner things become outer things—blood is seen, but dream is felt. Love is a meaning so acute that life begins to feel merely and elaborately euphemistic, burning with symbols, as if prophecy were as simple as opening your eyes. All roads lead to romance. (This so-called 'coping mechanism,' what I would call a compromise with life, is not, of course, a cure-all, and has led, often enough, to all manner of dead ends. See: four hours earlier on the living room floor, looking into Stella's eyes. See: months later, looking into Stella's eyes.) But most of all I was disgusted, distantly, like an aftertaste, because I never feel my seams more painfully than when you make me play your sexy little specimen, whether I'm in an exam room or bedroom, whether you're a man or a woman, whether or not you're a tgirl. But it's kind of worse when you are, like one girl, who, a few days after we first kissed, texted me *I'm obsessed with your vagina* and then, when I called her, said she meant *medically, as a friend*, because she wasn't looking for lovers; who said *fascinating* a week later when I came all over her fingers; a tgirl who, having dated tgirls, said tgirls are too insane, too intense, too complicated for her to date, at least for the next few years, but were welcome to be her friends, her sisters, and to sometimes share passion like nuns in the offhours, opening one another's prayer books. That last bit was fair enough, and the rest, I guess, in part proves her point, if the rest of this book hasn't already. The point of complication. *I only achieve simplicity with enormous effort.*

So the resident chaser wanted to see my cunt for free and I was too tired to refuse. I decided right then to think of it as a way of repaying my debt to him for breaking hospital rules. I was compromising my heart to make life bearable in an unbearable present, telling a fairytale to breathe through the nightmare. Besides, I knew that there, in the hospital, no one would question him if he claimed later that he wasn't sexualizing me, because every transsexual knows what it means to be desired *sub rosa*, or, really, sub revilement. I knew that there would be another beautiful transsexual woman in that hospital, and another, because there were men who broke our cunts if not on purpose then from the force of a hardly subterranean sadism, so I thought maybe he's not a chaser, maybe he is simply a passionate doctor who wants the best for his future transgender patients, maybe if he sees my cunt, he will be satisfied, just like when I was on a yearlong government scholarship at a high school in Shanghai, where one of the other American students, my closest friend, a girl with whom I had spoken intimately about my evolving sense of my sexuality, my evolving sense of my attraction to men, was cuddling with me on a night train to Xi'an, when, without foreshadow, she suddenly began touching my cock, at which point my body tensed fearfully, at which point she said something I don't remember now, something like "are you going to get horny or not," at which point I said something I don't remember, something apologetic, something yielding, at which point she began jerking me off until I orgasmed onto the cot silently. That was the first time I orgasmed from another person's hand. It felt possible because I did not want to have sex with her, which allowed me to be secure in the knowledge that she desired me, so that I was not anesthetizing my body worrying about my desirability, which had often prevented me from cumming with lovers; or like, so I was anesthetizing my mind rather than my body, in fact silencing my mind entirely and phaseshifting to neutral. I made my cock orgasm like a mechanism. The next night, after a long walk to see the sloping turquoise tiles of the Great Mosque, first consecrated in 742 during the Tang Dynasty; after walking along the ancient city walls, built under order of

155

Zhu Yuanzhong, the first emperor of the Ming Dynasty, after walking in the markets buying presents for friends and lovers—the next night at the hotel she wanted me to eat her pussy, and I thought maybe if I eat her pussy the best I can, then she will be satisfied. I don't believe that sort of thing anymore. I left the program within a month. She asked if we could have goodbye drinks, so I met her at a small empty bar where she got wasted and began to kiss me, grabbing the small of my back, pressing her lips into mine drunkenly, wetly, passionately—until I said I had to go.

Why am I so passive? When did I learn silence? I know, I know...but the question haunts me still as if the obvious were so obvious it couldn't possibly be the answer, because that's so sad, there is nothing for me to think about, nothing to make a language from, there is nothing for me to do except face it. Writing this book is a way to survive, because events keep happening, they started happening and they didn't stop, the car crash, the proliferation of breakups, the slicing down into the muscle, the slicing again, the psych wards and the events in the psych wards, the postsurgical complications, the knifing, the broken pussy, the et cetera, the broken fingers from punching a mailbox against which another ex was sitting, just after they threatened to call the police on me, just after they threatened to call an ambulance to have me taken away to the psych ward (like my grandma's best friend, who disappeared from the playground one day when a white van appeared and ejected medical men who wrestled her to the ground, lashed her into a straightjacket, and drove away) just before they stood and grabbed me, choked me with a headlock and threw me to the ground, whispering "bitch" as their lips brushed my ear, as their hair fell over my cheek and I smelled the scent of it like hay and hot prairie breeze—and all at once I wasn't angry or frightened, because all at once I wanted to kiss them, because I remembered falling asleep smelling their hair night after night, remembered when they whispered "I love you" in my bedroom with their fingers in my pussy, how for months they swallowed all my piss and it was better than an orgasm, my knees sinking into the red fabric of my pillows, my pussy resting on their lips, pissing straight into their mouth, recklessly relaxed, gushing, surging, in a sort of mouth-to-mouth drowning, the inverse of a resuscitation, and I remembered how they had choked me in my bedroom so romantically that I saw stars and fainted for the flicker of instant, falling limply into their arms like a damsel in distress; how their pussy had been made by the surgeon who taught my surgeon, how we felt each other's miraculous wetness for the first time one October dusk in Prospect Park, how it was the first time either of us had touched a ts_pussy other than our own, how beneath the hanging branches of a weeping willow we realized we were not errors but kin, not specimens but twin fountains in an enchanted rose garden, not solitary travelers but nymphs, dancing—just before they threw me into some restaurant's aluminum shutters and pinned me there with their forearm pressed into my neck, holding their other fist to my face like a weapon, saying, "don't make me hurt you, don't make me beat you up," before I grabbed onto them, holding them back as they started to walk away, before they kicked free, saying they owed me nothing, saying I was a child, a hysterical tranny, and returned to their apartment.

But before all that we had been arguing on FaceTime, because I was confronting them about how often, apart from sex, they forgot my pussy, because their pussy was suffering a drastic complication, their pussy was giving them searing pain, and the doctors were ignoring them, and I was emailing Anastasia, I was waking up in the early morning to go with them to Mount Sinai and help advocate for the pressing necessity of surgery; meanwhile I was talking with them every day about their pussy, and every day they spoke to me as if they were unaware of my pussy, as if I had no basis for comprehending their pain. Once, when I mentioned how my pussy had been broken two months prior, when I began to explain the pain of that man thrusting, they said they didn't have space to talk about my pussy. And when I confronted them on FaceTime, they hung up, so I took an Uber to their apartment, from which they appeared and said, "I'm breaking up with you, are you happy?" to which I said, "I don't care, I want you to listen to what I'm about to say," to which they said, "you're being childish," before storming off, up then down the street, before I placed myself in front of them, before I placed myself right in their path because I was tired of orbiting their Ptolemaic cosmology of pain, I was done and I didn't care if coming over meant breaking up because more than anything I needed them to take responsibility for their selfishness, without any further delay, I needed them to say it, needed them to hear themselves say it in their own words, like an incantation, in order to break the spell of their delusion—but to tell you about their delusion I would have to tell another story, do you see what I mean? There are too many events to weave into the constellation of my life-shroud, too many events and only so much meaning, so I'm writing this book of wounds, of events outpacing meaning, and I hope it can help you survive, otherwise what's the use? Otherwise, by my speaking, I'm just offering my particulars like the contents of my purse. Otherwise I'm just giving away more raw data to Empire.

// After reading my story *Ezekiel in the Snow*, Velvet wrote me an email:

Hi <3

I'm writing you on your birthday because I'm thinking you'd much prefer that over me joining in the barrage of calls you are inevitably fielding. I wanted to finally respond to Ezekiel in the Snow! We never really got to talk about it, and I feel like these emails go over really well with you, so I want to add another :)

Ezekiel is the one story in Unsex Me Here that is written from the perspective of a normie. To me it's like the bridge of a song, or maybe like a cross-examination. What I see you doing is smashing Elizabeth's minimalistic, quietly devastated voice up against Ezekiel's luscious, maximalist, unsexed one. You're pretending to behave at the beginning, pretending to write an MFA story. But at the center of the story is a character who won't comply with hushed, poignant dialogue, neatly woven plotlines, tastefully placed motifs...she won't comply with the humanist agenda of the liberal arts...I mean, she's not even human.

This is not to insult Elizabeth. I like her, she seems like a good lover and good sister. Her square-ness aligns me with Ezekiel, because I want her to loosen up and give up on this dimension with us. I also see her bringing some accountability to Ezekiel. After all, she does seem to leave a bit of a trail of devastation, of the heartbreak variety at least. Elizabeth and Aurora share that history. Of course, as a sibling, Elizabeth has to pursue. But Ezekiel kind of shits on their kinship, makes it conditional on their relation to a mermaid. A story Lizzie can't stomach, leaving them in different dimensions. She doesn't want her name returned. She stops hearing. Her fate, I think, is almost a threat to the reader. You might reject every dazzling word...but you'll never look at orchids the same way. Sorry!

I'm being called to help cook dinner, but I may send along more thoughts as they come to me. I also want to note that I saw two bears today, in broad daylight. Just lounging on some rocks.

Love,
Velvet

// After reading years of stories where my particulars were only elongated echoes in the static of a fantasia (*Via Crucis*, *Ezekiel in the Snow*, *I Carry a Peach*); and after reading an early draft of this book (*The Fifth Wound*) where the fantasia is nearby, where the fantasia is phosphorescing in our peripheral vision while the facts of my life are blazing, reflected on our corneas like sparks from the blaze of a campfire, Velvet wrote me an email:

I feel awkward writing this, because I basically never write anymore, except in one iPhone note where I painstakingly collect thoughts like:

"A needle is more phallic than a penis
A cock has never pierced my flesh"

Which might one day be a poem if it's lucky. Not any time soon. But I'm pleased that the drive to respond to your stories makes me want to write. Reading your writing has always been one of our most cherished forms of intimacy, that has become more dialectical now that I have been personal witness to many of the moments that have turned to image in your stories, as well as witness to actual moments of writing...not to mention how many of the ideas in these stories, I heard first as pillow talk.

I guess I'm naming all that because for me both these stories present reading and writing as per-haps the only way to really understand or to even DO relating at all. And then there are forms of speech-relation that are both-and, like weaving a dress of peacock feathers--is that not reading and writing simultaneously? And don't we always? And haven't we lived that, together?

It's funny that Via Crucis almost seems so stern and stark compared to Fifth Wound. Obviously it's a story that partakes of faggy extravagances, but there's an underlying tone of quiet devastation in it, like when you're done screaming or crying and you can barely talk anymore, and you also don't have to because you're satisfied with the sounds you've made. What I'm getting at is that it's serene. And I think the combination of camp and serenity is mind-blowing. Ultimately, I guess, it makes the angels explode, but not before ringing a very clear note that I still feel reverberating.

Via Crucis exists in the world of The Fifth Wound, since you reference writing it, which I guess you do with I Carry a Peach as well. So The Fifth Wound is maybe the outer layer of the dream that we have awakened in, where your room looks like your room, and Noel is there, and there I am, there's Loretta and Old Milk...

Something I want to acknowledge about the Fifth Wound, from my perspective at least, is how much it's actually an act of self-negation to include such personal stories in your writing, and how hard you usually write against that (that being the call for trans women to confess pain that may well be enjoyed by the confessor, to reveal details that are bound to be received as sordid, to tell the absolute truth so as not to be accused of fraud or deception). But I sense that perhaps you came to an impasse, where the most direct confrontation with Empire was in this exact story, and so you swallowed your ego and showed yourself. I guess maybe it's also that that project (confession and self-mythologizing) had been on instagram, where it is so encouraged, and ultimately that needed to be swallowed and digested by this story. I think Old Milk would like that.

Signed in blood & lipstick, your lover,
Velvet

So they wheeled me away from that cramped room with computers and without curtains, they wheeled me away in my T-shirt and single-use gauze hospital briefs while I tried not to bleed on the chair, because the gauze was already saturated, because the dream was spilling: I turned around one last time, looking. To remember. That was the last time I saw my underwear and shorts, mixed up in the bedsheets. My clothes were disappearing. Vanishing reality strip poker.

"Lie down on the examination table and open your legs," said the Obstetrics resident. It was sea green, tall as an altar. She examined my pussy while the man looked over her shoulders, but there was too much blood for them to see clearly, so they left to get a speculum. I was alone now, in a very small room, in silence, dripping—faster than a stalactite, but slower than someone weeping.

The woman inserted a speculum.

The man said, "Find her cervix."

I said, "I don't have a cervix."

My cunt was burbling like a freshwater spring.

The woman lifted her head from between my legs.

"Is your flow normally this heavy?" she asked.

Later an Obstetrics attending came to see me. The residents stepped out of her way. She examined me with the speculum but couldn't see my cunt clearly because of the blood. Nonetheless she told me calmly that she was going to sew the wound shut and that it would take about thirty minutes, but that they would put me under anesthesia because of the delicacy of its location.

Later I was taken to a perioperative room. I put my shirt in a bag and dressed in a hospital gown and a blue gauze bonnet, then I took a cute selfie on Noel's phone and sent it to Velvet along with, I believe, a text letting them know I was about to have surgery because my pussy had been broken while I was having sex with a cis man, and asked them to text Noel on my phone when they woke up if they needed anymore information, but that I would be okay and I cared about them and looked forward to seeing them soon. I must have also texted my mom and Noel, too, to say I love you. Then I turned off the phone and put it in the bag.

Later I was wheeled into the operating room. The IV drip of anesthetic was leaking on the floor.

"Why is that leaking," said the surgeon to the nurses.

No one answered.

"Why is that leaking," she said.

But no one answered, so the surgeon looked down at me and said,

"I saw in your bloodwork that your white blood cell count is high. Why would that be?"

"I don't know," I said. "I didn't know it was high." I was recumbent upon an operating table while nurses fluttered about me like I wasn't there, or at least without acknowledging me, so that I felt them as obliquely as blue moths. I was alone. My surgeon did not know why the anesthesia was leaking, nor did she know why my white blood cell count was high, which

163

later, after researching online, I realized was likely just due to post-traumatic stress and Lithium; nonetheless she kept asking, and I kept offering answers, my heart rate increasing each time she refuted me, until, at the peak of panic, I vanished. I traveled to Anesthesia. Bubble too small to call a dimension, wedged between the present and the future. Tiny abyss of air. What happened there is so secret that it didn't even happen, at least not to me.

Afterwards I nodded groggily in a postanesthetic haze. My surgeon told me she'd repaired a threeinch tear at the back of my vagina. As if that man were trying to break in. Grave robber. A year and a half passed before I could be fucked like that again. A year and a half, and only twice, briefly, and with too much effort, and not like before, not at all, really just halfway to fucking, because my pussy is so tight, because every time I dilate I feel that man thrusting. Every time I dilate my pussy clenches like a frozen pond. Ultimately I'm probably going to need another surgery, because he wounded my cunt and then fucked the wound, fucked the wound and fucked it harder, slicked his cock with my blood, splashed his cock in my blood, made my cunt bleed and then fucked my cunt with my blood, fucked not only inside my cunt but through it, into my guts, pleasuring his cock on the wound he was making, on the bleeding flesh of the wound he was making, on the ribbed mucosal wetness of the wound he was making, and at last squirted his warm cum inside the wound, bucked and squirted his bitter cum into the rift he had fucked into my cunt, his small buttocks quivering flaccidly before none other than the eyes of angels.

By fucking me there the man had fucked my fifth dimension, had forced his cock into my fifth dimension and so had fucked me once in many times and places, in one thousand instants at once the man had fucked the wound he made in me. His cum was reverberating through my fifth dimension. His cum was spreading transversally. His cum was making the future opalesce. I didn't see his cum but I felt it, just as I did not see the future but felt it, like a premonition of silver rot. Even Stella could feel it months later when we talked about that night, when she shivered as if sensing the substance that was rotting so many seconds, so many hours in so many times and places, the rot that was even licking the fringes of my fantasies, was even decaying my dreamworld, because there is no dream without my body, because my body is the place where the dream hides, because fucking my cunt is a timefuck, because my cunt is a cat's cradle, my cunt is woven from nerves and sutures and instants, from threads of flesh and time, not a matter of archangel Gabriel but a matter of the Angel of History, not a matter of predestination but a matter of interruption, a particular six hours on a particular morning, six hours offered by means of an anesthesia, six hours paid to the spirits that tend on mortal thoughts, six more hours of life on earth. Lost time is the foremost drug. My cunt is a cat's cradle. My surgeon wove it and that man unwove it. That man destabilized time.

(Two months later, in October, I was working as a hostess at an Italian restaurant. I only worked there for a season before I was laid off, but the courtyard is sentimental for me because one day in November on my lunch break, seated beneath its trellises of hanging vines, I would receive, from my editor, who I had met on Instagram, the email that led to this book. They read an early draft and brought it to their publisher, and it's because of them that it's now in your hands.

But the courtyard is also infuriating for me because one night in October, following behind a cis woman in a patterned dress or maybe in overalls, I can't remember clearly, can only remember the sense that would suggest to my memory a patterned dress or overalls—one night, following behind that woman, the man walked into the restaurant. I saw the shock register in his eyes. Mine were blue and blank, because even though my thoughts were breaking, even though I could hear the buzzing of my breaking thoughts, I decided to remain calm, remain opaque and smile and take them to a table, at which point I said,

"Welcome, your server will be with you shortly," and, straightfaced, without meeting my gaze, he said, Irishly,

"Thank you, ma'am."

I left and poured their beers without realizing, then, on my manager's request, went to get a bottle of wine from the attic. While I was gone I decided I would confront him. By the time I returned, which was after about fifteen minutes, because in my state of shock I had difficulty processing the names on the wine labels, they were gone. I went to the bathroom and sent him a text and told him he should have fucking paid me for what he did to me, that he should've paid me and should at the very least have asked if I was okay, and that if he ever came back to the restaurant I would spit in his drink and punch him in the face. He sent me a text saying he didn't know I worked there and wouldn't come back, nothing else. That was the last time we spoke.

A couple weeks later I went to see Anastasia at her office, seeking the comfort of her expertise and distant warmth, which reached me like the certainty of a future tranquility, the certainty of realizing, someday, my dream of easeful embodiment.

She said she couldn't see it clearly but the sutures looked good. So apparently no one could see it clearly, neither the woman who made it nor the woman who sewed it shut, nor nurses nor residents, residents nor attendings, angels nor demons, Sirens nor saints, not even me. What are you? I am a blurry object.

The only one who saw it clearly was Velvet.

The only one who foresaw it clearly was Elean'r.

But in Anastasia's office I was alone. Because when I told her how they hadn't given me pain meds, how I was in the worst pain of my life and they gave me Tylenol simply because they couldn't see it clearly, simply because they didn't believe in a wound or didn't believe in a transsexual woman or didn't believe my cunt was what I said it was—when I told her my cunt made them think I was a cis woman, Anastasia laughed.

The nurse standing next to her laughed. The nurse's name was Alyssa. Alyssa and Anastasia laughed riotously.

// Because they were delighted by the success of their surgery.

// Because it was so funny that doctors—medical professionals!—had thought I was a cis woman, so funny that she had done such a good job, she even fooled her peers! Because it was so funny how thinking I was a cis woman had led doctors, in the matter of my cunt, to dismiss blood and searing pain as status quo. How doctors would show such little respect for a cunt they didn't even know was transsexual. How doctors don't give a fuck about cunts.

I was alone, in a bright exam room. I was naked. My legs were spread open like a woman in labor. My injured genitals were exposed to the surgeon and the nurse.

I wanted to know I would be okay.

Anastasia and Alyssa were laughing.

I stopped breathing. I felt dizzy. My vision dimmed.

The laughing, the bright lights, my nakedness, everything was nauseating...

and then the man was thrusting. The man is thrusting. So I'm telling you the story of a few precious fluids, I'm giving you all my priceless errors because I cannot stop the bleeding—now I'm telling you everything because I was too afraid to tell a stranger to stop breaking my cunt.)

The next morning, Noel came back. They brought me underwear, pants and shoes. We spoke quietly in our little language. We held hands and shared a breakfast tray.

"No sex for a month," said the surgeon.

"Bad girl," said the nurse.

The sixth wound gave me ink, but no vision. It gave that man a way into me, but me a way nowhere. Nor did any saints rise from my pussy.

So I flew back to Anthemusa, where I am now, writing to you. And when I run out of blood, that's when I'll start singing.

BOOK THREE

NO LONESOME TUNE

I.

Poet Laureates of Scorpio Season

Say Severo Sarduy was planning a 'Eucharistic heist' at the Notre-Dame de Paris; say a fauxpearl rosary was hidden in his ass; say he was painting, with his powderbrush and a palette of eyeshadow called 'Whiff of Salvation,' a portrait of the Brazilian wandering spider who emerged once a day, at dusk, from the root system beneath the keys of his 1926 Royal typewriter, to hunt for one of the intoxicated moths who dined, luxuriously, on his innumerable silk thongs; say he called up a lover, gesturing, glossolaling—scribbles of smoke swirling from the tip of a long black Nat Sherman cigarette, always almost forming the shapeshifting letters of some Seraphic language—and suggested they pilfer a few sequined veils, silicone breasts, Kit Kat bars, false eyelashes, bone corsets, medieval manuscripts on the sacramental applications of pus collected from the stigmata of saints, and, of course, vast crinolines beneath which a few carafes of communion wine could easily be spirited, incognito, from the sacristy, especially because the breathless priest and his ruffled, clucking parishioners would be distracted by the infernal and infuriatingly selfserious pomp and circumstance of the pair's wordless Royal procession down the aisle—for the duration of which, and despite the Leaning Towers of their Bluebird-Nested, Cotton-Candied Coiffures, neither would so much as crack a smile—and back to his lover's kitchen, where Madame Sarduy would then, with syringe and needle, inject the blessed Blood of Christ into a dozen halfbitten peaches, retrieved from trash cans in the Tuileries Garden, and thus hoodwink the Holy Ghost into laying her Tongue of Fire upon an apostolic pile of rotten fruit. Say all of this had come to pass, and rising from the saccharine smoke of the Knowledge of Bad and Worse, the Christ,

171

dressed in her best Met Gala attire (woven, perhaps, from the layered petals of some heavenly flora—as brittle and mutely glittering as silver flakes of mica—sprouting from an overgrown median strip between the two narrow lanes of the Heavenly Highway) appeared before the dolledup Floating Signifiers (as she had once appeared, floating on a little cloud, at her Mystical Marriage to Catherine of Siena) to bestow on them (as she—the Christ—had once bestowed upon the Patron Saint of Pus-Sluts the bloody loop of her own Divine foreskin) a sugardusted Peach Ring, which, when licked by Sarduy's pinkly eloquent tongue, had, like some Proustian morsel in reverse, revealed to our favorite fairy a foretaste of the future:

Dozens of pickups, parked at the fringe of a field of wheat. A few horses stamping in the dust. One pink '73 Alfa Romeo spider, ventriloquizing Patsy Cline.

Beyond them, a crowd of strangers, haunted for months by a recurring dream, wade into the rustling stalks, seeking a clearing. When they find it, they lift their heads to the sky.

Now. Streaking forth from some unseen source, a spray of cerulean light. A blade of blazing, ultraviolet atoms slicing through a solid, pitchdark block of night.

Now, all at once, halting, hovering: a glitchy, shapeshifting blue fog, billowing over the field, the whole mass—restive, perturbed—shuddering like a sea urchin, rotating, erupting in unpredictable clusters of azure spines, which burst out, firm, cartilaginous, before abruptly melting back into smoke. One after another, three silver pulses shimmer across its surface; then, somewhere in its core, a swell of gravity shifts, drops, and—disintegrating in midair—swoops down the sky like a vast rusted scythe. Showering the earth.

The atoms are sucked back to a central point, where—globed, compacted, as dense as polished lapis—they spin, breathless, for a moment, before a gravitational exhale discharges them once more into the night. The dreamers stand, wait, murmuring under their breath.

172

Eventually, collecting in streams and rivulets, the atoms flow back, spilling over each other, rustling the wheat, climbing, rising as if atop the spout of a fountain, before splitting and swirling into a pair of elongating neon whorls.

They tremble and writhe, flattening stalks, scorching kernels, before chasing each other further, higher, while popcorn rains from the sky, and microscopic threads of humming silver gauze—arcing like heat lightning—weave and thicken into a web between the whorls, binding one to the other in a double helix whirling ever upward, skyward, bearing the souls of the Highway Kind♥ to the honeycombs of lost time, where seconds, thick, deep, sweet, are as bottomless as hours, as timeless as weeks; where the relation of present to past is no longer durational, and therefore irrecoverable, but simultaneous, and therefore substantial, as fine as a faroff constellation, as solid as a chunk of iron, so that the fifthdimensional wayfarers, bathing in honeyed hot tubs—their breasts rising, like lily pads, to the surface; their cocks hovering underwater like pink corals—begin writing verses to the tune of Time Regained, in the force field of a language freed from the fatal, inevitable twists and turns of a grammatical sentence: where cause and effect were, like the flowers in a garden, a question of relation, rather than, as in a geometrical proof, a question of logic. Let us take a moment of silence, then, on behalf of Kafka, who was so confounded by the complicity of storytelling in the tyranny of time that he could not bear to finish any of his novels, offering instead an *image*, that is, an irresolvable riddle, that is, a Little Fable:

> *"Alas," said the mouse, "the whole world is growing smaller every day. At the beginning it*

♥ Afraid of still waters, the Second Coming, Roman ruins, strangers attempting to tell stories, and drugs running out in the middle of a party; partial to dusk, dreams, poppers, acrylics, whiskey, Spring and Autumn, breast enhancement, train whistles, opals, candleflames, the Decline and Fall of the West, Dickinson's dashes, unsaddled horses, commas, cockslapping and cataclysmic infatuations; seeking nothing but transit, the sense of *going somewhere*, which always, immediately, evaporates as soon as the wheels slow to a halt.

was so big that I was afraid, I kept running and running, and I was glad when I saw walls far away to the right and left, but these long walls have narrowed so quickly that I am in the last chamber already, and there in the corner stands the trap that I must run into."

"You only need to change your direction," said the cat, and ate it up.

But Kafka was unlucky in love. Hans Christian Andersen was unlucky in love. The Little Mermaid was unlucky in love. I am not unlucky in love. I may, at times, dissolve halfway into seafoam, but so does any passionate woman after she turns off her camera. She might tell you about it, but she won't show you. Don't ask to see it. You wouldn't appreciate the iridescence. Sorry...

It's just that no one ever falls in love with seafoam, even if it looks pretty from a distance, even if it sparkles, because people think of seafoam as something already gone...no one would think to hold it...no one likes to hold something unsubstantial, it's awkward to clutch, too much responsibility like a butterfly: so if what you want is the dream, don't ask for seafoam, just read the book, because I placed the dream inside a book so that my seafoam wouldn't interrupt anymore...

But then, all of a sudden, I realized I am living with the book, as if the book were my bed, and sleeping on it would be a way of slowly perfuming the pages, because I couldn't describe the scent to you, can't photograph it, can only live with the book until it takes on some of my warmth, because the dream wasn't ending, I was drooling clusters of transparent pearls...

I needed to not live only in reality because reality was like a corset tightening continuously...there was so little breath for me in reality, so I needed to expand the width of the instant, I needed to bedazzle reality with the dream, as if sequins were seeds, bursting open into weeping willows made of sugar glass, because in the dream, in the meadow beyond the willows, I am a nymph telling a lullaby to a field of sunflowers, and the more I tighten my corset the easier it is to sing, as if it were forming me into an instrument, as if I were a kind of dragonfly and at the same time a flute, because in the dream I possess not only breath but melody, in the dream I am the daughter of the Ninth Muse and Aphrodite, and in the dream I have one implanted lung of a seraphim, a seraphim who gave me one of his lungs in exchange for my cryofrozen cum, which can, apparently, in the magmatic ruins of Heaven, be compressed into extraordinarily beautiful prisms that angels like to hide behind waterfalls or in quiet parts of forests where intersecting leaves hover like a heavy green consciousness—or at the center of an ant pile, in a crater of the moon or the knot of a tree trunk. This was an inadvertent book, I folded stories into it like nested gardens hiding prisms that allow a woman to timewalk, to timewander or timesing: I wrote the instants as I lived them, and then later I widened the instants as they emphasized themselves in relation to what came after. Then I wrote what came after; then after months and months, after each instant was no longer a flash of time but a foreshadowing of implications spreading like briars of shadow, I returned to the first instants and their later kin, I encrusted the instants with sapphires of reflection and emeralds of revelation whose every facet transmitted a thread of glow, twining with the others, until they emanated, together, an aurora of lost time.

I thought I was telling a story about a breakup, or the story of how a fairy disappeared into the forest with my peace of mind, not on purpose but in a sort of confusion, less as if he were taking it from me than as if he were tangled up in it, like someone caught in a thicket of thorns and cobwebs, ripping bloody vines from the weave of her cloak: I thought I was telling a story about how he vanished, tormented by my pieces of mind, because one woman's terror is another woman's treasure, because one woman's baroque thrill is another woman's nausea after tightening her corset too much, which is like eating too much hard candy, or drinking liquor in the morning on an empty stomach, or a lover saying something harsh without any inflection, as if they were texting.

I thought I was telling a story about a breakup like waking up from a dream into a nightmare, from a saturated reality into an arid unreality, the difference between an oasis and an abyss; a story about how I accidentally lost my meaning by tangling Ezekiel in it, by constructing it around Ezekiel like a diorama, like a diorama installed within the plexiglass shell of a spacecraft, whose thrusters would carry us both off the surface of the Earth and toward Saturn's rings.

In the course of trying to become beautiful—which was a way of protecting myself from everything that happened after I started wearing lipstick, and a way of proving everyone wrong, because my father said 'you don't look like a woman and no one will ever think you do,' because Ezekiel said 'you are pretty, but not beautiful,' because so many people said so many things, and because I had always admired the beautiful women in perfume advertisements—I became afraid, and I disembodied myself out of fear, so that my body became a silicone angel while my soul remained half awake, half in Anesthesia.

I mean I thought I was looking for my body, telling the story of how I went back to certain instants, intentional or accidental, intimate or traumatic or both, when I was word made flesh. But refusing the abjection of meaning as pain: accepting pain rather as a form of extreme embodiment, which suggests a route by which pleasure might travel to seek the same, which suggests a shape pleasure might take, as if Hell were also the mold of Heaven.

But all along another story was accumulating in the folds, all along and I didn't even notice because I wasn't writing it like I knew what would happen, I was writing it like the angel of the present instant, writing it piecemeal like a pigeon collecting breadcrumbs, adding just one more dash of sugar, assuming each would be the last. But two weeks ago I realized, almost in disbelief, that this book is half a romance. That the instants had been accumulating meaning, forming a constellation that was converging on another instant, when Ezekiel called me this very autumn, at the end of September. He told me he was in distress. ██████████████████████████████████████▾ I told him to return to Texas, to go see his sister and mother. Then the next morning, rapt, corseted, braless, whaletailed, freshly single and reading *Bad Bad* by Chelsey Minnis▾ in one sitting at a local coffee shop while light through the trees spangled the pages and reflected shadows of flowers, I sent him a text: "U can always feel free to stop by New York on your way…"

"okay Aurora it's truly in the air," said Ezekiel. He'd texted his sugar daddy, Alex, at six in the morning. Alex bought him plane tickets. A few days later he was in the city. What can I say…

After a year and a half of twirling his hair, a year and a half of daydreaming during our bimonthly phone calls, a year and a half of exclaiming, unprompted, how much he wanted to come to New York, but perpetually deferring the date of his arrival, perpetually selecting a date and then apologizing, selecting a new date which itself would pass unnoticed—so that I didn't expect him to come at all and took his exclamations for what they were, an expression of desire, the skittish expression of a desire uncertain of itself, that is, uncertain of its meaning—which was itself satisfying like tiramisu because I had already decided not to cast a spell upon myself, had already decided not to cast the spell unlocking the reliquary where I kept the wrath of wanting, because the book was enough, because thinking about the Ezekiel and Aurora of that ambered era when we briefly surpassed reality in the subatomic storm of a shared dream of two sleeping beauties writing stories on the petals of pink evening primroses and scattering them into the Pecos, mixing our mysteries into the mysteries of the world…thinking about the Ezekiel and Aurora who were neither one of us online much and therefore neither had the impulse for much of an audience beyond ourselves, each other, hypotheticals, a few friends, whatever spirits haunted our bedchambers and

▾ redacted quotation: verse two, lines three and four from "Flyin' Shoes" by Townes Van Zandt, about how autumn makes him feel.

▾ Given to me by Velvet over a year ago now, though I only began reading it, just as I only began writing about our romance when our reality ceased.

the extraterrestrial primroses that may or may not be growing on one of Saturn's moons…thinking about it all was sensitizing my dreamworld with nerves and fresh sensations, rippling through the starfluid birdbath where my memory swirls, churning within the waters of the belladonna lagoon beyond the sleeping straw-berry glade, phosphorescing its narcoleptic depths and revealing wingless angels with melodious gills, technicolor ghosts of jelly-fish, bleeding nymphs suturing one another's wounds with needles from the carapace of a puffer and thread spun by a blue spider among the petals of water lilies…

I've been thinking of you so much during this summer inevitably heavy (for a flit-hunger like me) cancer season, here at the brink of a more serious wildness I hope?

I've been thinking of you as I read Near to the Wild Heart, my favorite scene was when Joana was staring at Antonio as he was sleeping & the opacity of love/being emerging in its full strangeness, peril, & mystery … It's making me think of when we dreamed side by side together & apart & were in a very "I'll be here in the morning" giddiness despite the sublimity threading to crush our little fairy hearts

...and my phone calls with Ezekiel were a feverish pleasure, breathless like my conversations with Velvet, thrilling, almost manic but at the same time a form of slow flirtation, so much slower than the first night in the flowerbed, slower too than the Hounds of Love, so while I longed for him from time to time, I didn't ache: after a year of Ezekiel sending me his poems, reading my stories, sharing his secrets, stepping sideways into a pocket of duration, neither book nor world but song, not song but dialtone and hymn, not hymn but hum—after a year of what you might call 'getting reacquainted,' or (extrapolating from page 104) what Ezekiel might call 'swimming in the pool of reconnected light,' all of a sudden and all at once, on the run from reality, or maybe in search of the superreal, chasing the impulse and sweet chaos of a happy ending, Ezekiel was asking where to meet me, so I suggested the same coffee shop where I'd read Velvet's book conspiratorially as if breaking up were a way of falling in love again, sneaking back into the garden after dark, alone, under cover of delicious ferns...

Aurora: cutoff jean shorts, patent leather corset, gray crop top so gauzy and mothbitten it resembled a shredded segment of shroud. Freckles, blush, twinkling gloss, shadow of shadow. Extra Adderall in the right pocket. Scanning the courtyard like a woman who appears delicate, strong and tranquil. Because stillness—on a hot day without a breeze, like a flower reaching its sentient petals sightlessly into the glittering mesh of an experience of heat—stillness is desire pooling like perfume in the warm throats of honeysuckles, condensing with sweetness into a single drop...because there is no breeze to bear the sweetness away...

Ezekiel: baseball cap, spectacles, flannel, satchel full of cigarettes and books, seated at a rickety steel cafe table, chair and table both on little steel stilts like the legs of flamingos, but powderblue, and Ezekiel...my mischievous deep forest kink, my flickering candle, my candy lasso, my fairyvibratory exboyfriend: wearing what I used to call his 'poet's shoes.'

At the coffee shop: bunnylike reticence, hallucinogenic eye contact, peals and shrieks of laughter. Bubbles everywhere.

Afterwards Ezekiel took me to see a water fountain—full, brimming, but still and glassy as a mirror—in a park across the street.

He was taking a puff of a Camel Blue. Angelrouged, giggling sweetly, shivering a little,

"I saw this fountain in a dream last week," he said.

We were breaking open our night together. We were beginning. I was distracted by intrusive thoughts about time. I was distracted by memories of the paintings of Hugh Steers. I was distracted by the question of whether or not my body would allow me to experience Ezekiel, or whether hypotheticals would suffocate my senses. I was afraid that even though Ezekiel had come to me at last, he had come too late. Because the only way to survive my love for him, which was like thinking the same thought for hours and then sleeping and dreaming of the thought and then waking and continuing to think the same thought, some memory of Ezekiel's voice saying something opaque, something which, if I could clarify its substance, would settle the question of whether he had loved me, which meant I was beautiful or whether he didn't, which meant I was ugly, unfit to dream of flowers and topaz, because fairies who dream of flowers and topaz are the kind of fairies other fairies dream about, and if I was ugly then he wasn't dreaming about me, because even though I knew he believed I was, if not the daughter of Aphrodite, then at least the daughter of the Ninth Muse, romance is more than musing, romance is a matter of two bodies in motion, because movement is meaning, because when we are moving, we are accompanying time on its passage, we are following together in the flightpath of a god, we are the attendants of Hermes on a sacred mission, shod in wingtipped heels and sipping liquid mercury: whenever I imagine nymphs, they are dancing in a circle, holding hands—but to be a nymph meant being recognized as a nymph, meant other nymphs recognizing you as a nymph, not as an aspirant sipping from the sacred spring alone; so every day of remembering Ezekiel involved the intricate examination of one instant of recollected sound, like a torture because I couldn't remember precisely how he said it, couldn't decide on the words or on the tone, and each conjecture when reeled in his voice and visage seemed as possible as any other, so it really came down to the question of whether I believed I was beautiful or ugly, which meant realizing that I wanted to be beautiful more than anything else, my vocation on the earth was to slowly prove that I could be beautiful too, the only way to survive my love was to become so beautiful that no one would know how I felt the night he had looked at the moon. I became beautiful like a tomb for my love, I buried my love inside my beauty so that now it was only possible to love him with the ghost of love, like a voice accessed through prayer, a voice through the clouds...all this because he had been the first fairy I ever loved, I had sworn never to love a fairy but at last after seven years of daily denial had decided to die loving fairies and no one came, for two years no one answered my call of love, I sucked dick in search of meaning, tasted one thousand flavors of cum dreaming of a sepulchral doeeyed West Texas pixie, watching the horizon, waiting for him to appear from the mists of our future, my nameless nymph who I would recognize not by name, but by slant. Before I saw him, I felt him coming, felt him writhing and tangled in a net with translucent seahorses and the fossilized jaws of prehistoric sharks. Then one night, on a whim, I met up with an old friend from middle school who I hadn't seen since 2006, in Dallas. He shared his coke with me and his friends, and we caught up on the porch, then left together for a party at a little house in East Austin where a ~~boy~~ approached me and I recognized him as the fairy from my foresight, just as he (having, that night, already offered to blow two

181

straight boys, of whom one had said no, and the other, maybe later) recognized me at once as a stranger lately blown in by a swerving angelic gale—a silvertongued sweettoothed ~~boy~~, a sapphirereflecting intertemporal figment of effemination—to rescue, without premeditation, a damsel dying of men in a blue kitchen. The only way to survive my love for him had been to suffocate it.

But I wanted to be simple, so I chilled my mind to zero. I breathed in and out. In and out, baby.

As we wandered out of the park, I converged into the instant. I said,

"Can I take your arm," and smirking from shy surprise, he said,

"Yes."

Our romance beneath the green trees was restful, the leaves rustling, slowly heaving silver, pouring waves of silver into green, like silver rain dissolving eaves of green: me and Easy walking down the sidewalk for the first time in a century like two lovers...our bodies remembering, silent, skin to skin, conducting an infinitesimal heat transfer, because when your blood communicates like wine, when meaning is matter, when leaves flutter like hummingbirds trapped in the rafters, it's enough to walk down the street as lovers...

Our bodies were not only remembering, but sensing, palpating the passage of time. Our bodies were firmer now, hardened by the subatomic breezes of thousands of hours; but softer also in unexpected places. I felt a scatterplot of microscopic drift stippling my skin, an immediate intuition of the almost cellular shifts in his stature, his texture, his scent and sound since I had held him last, as well as an unanticipated ease with the syllable and decibel of his silence, that is, the manner in which he meant his silence, whether it was communicative or pious or personal or phantasmagorical or merely rhythmic, like the interval of oasis between stretches of sun. They were too many to name or know, but easy to feel. Our bodies were communicating by exchanging warmth and, in brief and fragrant telegrams, scent, enough to provoke a crowd of memories to rush and blur together, to condense halfway to clarity and then evaporate all in the space of an instant. There was no reminiscing, no crushing of butterflies between frantic fingers, as on those occasions when light haunted everything like a paranoia, when love was a noontime sun, because I had sometimes felt that if I didn't expose my every sensation as if my soul were exploding, as if the echo of the explosion of my soul resounded like an endless wave of confession—then I was lying, I was only creating for Ezekiel the illusion of a uniform love, which, for those intervals of mirage, I believed to be the ultimate betrayal: deciding for myself which substances to breathe into our shared secret glade and which to keep in my own lungs; responding to the needs and generosities of the instant, exerting in intuitive tandem with Ezekiel the shapeshifting impulse of vision over the composition of our atmosphere. I had not yet learned respect for the form of the helix, the parallel swirls laddered by bridges, or how to divine within that form a record of the movements of nymphs dancing with intertwined arms in the ancient future. I had not yet learned respect for the opaline seed of mystery which gives, to love, its pulse; had not yet learned that there is a reason for a skull, for a flesh, for a shocked cerulean cornea; for a braided mass of muscle, for a weave of nerve and blood vessel, for organs pendant and clustered like pearls, for the polymesh of sacred senses, as if our souls were spiders, burying themselves, on purpose, within sensitized hives of silk: there is no good reason to wound a lover in search of a glimpse of their soul, nor to wound myself attempting to offer a glimpse of mine; there is only the proliferation of mysteries, pressing up against each other; only the density of the knot, of the knots within the knot and within the knots, more knots, like a record of the flightpaths of two angels weaving light as they fall from the collapsing Heavenly Highway through atmospheres and layers of sediment and into the Morning Star Lounge, that honeycomb of subterranean opaline caverns where Fleck of God wrote the first draft of *Bathing in the Dark*, edited an anthology of angelic choral echolocations, *Songbook of the Seraphim Roosting Among Stalactites*, and— having at some point, perhaps by ingestion of magnetite atoms, developed magnetoreception—created tapestries whose textures mimicked the murmurations of those divine somnovolant flocks of flittermice on their flights of fancy.

Together we were glittering, glancing and sniffing with bunnylike exuberance. We were stopping in the bodega for sweets. We were sharing candied oranges and redtranslucent cylinders of strawberry licorice, sipping from silver canisters, like motorcycle exhaust pipes, of Red Bull. With hushed wonder, as if consulting a psychic, fearful of shattering some rare substance, we shuffled hesitantly among late autumn liqueurs and golden aperitifs, the blood of the Bordeaux and the pulpy milk of unfiltered sake; selecting a portentous honeywine, which tinkled like a love potion as I lifted it carefully from the tight rows of bottles blazing in luminous hues of amber.

"You're such a babe," said Ezekiel, while the trees reeled softly silver and green above us. As he followed me through the tall doors and up the narrow wooden stairs of my building, I imagined him watching my back, as a woman does when she is in the public of man or fairy, whether her swaying hips symbolize the sanctuary of femininity, like, *thank u goddess!!!*—or when they inspire a sunset of desire, wherein forms become more reminiscent and more vague, wherein the world becomes intimate, shadows catching like flames among the intersecting leaves; wherein desire becomes more a matter of scent than sight, a matter of blur and whisper, mischief like a bubble bath and passion like psilocybin, the romance of watching what you know dissolve in the burning pink phantasmagoria of dusk and the blueberry haze of twilight,

Soon we were in my living room. I was pouring Ezekiel a drink. I keep, in a cabinet beside my bed, as if they were crystal heirlooms, a set of four tiny and translucent glass teacups bought by Noel in an antique shop, one of which I filled with honeywine and brought to him, blazing azure like a fire opal, faintly tinkling atop a waferthin saucer. Despite his bashful, flickering sweetness, he handled the glass with grace.

"Aurora..." he said.

Because he was delighted by my infernal daintiness. The dream was always more than a language. The dream was not a museum or an archive, but a way of relating to time through trinkets and old treasures, bearing on their surfaces the traces of other rooms, other afternoons and other passions; records of the sudden or ritual movements of romantic, furious, frenzied or spiritualized hands in the smooth and faded spots, the bruises on the fruit, in stitches or mended cracks, in wounds or errors, in stains, dents, chips, scratches, creases, etchings or marginalia. Objects are marked by specific instants, whose particulates remain embedded forever in each perfect defect. A defect is a nick in time. So when I place dried milk thistles in a vase; when I arrange, beside a miniature silvering vanity (reflecting, in its dim glass, the slumbering ruin of her form) the lower half of a porcelain mermaid—found by Noel one afternoon in the refuse sands of Dead Horse Bay—atop a matching wooden attic bed, rickety and sheetless, designed to furnish a dollhouse almost a century ago; when I pass the teacup to Ezekiel, asking him to meet me on the back porch, then return to my room...circumventing chronology by collage or constellation, what we call 'decoration'...

- one window, eight feet tall, set into an alcove with antique white shutters. The lower pane environed by a green profusion of leaves, as if I lived within a treehouse, a lady's chamber suspended among creaking branches, floating on clouds of foliage.

The upper pane, meanwhile, was a rectangular depth of infinite topaz across which clouds drifted. My ensconcement in the skies. Reminding me, more often than not, of one of the final lines of Qi Biaojia's introduction to *Footnotes on Allegory Mountain*:♥

此在⋯雲客宅心

here the Cloud-Guest♥ can seclude [his] heart

- beneath the window, a cinnabar blanket spread over the mattress, topped with a technicolor quilt and a powderblue throw. Piles of blue and yellow pillows.

- the stacks of books I'm reading now, or beginning to read, or want near me to consult or reread (*Gravity and Grace, Soulstorm, Mucus in My Pineal Gland, Sun of Consciousness, Mimesis, An Apprenticeship or The Book of Pleasures, Popular Garden Flowers, I and Thou*)

- a powderblue bed tray Noel bought for me at an outdoor flea market in Cape Cod, on the underside of which is etched, in cursive, *Please Return to Mrs. Chester Martin*, above an address in Texas, a town by the same name as Noel's surname. I looked it up on Google Maps. A tiny house on a small ranch. Possibly a figure was staring out between the curtains of one dim window, or only a shadow hovering within a shadow—but when I saw it a shiver effervesced up my spine. I sensed a haunting to my left, as if an object were a portal between rooms.

♥ an essay he wrote in the 1630s to commemorate the garden he had built slowly, during the nine years of a midcareer retirement—having returned home to Zhejiang to care for his dying mother and to organize his father's manuscripts and library—in order to surround his scattered attentions with perfumes, to frame his mind with foliage, and hopefully recover the piece of mind requisite for reading a book. Years later he was buried therein, in a coffin he had himself prepared. His biography records the last words he spoke to one of his sons: 'Although your father did not fail in his family duties, I was however somewhat too addicted to the springs and the rocks. I was lavish in constructing my garden and this was my failing.'
♥ 云客 (cloud-guest or cloud-visitor) is a euphemism or epithet commonly translated, simply, as 'hermit.'

Objects don't die like we do. They are silent and eerily immortal unless acted upon.

- the altar with two wooden reliquaries (one glazed with green leaves and golden flowers, the other matte buttercup and chipping, protecting a fragile and complete opalescent shed from Old Milk, old postcards from Belgium, a birthday letter from Noel, dry cassia petals and a scythelike shard of bloody glass), an alabaster dish filled with a strain of weed called "Dead Hot Strawberries," a bottle of Double Scorpio, a deck of tarot cards, a chainmail protection amulet (now Ezekiel's), an empty pack of cigarettes from a Parisian lover, two cigarette butts with her lipstick traces still fresh, a needlelike chunk of quartz from another lover and a bundle of dried lavender.

Aurora: undressing. Hook by hook, lace by lace, like unlatching armor. Leaves rising and falling liquidly out the window.

Clutching my stomach. Eyes dim.

A feeling like a wedding day.

Plunging her hand into the softness, reaching for the few dresses at the back of the closet, selecting the gown I'd bought three years ago with Noel at the vintage store in Provincetown (more the dream of a gown than the gown itself, the possibility of wearing a dress like that), worn once, assumed lost, in fact stuffed into a bag in the basement, then found, like a demand. The demand for an occasion, for a twilight and a floating, because this evening gown—sleeveless, airy, with accordion pleats fanning from the bodice—this periwinkle evening gown from the 1970s, draped with a diaphanous chiffon capelet curling like blue mist, rolling, sloping into the suggestion of sleeves as attenuated and gracile as the petals of a ghost orchid, was hovering before me, hovering like the holograph of a sylph descending from a cloud, the spirit of a sylph returning to her body:

Never ran this hard through the valley
never ate so many stars

I was carrying a dead deer
tied on to my neck and shoulders

deer legs hanging in front of me
heavy on my chest

People are not wanting
to let me in

Door in the mountain
let me in♥

♥ Jean Valentine, 'Door in the Mountain,' 2004. After Jean Valentine died, Ezekiel read this poem to me on the phone. When we were first lovers, he was silent so much; now—less evasion than enchantment, the possibility of speaking with beauty and mystery, but without the shame and vanity of self—he spoke to me in poems. And I speak to you in poems because there is nothing more miraculous than finding my own feeling as an artifact, as if proof that dreams were more than a furious static of meaning, but formed a genealogy as hard and porous as bone. As if recitation—in the instant of confession—vaulted feeling to its own fifth dimension, activating a wellspring of ritual and extending the slake of an oasis spell.

I decided I would show Ezekiel my secret glade, my secret waterfall and the secret pool whose waters could transform us. The meter was expressed in patterns of hesitation, revelation and rippling.

Ezekiel: leaning on the porch railing, smoking a slow cigarette, surrounded by silence and a rustling, seagreen plash of trees rolling like waves, gilded, capped in a golden foam of October light; lost in thought, really in a well of dissociation, what he called his 'burial zone,' a grief dimension perpetually collapsing in on itself, that is, perpetually rotting from the inside out, because it is touched, perpetually, by death—then, hearing a rustling (first faint, then magnified) he turned his head, knocked suddenly breathless as I settled beside him within a haze of swirling periwinkle mist. Later he would tell me this was when we entered what he'd called, in his diary, our 'angel realm.' His eyes were already gleaming...

He was dazzled, almost demure, averting his gaze, struck shy by the fluttering of his hummingbird soul; then his long sloping lashes fluttered against my cheek like little wings, his lips brushed my lips, deep, warm and plush, embowered by a moustache whose bristles were rough and pleasant like dry grass. We were kissing again.

"You are so beautiful," he said, when the breeze was in my hair.

a Route of Evanescence,
with a revolving Wheel –
a Resonance of Emerald,
a Rush of Cochineal –

Soon we were sitting beside each other in yellow canvas chairs, sipping fire opals.

"What were you thinking about, baby?"

Because when I had first stepped outside I saw a hazel ache in his eyes, even in profile, which had receded when he saw me but remained beneath the surface, swirling slowly.

He smirked.

"Could you tell?"

"I can always tell."

His smirk widened:

"Did I do it back then, too?"

"Yes," I said. "Of course. We would be in the middle of a conversation and all of a sudden you'd disappear for like, an entire hour...like you'd be sitting beside me staring intensely at, like, a candleflame, elsewhere."

Ezekiel laughed giddily at my memory (not just

mythographic but pointillist in matters of romance) and at his own forgetfulness (perennial and for him, perennially bemusing, amusing, or both), then glanced, sweetly pained and smiling with retrospective tenderness at the inchoate Ezekiel who had nonetheless suffered from the same predicament, a sort of blur in his perception of time, as if dissociation were no different than a night terror, than the weight of a demon on your diaphragm.

"I was thinking about withdrawal," he said.

"Like about your dad?"

"No," he said. "Or at least not actively...but I'm sure I was, without realizing it..."

Because when Ezekiel was thirteen, his father had gone to rehab. Withdrawal was fatal. One afternoon, alone in his bedroom, an aneurysm ruptured his heart. And as Ezekiel always says: he fell.

"I was thinking about my tendency to withdraw."

> about withdrawal from substance & the danger / shakiness / destabilizing nature of that ~~~ & the impulse to withdraw from people, friends, relationships, when I'm depressed & fear I've been "using" the magical substance of love to fill an appetite or as a subconsciously desperate attempt to avoid withdrawal from the earth, the poetics of relation, the stakes of it

He paused. Took my hand in his gentle hand. We were older now. His eyes were tired, but glittered dimly, almost kaleidoscopically with presence of mind. So unlike seven years ago. But I couldn't meet his gaze. I was afraid of feeling nothing. I was afraid that he wasn't Ezekiel, that he was a mirage, that unseen demons were attempting to make a fool of me. Too often I overdetermine an instant, imagining the future as if it were already a memory rather than experiencing its volatile glamor without the guarantee of a story. I can be too concerned with convincing Ezekiel that our love was prophesied, arranging symbols not as a means of communing with the mystery of my love, but as a proof for his. Intrusive thoughts reach a fever pitch in the presence of pleasure. Love is my vital glitch.

The next instant: do I make it? Or does it make itself? We make it together with our breath. And with the flair of the bullfighter in the ring.

"Tonight I want to show you that I love you," he said.

II.

Now You Be Emmylou and I'll be Gram

The setting sun was lighting candles in the leaves of the trees. The candles were flickering in the branches without burning the leaves. Clouds blazed auroral. None of the men who loved him, none of the men who'd known him—no one had protected the twinkle in his eye. No one had even noticed. They had wanted his attention; they had demanded his desire. They had wanted his starlet exuberance, his starlet fitfulness and his starlet confusion. They wanted him like an unbroken stallion just so that they could break him. But a horse will not stay in a house. A horse will not stabilize your life. The only place to meet Ezekiel is in the twilight of a meadow, near the shore. Where wild luminous horses graze by moonlight, striking their hooves against the sand.

"I was jealous and manipulative and far too demanding when we were younger," I said.

What I was now recognizing as vital and selfconstructed adaptations (rickety, ingenious) to grief and solitude—which were sometimes sudden swoons of dissociation, but were sometimes also sudden swells of starfluid, radiant ripples of his fleetfooted flightsteps, his glittering dance among dimensions, his teleportation among rooms and moods, spinning supersonic mazes of knotted light, on the run from time—I had once interpreted as proof of cruelty or capriciousness or carelessness. So much of my love had been a kind of doomsday preparation, because the instant is an open wound on the verge of being sutured by the reeling needles of the clock. But one day the needles would cease. The past and the future are when

193

things are happening, but the instant is when things happen. The instant has no story, because the instant is the event itself, like falling headlong. I had preferred the certainty of a future to the uncertainty of the instant. But Ezekiel vibrated with uncertainty. Ezekiel was the instant. He was repercussive and evernew. Ezekiel had no future because he was always about to happen. *I am before, I am almost, I am never. And all of this I won when I stopped loving you.* I was infatuated by his vanishing acts; his simultaneities and airy leaps; his glamor, which was a kind of resplendent gloom akin to lighting a candle in a sunless hall of glittering stalactites, and by the foamy iridescent glitches which intermittently interrupted his broadcasts like sylphs screaming from the inescapable heat of their haloes. I wanted to be like him. I was a serial zealot. He was a shapeshifter. The wind was always in his feathers. A perpetual fall is as good as flight because, like flight, it has no end, and what has no end has no direction. Paradise is nowhere.

"But you were going through a lot, too," he said.

"Well, sure, baby. I was going insane. I'm not saying I blame myself, just that I don't blame you at all."

I lit a joint. Smoke curled off the burning tip. I took a puff, then pressed my lips against his, and, to his surprise, exhaled into his mouth. Ezekiel and I were sharing breath.

"You'd had your heart broken for the first time like, literally a couple months before we met," I continued.

"And I thought your heartbreak meant you didn't love me, because back then I hadn't begun to experience the minor and the major passions, the heartbreaks and the holy patterns, the transformations and the repetitions, and the seasonal intimacies, the accumulation of exlovers. I thought that true love inspired confession. I thought love was a euphemism for absolute transparency. But transparency was only a euphemism for surveillance. Surveillance is the inverse of love. What you needed was patience and I offered only paranoia. You were a fairy from West Texas who grew up in a small desert city and never met another fairy except your best friend. Romance was not an option. Your dad was dead. Your mom was ashamed to have a fairy son. An evangelical cult was vampirizing your grief. You publicly declared yourself an atheist, which in Odessa meant something. Who protected you? Then you moved for the first time in your life to start college and fell in love, improbably, your first semester, with another boy named Ezekiel, your new best friend, who made out with you when he was wasted but said he was straight once he got sober, who called you a faggot and confessed his love to you. More and more I relate to how you were then. Especially after these past couple years, half my mind is seafoam…"

I took another puff of the joint and offered Ezekiel a powderblue Adderall. He handled the pill like a pearl, with aweful vigilance.

Tapping ash into a translucent glass saucer,

"Anyway," I said, "I love you too darling and I never noticed before but you have the prettiest lashes…"

Ezekiel blushed. The light was fading.

"I want to do your makeup," I said, exhaling a blue plume of smoke.

In my bedroom we poured more honeywine. I rolled another joint. He was taking photos of me. I was wearing a thick white cotton shirt, buttoned low, and a necklace Velvet gave me for my birthday, an orchid with golden articulated petals made of waferthin metal. And thin cotton panties.

"No one has ever said my eyelashes are pretty," said Ezekiel, nestling in my pillows. We kissed again, his breath like smoke and pomegranates.

Or cool blue dawn: Horses galloping back from the meadow beyond the meadow, beyond the meadow, beyond the meadow.

This woman's work: to say the things they'd never said. To do the things…

"Wait a second," I said.

I plunged a hand into my closet and pulled out a sleeveless, unselvaged dress, whose handdyed fabric, rough but thinning, almost threadbare—a pale mottling of apricot, coral and rose—with lustrous rungs of stiff purple stitches rising up the spine and spreading in Sashiko crosses along the seams, like an underworld shroud ripped apart by bats and repaired only by a route of spider silk, spun by the nimble pomegranatestained hands of Persephone: a dress, that is, whose airy fabric, particularly the neckline, was always on the verge of further ripping, especially from the repeated impact of unsaddled breasts. Its train, however, was bustled, so that, floating across a meadow to greet the morning horses, a patchwork of scraps, gathered like the folded membranes of a bat, reinforced with narrow ribs, would fan out behind me in lurid flickers of magenta, lipstick, hot pink and blush, sparking, catching, blazing into a bubblegum conflagration, half Old Testament angel, half *Oops I Did It Again*—one more premonition of strawberry rapture.

"It's beautiful," said Ezekiel, with a voice like someone whispering, lighting a candle at the foot of a statue in a cathedral.

"It reminds me of everything you make me feel about glades and waterfalls," I said,

draping the fabric over my forearm:

"It's my favorite dress. You can try it on if you want."

Suddenly Ezekiel paused; unsouled his eyes, saying:

"And actually live by my own poems…"

He was staring like a deer into the middle distance. He was abstracting in absolute stillness. The valves of his attention closed like stone. But this time I wasn't afraid of him; I was worried for him. The choice to exalt or elide was his own. The dress was or was not the veil between dimensions. Ezekiel didn't know he was beautiful in the sense he reserved for women. He approached the Garden like a postulant or pious trespasser rather than a bee, butterfly or one of the Hesperides.

It was autumn. Season of mists and mellow fruitfulness, when yellow leaves, or none, or few, do hang. Season of Libra, sign of my Venus, claw of the Scorpion, close bosomfriend of my maturing Sun—her next of kin, mother of snakes, archangel of the final fluid. The seventh anniversary of our first date.

Ezekiel was gathering honeysuckle flutes. His anesthesia was fading. His lashes fluttered like passing instants.

"I would like that very much," he said, smiling at me like he was in love with a nymph.

And when the Dews drew off
That held his Forehead stiff –
I met him –
Balm to Balm –

*

Within a shallow pit of sunrise silver, the brush was tapping, sweeping and rolling, like a sparrow bathing in dust. Easy was wearing Persephone's gardening gown. Overspilling her collarbones, that chainmail amulet within whose translucent pendant the fragment of a petal is sealed, occluded within the etching of a rose:

"Keep your eyes still, baby."

My fingers formed a scaffolding upon his cheeks. I grazed his lids with skifts of powdered pearl, smoked his creases in a haze of ultramarine and extended the curves with silver wings. I smeared his cheeks with sheer shimmer and saturated his lips with cochineal, close bosom-friend of prickly pears. Last I amplified his lashes, like silhouettes of grass elongating in the setting sun.

I told him Best – must pass
Through this low Arch of Flesh –
No Casque so brave

It spurn the Grave –

I told him Worlds I knew
Where Emperors grew –
Who recollected us
If we were true –

And so with Thews of Hymn –
And Sinew from within –
And ways I knew not that I knew – till then –
I lifted Him –

Easy was in no rush. He sat still and gentle, alert to the fresh
sensation of sweeping (rubbing his bleary eyes—the closest he'd
come before—was heavy, but the pearl and ash and azure fingers
were light, were the telegraph taps of a fairy princess dying of
men in a blue kitchen, on the other side of his lid) squinting every
so often to glimpse which lurid pigment was clinging to the tips
of the bristles, the better to imagine the birth, felt first within his
body as a sweeping, of the nymph herself. To her I whispered:

"Open your eyes."

As if we were sitting beside a creek and I had dipped a basin
in the stream—borrowing, like someone taking a photograph,
a volume of its duration—which I now handed her to use as
a mirror, I handed Easy a mirror. The creek was warbling.
Nearby a swarm of hummingbirds was piercing the hearts of
a strawberry bush. We were reclining on a bed of moss, not
damp but not dry, not parched but cool, verdigris and almost
velvet, like fungal marble. Our ribs were glowing with phosphorescent scripture written by the inkdipped pterodactyl
beak of Our Lady of the Goodbye. We were wearing honeysuckle diadems.

"Oh my god," she said, twinkling.
"Oh my god…"

Looking up at me in confusion, beatified by surprise:

"I'm beautiful," she said, like a question waiting for an answer.

Stepping from mossy bed to beach of pebbles, she sought the timewrinkled waters of the creek itself. Beneath the surface she saw a mermaid with crimson lips. The mermaid was humming a song…

"I'm beautiful," she said, as if trying to explain the existence of the mermaid. The mermaid mouthed silent words, which rose as bubbles that broke when they reached the surface. Starfish crawled from the waves like shipwrecked sailors. They crawled laboriously up the shore carrying a length of kelp, which, if consumed, forces gills to split the skin of your neck silverly. The mermaid was offering to take us to a cave on Saturn's moon Enceladus,♥ where Dolly Parton once played a full set in a mother-of-pearl three bolt diver's helmet, with matching acrylics; where the Siren sometimes sang in the offseason; where Sappho wrote her infamous midcareer ode to Deathless Aphrodite *of the Spangled Mind* and where I will one day write my infamous ode to Instantaneous Aphroditos *of the Spangled Boudoir*. I folded the kelp delicately, then wrapped it in pink organza and slipped it inside a spiked conch shell for us to use another day, because today was only the first glimpse of the mermaid, whose translucent seahorses I feel galloping like…right now…at this very instant…but in the future…

"I'm beautiful," she said, as if she were experiencing a depressurization

♥ One of the many moons of Saturn, Enceladus, sprays the vaporized water of its global subterranean ocean through fine cracks in its frozen surface, covering the particulate matter of Saturn's rings in a fine layer of ice, rendering the rings reflective, and therefore, unlike the rings of Jupiter, visible from Earth.

of the mind (bluejays swaying in the boughs of gnarled oaks; angels wandering aimlessly in search of their absconded god; streams and moss; mushrooms bursting into puffs of gray fog; deer in silent contest, pounding, crackling the underbrush with their hooves, huffing, bowing their heads and commencing the arid clatter of their antlers); a sudden elaboration, a recuperation of ambit.

"Easy," I said. "I knew you'd be beautiful, baby."

She was beautiful like a will-o'-wisp awakening, like a halfboy nymph weaving emerald embers in the ruins of a marble tomb.

*

We disappeared into the deep woods. The trees trelaxed their distances; became a twilight, a velvet net. By the time light met the forest floor, each shaft was attenuated, almost translucent, like a fallen icicle—for the trees had banqueted on its luster. The sound of the creek was fading. We were leaping among ferns and branches and thickets of thorned flowering plants; through cobwebs and Spanish moss; bounding like deer over amber pools of dead and liquoring leaves, running as if diving slowly into a nondimensional zone of boughs and shadows, as if sinking through a plane of universal canopy, falling diagonally across the green and heaving gloom—as if passing briefly through a painting, silently flittering the silver wings of our sandals and vanishing at the bottom right corner of the frame.

> *We are always halfway there*
> *when we are here*
> *but we make nocturnal missions*
> *into the dream of heavenly completion*
>
> *It is blessed, I am blessed*
> *when I walk over the bridge*

with an angel
into a strange party where
the group's president, with his words
hurts the angel's impenetrable—

but tender!—skin and ruins what for me
could have been the time
of my life, mutual but unfulfilled passion

Then the angel informs me, always,
with a pleasure I can't imitate
and eyes ringed with pain
that we are only halfway
on our way to such a communion.♥

In the deep woods there is a dell where three small waterfalls spill. Between intersecting streams of pearly foamy water, on one of the eminences of mossy limestone clutched by the roots of a family of weeping willows, there is a halfruined house, a tworoom stone cottage whose roof and rafters—forever damp and on the verge of irreversible rot—are infested with honeysuckles, tumbling voluminously off the far side like a waterfall of yellow flowers, but spilling so slowly that to experience them as a cascade would require the attention span of an angel. The house is built on the edge of the cliff. Every so often a loosened shingle slides down the roofside and shatters on the wet rocks below. You can see one of the falls right outside the kitchen window. The kitchen is warm with a dim golden glow. The cabinets are full of preserves, canned peaches and candied jalapeños. The fireplace is always flickering in the living room, across from a small bookshelf which, in order to avoid fungal blight, we must keep within a halo of heat.

Ezekiel and I danced in our diadems in the front yard, while *This Kiss*

♥ Fanny Howe, 'By Halves,' in *Poetry*, April 1973. I read it to Ezekiel on the phone in late November. He said he would print it out and hang it on his wall.

201

by Faith Hill played from my portable radio. We were singing along, slurring the words with kisses while the waterfalls filled the air with blue mist. I've never seen him so happy.

'It's – the way you touch me
It's – a feeling like risk
It's – perpetual motion
It's – centripetal bliss…'

Soon we were recumbently almost naked on a crimson quilt, in the shade of a willow, smoke curling from his fingertips. He was reading me poems while I rested my head in the crook of his arm, while I ran my hand through the copper drift of hair on his chest. Slowly my nose sank down into that warm cleft: tickling, brushing, coyly nudging: I could smell the soil, the galloping, the sunbaked musk, the density of a season— could smell the fine grains of an Et Cetera my body has understood from the beginning, which means I do not need to. Of all the senses, scent feels nearest to prophecy.

"Oh my god," I said. "Easy…"

Ezekiel lifted his arm.

"Come here," he said.

He grasped my hair in his hand and pushed my face slowly and firmly into the bronze undergrowth curling slickly from his armpit. I moaned. I pressed my nose into the musky damp depth of him. I was wild for the scent.

Meanwhile Easy's cock rose firmly into the air, like a plank. His thick plumpink cocktip was waving back and forth with the thickening beat of his pulse.

"That's good, baby," he said. "I don't want you breathing anything but me."

My hip brushed against the thick lip of it and I felt a cool burst of incandescence in my cunt. I was moaning, bucking my pussy against his leg. I licked him clean with my whole tongue—long, thick, deep strokes, saturating my mouth with his hot smut valentine tincture: with what can only be experienced, but not remembered, or what can be remembered only by experience, but, by its heady concentrate of *eau de Ezekiel*, brings all memory nearer. Call it my madeleine.

"Good girl," he said, petting my head.

I remembered how excited he'd been the first time we brushed our teeth together, because domesticity seemed to him and me like an impossible fantasy; remembered holding hands in the dark at the movie theater; remembered giggling, remembered screaming; remembered the grit tumbling within the round full syllables of a mourning dove's warble; remembered everything:

I sank my teeth in his neck, sucking him bruised like a peach, then traced my tongue down the rungs of his ribs and between his hips, pressing my mouth into his taint, his ballsack draping over my nose as cool as marble, as wrinkled and soft as a length of crepe.

"Good girl," he said, moaning.

I sucked and drooled on his bulbous plumpink cocktip, whimpering, pleading, slobbering like a sweet slut so that my spit rolled down his shaft—then slowly and continuously, in a single plunge, swallowed his seven inches to the bush. Easy furrowed his eyebrows, began to smile, exhaled sharply. Then he looked at me, tilting his head, saying,

"Mommy's choking on Daddy's cock, isn't that right?"

I smirked.

"What's funny?"

I shook my head.

"What's funny, baby?"

I shook my head again, doeeyed, as if I couldn't possibly...

"So say it then."

Like a dare, flagrantly, feigning innocence, the hint of a smirk flickering across my face, I nodded, humming

"mhmmm,"

because I wanted him to make me say it. He raised his brows like, *oh you think you're clever?* then took my hair in his fist and lifted my face slightly, saying,

"Look me in the eyes, baby. Say yes, daddy. Yes daddy I'm choking on your cock."

I spat him out to reply, but he said,

"No no no, baby," slapping my cheeks with his cock each time, before grabbing my head with both hands and holding it in place while he fucked it.

"Don't ignore me, baby," he said, laughing.

"Say yes, daddy, I'm choking on your cock."

We were trespassing in the language of men and women. Our eyes sparkled with incorrigible mirth.

"Yes, daddy," I said. "I'm choking on your cock," I said.

But I didn't say a single intelligible word. Topaz spit was oozing from my lips, streaming through the folds and crevices of his ballsack, tickling his taint.

Looking him right in the eye, I spat into my cleavage, pressed my breasts together and took his cock into their soft mass.

"You're so fucking sexy," he said, moaning.

"A LITTLE PATH JUST WIDE ENOUGH FOR TWO WHO LOVE." — E. D.

Then he was on top of me, burying his face in my breasts, spitting a stream between them and licking it up again, nibbling my nipples, slapping and squeezing with a pleasure multiplied by its novelty and by the sweet surprise of its straightforwardness, not because of its Trojan horse of heterosexuality, but because our bodies, more directly than our shy and wary minds, already remembered how to want one another, not without complication or dissociation or pain, but with intensity, because years ago, raining hot spatters of opal five times a day over one another's mouths, we had experienced, like an oasis deepening,

204

ripening without widening its circumference, not a gradual attenuation, but a tidal accumulation of pleasure, so in the intervening time our bodies had not forgotten how to weave themselves back into the lurid sensorial mesh of this frayed fairymoan pherotale—but, having changed so drastically in form that we could not even pretend to reenact the past, there was no possibility of an *auld lang syne*, we were making ourselves vulnerable to our story, which meant making our story vulnerable to us in turn, risking our meaning on a double or nothing, destabilizing our weft with vibrating golden threads, honeysuckle vines and the possibility of flames. 'Weaving back' meant having a second chance for desire in chronological time, not as exlovers but as if our first love down in Texas had happened in a kind of early Cenozoic era, as near and irrecoverable as the memory of a wooly mammoth—and just as soil and ice bear sacred traces of fur and tusk and genetic code, so flecks, fossils, footprints and loose threads mark our meadow, that intermittent paradise where worlds of wanwood leafmeal lie.

We were trying to live in what Easy called 'the upper ruins,' or in his manner of inflecting, 'the upper *runes*,' halfway within a dream of romantic domesticity, and halfway within a forest consciousness, like nymphs on the verge of transcendence, I mean on the verge of transforming into a garden rooted, sprouting from the springs of a mattress:

"I've never been with a woman before," he said.

He was horny and mischievously delighted. The last shall be first, and the first shall be last. Ezekiel was a virgin with women. And I was a virgin with fucking a gay boy who fucked me when I was a fairy. I felt like we'd never fucked before, or had only done so in another genre left in traces within our story like a palimpsest, a déjà vu. We were whirligigs of time, two whirl-o'-times illuminating, by our feverish orbit, the fresh ambit of our fairy circle. We were hornily mocking the men and women who had tried to convince us of the impossibility of our love, the impossible brokenness of ourselves; protecting each other from the heat of the spotlight, eclipsing the solar glare of shame with the sudden diorama of a wedding roleplay, because we were exceeding together what we had once claimed as maximums, we were lifting sheaves of flowers, shaking perfume from bouquets, raising a distant portal from the soil.

For the first time in seven years, Easy was claiming me as his lover, was weaving himself into me like a chaos, a heath of grit and holy writ—but we both knew not to attempt describing, at that instant, the subatomic blue storm of our particularities and possibilities, lest we fray threads as fine as smoke curling off a cigarette tip, swirling a world together in the dark. Silence was narrating. Shadows were illuminating our minds. Our bodies howled with pain and pleasure. Leaping from cloud to cloud, we kept the secret…

Among the waterfalls, we kept the secret…

Easy reached into my underwear, feeling the soft give of my cunt lips. He had never felt a pussy before. I'm not sure he had ever even seen a pussy in person. A python was curling around leaves of paper in my desk drawer. Our tongues tasted like strawberries. Flaming swords floated on either side of the crimson quilt, preventing the encroachment of angels or demons.♥ While he kissed me, I guided his hand to the slit. My outer lips are plump and pillowy; I spread them apart with my fingers, revealing the rest. Already I was slick and trickling from the heat and weight of him. My legs began to widen and my hips began to buck. Easy's finger sank slowly down into pink…

He was careful because he loved me, because ever since the Irishman cracked my cunt, I need a slower start.

Soon he put another finger in me.

♥ If you've bought my porn, then you've seen my pussy. If you haven't, then you probably haven't. Certain passages in this book were first published as captions on my OnlyFans videos. Before they were poetry, they were poetry. If anyone in one hundred years finds this book and reads it, I wonder if they will know the taste of strawberries…

Soon his fingers were filling me up.

I was aching. It was a sweet ache. My cunt felt fuller and fuller. I moaned, clutching his neck. My eyes were brimming.

"Holy shit," Easy said between kisses. "You're so wet."

My pussy was sloshing loudly now. He leaned back to look. Transfixed, he sat upright, pulling me by my hips, rubbing his halfhard cock between my wet and pinkly swelling lips, watching them part into two mounds from the force of him and fold wetly around his cock as he withdrew. In seconds he was rockhard again; his cock was gleaming. And then I wanted him inside of me, even though I knew I couldn't take him, because I hadn't dilated in weeks, had only been cuntfucked twice in the year and a half since the Irishman, both times for no more than a minute, both times pleasurable, both times brief and most of all frustrating, because all my life I had always said harder, baby, I can take it… But—but even so Easy was here, we were playing in the garden beyond our maximums, and my pussy made him want me more, not less…

Soon I was on my stomach with my ass in the air, soon Easy was pressing his cock into me, slowly, slowly, because I was so tight…

and then he was fucking me, and every thrust was forcing me open, and I was aching with the possibility of pleasure…

But just as soon it was over, because I was still too tight, once again I was too goddamned tight, and my surgeon won't give me anything for the pain, she simply can't prescribe me painkillers, so every time I dilate, that instant comes sweeping back through the sixth wound like a blunt knife; every time I feel that man thrusting forever, so it was just too much trouble for twenty four hours, especially because it wasn't the last twenty four hours, there would be so many more hours? So we kissed and smoked and made little sounds like halfdrowsing kittens until, curled up in Easy's arms, I fell asleep mid-sentence.

III.

To the Tune of *Hey, That's No Way to Say Goodbye* by Leonard Cohen

When I woke the next morning, he was already smiling at me across the pillow. He'd been watching the end of my dream flickering on my face, like when you walk past a cathedral, listening to the faint buzz of an unseen congregation singing, in swelling chorus, the final notes of a hymn.

"Good morning, baby," I said.

"Are you hungry for breakfast?" he said.

Looking into my eyes, he pulled down his blue boxers, catching his cock on the elastic, stretching it forward like the mechanism of a catapult until its blue veins began to bulge with tension, then releasing it, so that in one parabolic flash the swelling plumpink tip slapped back against his abdomen.

I took him into my throat. I sucked the cum from his cock like venom from a wound. Afterwards we ate jelly donuts. He smoked some cigarettes on the porch. We were planning to go to a bookstore so we could buy little gifts for each other, honeymoon mementoes. But his sugar daddy was insistent, was texting and calling and sending a car and Easy was licking the tears from my cheeks and then he was gone.

Before he left, he took off his blue boxers. His favorite pair.

"So you don't forget my scent," he said.

IV.

The Woman's Face on the Other Side of This Pane—Paper or Fate?

The next evening he insisted on some time alone while Alex and his entourage went out for massages before dinner. He called me.

"I've been pacing around Brooklyn on and off crying," he said. "Yesterday was one of the best days of my life."

"Where are you?" I said.

I met him by the water at a park in Williamsburg, in my pink Persephone dress and cowboy boots. We smoked a joint in the sand and kissed as the sun set. The waves lapped seafoam against the shore. You could see all of Manhattan from there…

Analyze duration as you
wish to the world we are
from this moment forth

quick light clay dust we
dressed today in a hurry

I had read him that poem on the porch the day before, from *Souls of the Labadie Tract*. Now he recited it to me from memory, smiling, almost tearful, furrowing his brows with a look of sweet confusion. Then he pissed in the bushes, me holding his cock for him like I had that first night in the flowerbed. I pissed too, fanning the dress around me, wiping my cunt with a blank page from his diary. We danced in the grass. I gave him his first eyeshadow palette. We kissed goodbye.

V.

Written in Light, in Either Case

Before flying back to Iowa, Easy went to the beach one more time.

back to how I love you

VI.

BECOMING HORSE GIRLS

The room stank of semen and smoke and whiskey, of
saddle leather, shit and cheap soap.
  – ANNIE PROULX, *BROKEBACK MOUNTAIN*

Do you think all lovers feel like they're inventing
something?
  – CÉLINE SCIAMMA, *PORTRAIT OF A LADY ON FIRE*

Just before I flew to him, he said:
  —I need you to heal me.
  I was in New York. A couple days before I'd been
on one of the best first dates of my life, for twenty-four
hours. She wrote me a letter, a poem that I keep on
my altar. She covered me with bruises. We joined her
friends at bar after bar. At one dive, a reality star held
my tits. Like, my tits were out and she was squeezing
them slowly, saying 'you have really nice tits...' My
lover and I talked to a lot of strangers in between kisses.
We told everyone we met that we were engaged, about
to be married. Everyone was so happy for us.
  But she lived in another city, so we said, for now,
goodbye.
  And I slept for a day.
  Then Ezekiel called me. He had problems. Boy
problems and friend problems and, half on account
of the former, half on account of *the dream of heavenly completion*, problems with his soul. The sort of
problem that belongs to god in an unutterable opacity

217

far too crystalglittering to be printed here. I gave him advice that eased the pain, and promised him respite from the ruins of his circumstances.

He said,

—This is the first time in two years I'm having anyone in my bed.

And then I flew to him, and he drove me past fields of wheat and welcomed me into his blue house, where I held and kissed him with sweetness, and he took me to a bar in a red barn where we played Cowboy Junkies and Kate Bush on the jukebox, kissing, holding hands, him telling me the story of how he became a poet, the story of who he had become to the friends and lovers he'd met there, and who he would, later that evening at another bar, introduce me to, arm in arm, everyone wondering why a gay boy was romancing this mysterious woman from somewhere else. And I said,

—I will take care of you if you will take care of me.

On the second day, in a green field, near a handpainted sign that read *Pirates & Villains Only*, attempting to demythologize our discourse, foregoing any abstraction of shadow or obliquity, shedding my peacock feathers, I said, just above a whisper, because my throat was sore and my lungs were aching, and because I wanted to make it easy, to make it simple, just for once:

—If I get sicker, I will need you to look at me gently and tell me everything will be okay,

and he promised, he repeated our oath. His eyes were spangled and dazzling because I'd done his shadow again. We held hands. We were alone in the green grass. No one saw us. The wind blew. He read me part of a poem by Fanny Howe:

'Triggers follow feelings but precede acting on them
A feeling triggers a feeling, then the heft
Of the hand to work

A human face is pressed on glass; mirrors like armor
Break shapes into targets

The woman's face on the other side of this pane—
Paper or fate?
Written in light, in either case'

Back in his bedroom it was afternoon. We were something old and something new. We were covert like bunnies. We were perfect like swans. We were Easy and Aura and no one was watching. At last I was far from the city—far from all the eyes pressed against the glass of the hot girl hothouse. I was in love with him, in love with the fantasy of loving him in his quiet blue home, where he made himself scrambled eggs in the morning, where he wrote the poems he sent me, where his scent was not a dense and fragile trace left on a pair of boxers but the very air and atmosphere of all affection. I didn't care that I was getting sick. The afternoon was gentle and full of autumn. The leaves were gilded like illuminated manuscripts. Soon he would teach a poetry class to undergraduates, but just then we were rustling in his bedsheets, Easy flung back on the pillow, me between his legs, wearing his baseball cap backwards to hold my chestnut curls, sucking his cock like I was writing a love letter—wild and relentless and delicate.

He bucked hard against my mouth.

His cum was sweet, somehow, sweet as the juice of a pear, even after all his cigarettes.

—That felt so good, he said,

in a daze of surprised pleasure. Then he fingered

me for half a minute and, at risk of running late, left to teach his class.

When he returned, I asked for his help dilating, because Ezekiel wanted our sex to be spontaneous, experimental and fanciful, but in order to be spontaneous, in accord with the exigencies of my cunt, I have to prepare carefully, I require advance notice, because ever since the night a man broke it, I bleed every time I try to pry my pussy. Dilating alone is invariably more painful. *Door in the mountain. Let me in.*

I started reading a book aloud to distract both of us.

After a few minutes, he said, "I'm sorry, I'm dissociating…" Behind the twinkling, I saw sorrow in the lines of his face. I said not to worry, that it was okay, and we went for a walk to the cemetery instead. Deer pranced among the gravestones. We pushed against the stone door of a mausoleum.

—I fear death, I said, but I do not fear the dead.

But the dead said nothing.

Now all at once a perfect pain was brushing my skull like the soft noxious tentacles of a jellyfish, lacerating my forehead so delicately I was left breathless. My body shuddered. I clawed at the pain. Clawed at my breasts because my lungs were burning. I was howling. Ezekiel was halfway to Jupiter. He was looking at nothing with taxidermy eyes. He was holding me rigidly as if his limbs were the limbs of a deer. He wasn't speaking. My fever was rising.

I was afraid I had made a mistake by visiting my West Texas walker-after-midnight, recollecting the day, thirteen years ago, when my mother had confided in me, at the beginning of a three-hour car ride, that she feared, if she got sick, my father wouldn't know how to take care of her. I remembered her fear with nausea, because I was beginning to understand what she meant, was all at once realizing how, in matters of intimate idiom and amorous agon, Ezekiel (a Gemini) reminded me of my father (a Scorpio), and I (a Scorpio) reminded myself of my mother (a Gemini). Suddenly, far from my home and my life with Noel, sick in a strange bed beside someone I, in a day-to-day sense, hardly knew at all, I was realizing—one lover after another having placed their faith in my mysticism, having believed, because of the force of my believing, that I could echolocate the glade of dancing nymphs—I really had no idea what I was doing. Ezekiel was always complimenting my capacity for making meaning, but that night I was too delirious to mythmake. Pain was neutralizing me.

I couldn't override my confusion with visions. I needed to know which shadows of ours were boxing in the darkroom—needed to know what was passing unsaid between us. Because he still hadn't acknowledged having said, on our very first date, the third time we attempted to be lovers:

—You are pretty but not beautiful,

while we sat outside the Bluebonnet Cafe in Marble Falls at dusk as the world turned blue, having shared my secret favorite: banana cream pie. In the year and a half of our phone calls he had simply begun praying to me—and to the advertisements I posted on Twitter, the images and ten-second video clips of me sucking on a lover's balls with a full face of makeup, eyelashes elongated with tiny threads of cashmere; or dressed in a corset, playing with my pussy at my writing desk; or just after cumming, pressing my breasts like fresh dough, seducing the future with my emerald eyes, with my messy black eyeliner, with the burning pink blush of my cheeks, glistening, etherealized—had simply begun praying to me as if my butterflying mind were a religion unto itself, as if I were a temple of Aphrodite, more and therefore less than human, because he desired me, too, in the form of a fairytale (*I adore you, I'm obsessed with you*), rather than as a broken girl looking for her pieces of mind.

I was arriving at the questions I'd been murmuring to myself since Ezekiel reappeared: Why all those years ago did you tell me I wasn't beautiful? And how could you love me if I wasn't beautiful to you? And how can I trust you, how can I trust what you see in me now? Do I echo some dream of yours, do I fulfill a meaning? Does a part of me proliferate your fantasy of your own future self? *Which lover are you, jack of diamonds?*

But instead of offering my vulnerability, instead of asking what was passing unsaid between us or which shadows of ours were shadowboxing or any of the questions howling in my mind, I said, sharply, uncertainly, through gritted teeth:

—I need pleasure too.

and after a pause, knowing as I spoke that I had selected the wrong sentence, almost suffocating on my own words, uncertainly but sharply, I said:

—I want pleasure now. Tonight.

I had failed to meet the moment. I had disenchanted the angel realm under whose clouds we had been seeking a new and bodily form for our love, without the interruption of past asymmetries, without the intercession of a direct address. For me to put Ezekiel on the spot like that was a betrayal of relation, was reckless and destructive. Terror seized him. He disappeared into the shadowlands.

There's a certain Slant of light,
Winter Afternoons –

222

That oppresses, like the Heft
Of Cathedral Tunes –

He fell, he disappeared into silence, which is to say, seafoam, the inverse of sweetness, the roar and rot of an acute emptiness. A sort of Hell hidden in the body.

Heavenly Hurt, it gives us –
We can find no scar,
But internal difference –
Where the Meanings, are –

We were sending terrified transmissions back and forth like a fog of scarlet, as if wounds had their own perfume.
    —You're a taker, I said,
    like I was spitting.
    Leering down at me, he replied:
    —And you give *so* generously.
    In a single motion, I leapt up from the bed and grabbed him by the collar with my right hand.
    —Don't you dare say that to me, I said.
    But he flinched. Easy was scared of me.
    I saw it clear.
    I pulled my hand away, ashamed.
He went downstairs to smoke a few cigarettes on his front porch. I was reeling from fear and fever. I went down to the kitchen, found a knife and brought it up with me to bed. Whenever I am overwhelmed but I don't want to hurt myself, I get a steak knife instead of a shard of glass. A steak knife looks dramatic but is significantly less sharp. I stare at the knife until it takes the place of a wound. So I stared. When the feeling left, I set it among a mess of stuff on his powderblue bedside table. Then I turned off the lights and breathed in the dark. He returned soon. I wondered how to get

the knife back to the kitchen unnoticed. Thankfully he didn't notice it then, but he would the next morning. 'It stands for knife,' he would say. Which, truthfully, was fair. I can't expect a lover to know that a knife can, for me, by the dull sparkle of its own spectacle, mean its opposite. He turned a light on. He said my anger was a form of sexual pressure. I said that my anger wasn't about the present instant, but the accumulation of confusing and demoralizing exchanges of desire; I meant that it wasn't about sex, but about communication.

He said we had only hooked up twice since we became friends and lovers again: first in New York and now in his bed. And this second time had been unplanned, a sweet lark earlier that afternoon.

He suggested it was by chance that both times I'd sucked his cock but he'd hardly fingered me for a full minute. He said two times can't be called a pattern.

He said he thought I liked sucking his cock. I said of course I liked sucking his cock, but it was naïve of him to mistake my passionate cocksucking as simply and solely a matter of desire. Cocksucking was an exertion of love.

Easy sat in silence, with his hands in his lap and his head hung low. He was crying. I had never seen him cry. But he was crying, he was saying that he didn't know how to touch another person. It was one thing to accept pleasure. Accepting pleasure required remaining at rest, it was a question of building sensations in a Midnight Zone; the difficulty was internal. Giving pleasure was relational; there was no looking away. You had to stare down at someone desperate to experience pleasure, someone not pretending to be measured, someone whose desires were so direct that, from the distance of dissociation, they appeared (in fits and flashes of which I felt ashamed) frightening and grotesque, all the more so if you loved them—all the more so if desire was dangerous, if love was rare and precious, if you felt compelled to protect love from the danger of desire despite your equal and opposite resistance to that particular form of dichotomizing panic. Giving pleasure meant not being ashamed of reality, which required either transforming reality or allowing reality to be true without disbelieving in the dream. But mostly reality felt like a negation—total and inert.

—I don't have any sense of my own body, he said. And then:

—When we have sex, I imagine that I am you.

*

And when I finally asked, he said he didn't even remember saying it, couldn't believe he would ever say it.

—It's not true, he said. I never thought that. I always thought you were beautiful.

—You read it in my book. You knew.

—You should've asked me directly.

—I didn't feel safe asking you, I said. You had the privilege of setting the terms.

—I didn't want it.

—It's not about if you wanted it or not. You go, and you return. I had no reason to believe you wouldn't vanish if I confronted you. You didn't call me for two months after telling me you loved me.

I said he was always dreaming of a highway, I said he was always walking away.

—And Ezekiel, I said. You should've asked me directly before you started reading my Twitter every day.

(Fantasy is not in itself ethical, but it is the means by which an ethics is made.)

I said:

—Before you began developing an indirect erotic relationship with my image, rather than with me.

Then I said:

—I feel like you've been manipulating me for a long time now.

And he said:

—I feel like you've been manipulating me for a long time now. After I came to New York, your tweets took on a different tone…

He was right. Over time and despite my frequent discomfort and silent panic and every so often my genuine pleasure at his abstracted presence, I began speaking slantly to Easy through the mouth of @silicone_angel, especially after his visit in October, when I started expressing more passionate feelings and expectations about the kind of relationship awaiting us than I had the nerve to confess to Easy voice to voice, balm to balm. I tweeted about beautiful women who date femboys, transsexual sex goddesses who love fairies, being his garden of Eden cunt, etc.

—That was wrong. I shouldn't have mixed my feelings for you with my online Siren song.

(It was dissociative; more oblique than poetry, and more dangerous.)

—I'm sorry, Ezekiel.

My fever spiked in the early morning. After I convinced him of the urgency, we went to the hospital. Easy was submerged in a haze; I was experiencing a paranoia of attunement. Every so often we argued. Every so often we spat words. And though I kept my face calm and my voice even, every time I felt upset the monitor inevitably registered my racing pulse and began beeping loudly, at which time Easy would groan and mash the button repeatedly, in order to extinguish the sound of my heart.

In my hospital room, we stared for a while at a crucifix on the wall.

—The equation just doesn't make sense, he said.

I gave the crucifix the finger. Easy smiled.

—They should make statues of Judas kissing Jesus in Gethsemane, I said.

—That equation makes perfect sense, he said.

The next afternoon he woke numb, uncertain of me, and on the verge of influenza. I woke in a desperate terror, because I woke knowing immediately that we had lost each other. We had hurt each other too much. He read me a passage from Claudia Rankine's *Don't Let Me Be Lonely*:

'Define Loneliness?

Yes.

It's what we can't do for each other'

*

Later on, my mother called to tell me that my cousin had died at one hundred and five years old. He made sundials and gave me my first chunk of pyrite. I hadn't seen him since transition.

Then I was kissing Ezekiel and crying. I couldn't look at him. He pulled back once, then again a few seconds later, asking if I was okay, asking if I was mad at him. I couldn't talk at all, not a word—and my kisses, like little exorcisms, were too much for him to bear.

So I told him I was sad about my cousin and needed some time to think, then left with a full bottle of vodka and walked to the cemetery, where I stumbled among headstones and obelisks, singing in the moonlight to any dead who wished to lend an ear, to the wind and drifting deer, pouring vodka here and there as an offering, drinking it like water, singing *I dream a highway back to you...*

When I crawled into bed, desperately and somehow earnestly, with an ill-fitting sense of the sacred and a certainty, at that moment, of the holiness of our impossible passion; making a fairytale, instinctively, to delay the nightmare, the pain and terror I felt for myself, for him, for us, I said, for the first time in my life:

—I want to be your wife.

The next day he took me to the library to print out a copy of this book.

We napped through the afternoon.

We snorted Adderall and danced in his living room.

And then we held each other in his bed, gazing into one another's eyes, singing that song. I knew we had failed again. I knew he loved me and I knew it was over. The song kept playing. I cried and howled. His bluesilvering kitten leapt onto the bed and nuzzled my cheek slowly, meowing softly, purring.

—She's never done that before, said Ezekiel.

In the morning, wearing my Persephone dress and blue jeans, he drove us to McDonalds. We ate in a windswept field, then returned one last time to his blue house before I left.

*

On the phone a few days after I got home:

—This whole time I've been in a privileged position, he said. I've just been riding the high of our calls, totally oblivious. I feel sick, like I've been...

—Extracting from me?

—Exactly. How much of the last year have you felt like this?

—Not every moment, I said. But it's always been in my mind. I felt confused and frightened, Easy.

For a moment he was silent. Then:

—All this time, he said, I haven't been loved.

I was nauseated. It was another dimension of heartbreak. He could take his love from me, but he couldn't take mine from me. Please don't take it from me. My love is real, Ezekiel.

—I can be in pain and still be in love, I said.

And we went in circles like that for a long time, making ruts with the weight of our feeling, until at last he said:

—I need to be gone for a while.

—But you promised you wouldn't ever again.

—I'm the pretender, he said.

—Ezekiel please

—I'm not who I'm supposed to be.

Silver Soul was echoing in my skull.

—I don't feel safe, he said. I might even go to the psych ward. I was numb all week. I'm having a trauma response.

And then, shy but firm:

—I need to disappear,

trailing off like morning mist.

I felt a twinge of panic like a plucked string. But it only sparked; it did not catch or resonate. Because I knew what he meant. More and more as years went by, I was withdrawing from my life, myself; more and more I was losing faith in visions; more and more I was ashamed of exposing my lovers to my destabilization, to my blanks and manias and meltdowns, to the unmodulated sound of my mind. Reality was so brittle. I lost it every day.

—I understand, I said,

registering my acceptance with genuine surprise. I was heartbroken and furious, but I did not blame him.

—I understand why you need to go, Easy. I understand.

—Thank you, he said,

with a sigh of genuine relief.

—Do you know how long you'll be gone

—I don't know

—Can you promise you'll come back

—Yes. I promise.

—...Thank you for giving us another chance at love. I know how hard you were trying.

—I'm heartbroken. I've been heartbroken since you left.

—I know.

—I'm sorry we couldn't rise to meet each other this time.

—I'm scared, Easy.

—Please be safe, okay?

—I'll do my best, I promise.

—Don't die, Aurora. I need you. I need you there in the future.

—I won't, I promise.

And then, after a pause:

—Ezekiel...one day, will you rise to meet me?

—Yes, he said.

Our voices were cracking with pain.

—I love you.

—I love you, too.

And then we wished each other well.

When I was alone again, I drank a bottle of sake, took the old bloody chunk of glass from my reliquary and smashed it into shards.

Eventually Noel heard my howling and rushed to my room.

—Aurora please stop.

—I can't, I said.

—Please, they said. Give me the glass.

—I'm not done yet.

—You've done enough.

—The price is even as the grace.

Blood was making a puddle on the floor, rich and oozing. Blood had spattered a lampshade.

—Please call your mother, they said. I can't do this alone.

They said I couldn't stay at home, drinking and bleeding. In my case the next cut is always the deepest. Because that was the deepest wound anyone has ever given me—I did it with my own hands and with hours of drinking and slicing, all the while singing *Bleeding Love* by Leona Lewis and *Hurt* by Johnny Cash, or *Fields of Gold* by Eva Cassidy and *A Song For* by Townes Van Zandt. That same night I was involuntarily committed to the psych ward.

After a week I had two lovers. One of them, a nurse saw him kissing me. The nurse had already seen my chart. She shook her head. She turned to another patient and said, pointing at me,

—That's a man. He's kissing a man.

The patient told me what the nurse had said. I confronted the nurse. I said,

—If you're going to talk about me, do it to my face.

But she wouldn't look at me. So my lover was saying,

—What's your name. Tell me your goddamned name.

But she hid her nametag and left the ward, because she was 'afraid for her safety.'

One of the night staff said later that maybe if I wasn't sleeping with half the ward, I wouldn't be having problems. Another one of the night staff, Hector, held me while I cried. He was the one we all liked. He called the on-call, and asked him to come speak to me, to make it right. But the doctor refused. The doctor said I would have to get used to this sort of thing. When he hung up, Hector was crying, too.

—I'm so sorry, he said.

I walked over to the nurses' station and demanded an audience with the on-call. The nurses were behind a pane of glass. They pretended not to hear me. I pounded on the glass. The nurses called crisis. One of them said:

—Now he's coming. Are you happy?

I was wearing cowboy boots and I started kicking the front door of the ward.

My lover said,

—Baby you're going to hurt yourself.

I wanted out. I wanted to break the door so we could leave. I kept kicking but the door wouldn't cave.

Soon a group of twelve or more men filled the hall. The crisis team. Calmly, one of them said:

—You can speak with the doctor if you go to your bedroom.

—He's going to speak to me?

—Yes.

So I went.

But within seconds, the men closed in behind me, clotting my door and my room, parting only for the doctor to stroll through with a syringe in his uplifted hand.

—I'm going to give you a sedative, said the doctor. Then we can speak.

(But the sedatives they had given me before—my first five days in the emergency ward, on a stretcher with no pillow, no privacy, and twenty-four hour brightness in a room full of stretchers, of men and women, where one man told me how converting to Islam had brought him closer to God, and we spoke for a long time, not only because he had a glint in his eyes and I had a crush on him, but also because of his manner of speaking about matters of the spirit, and, after that first man was released, another man, this one cute enough, but glintless and convinced of his Christ-given genius, told me about his in-progress 'masterpiece,' a play, 'really a philosophical romance,' about his ex-girlfriend (not a genius like him, but so kind, so good), specifically about 'space' (what his girlfriend had asked for) considered as a condition of the soul, a psycho-spiritual state as substantial as Heaven or Hell, but about which he could say no more than that, lest his 'million-dollar idea' fall into the wrong hands—the sedatives the doctors had given me in the emergency ward, and of whose risks they had not informed me, had caused muscle seizures. My body twitched and jerked painfully while my eyes and mouth were stretched wide open, as if I had been surprised by joy, as if my face were frozen in an instant of joyful surprise; and my hands and arms were locked, aloft, my fingers half-curled and my wrists bent outward as if in twin gestures of benediction; soon my eyes were blurring and I could hardly speak. I was sweating profusely, weeping, garbling my words, trying to shout: "I'm scared, I don't know what's happening to me." Until my doctor happened to walk by and said: "Oh, you're having a reaction to the sedative. Easy to fix." And injected me with a counteragent that extinguished the fit in a few minutes. "At least your eyes hadn't rolled back yet," she said. Staff noted the reaction in my chart and wrote that I was not to be given the sedative, Q, again.)

So, naturally:
—What is that, I said.
But the doctor ignored me.
—What is that, I said. I'm allergic to Q.
He was walking toward me. The needle glinted, a drop of fluid globing on its tip. I jumped up from my bed, flashing like a diamond through the crowd of men while one after another sought to grab me until, as I reached the doorway, I fell. All at once, ripping my yellow dress and half my stitches, hands and hands were grasping at me, grabbing for me, a proliferation of hands were taking me, were bruising me with their tight grips, were lifting me in the air while I was bleeding, kicking wildly with my cowboy boots; while I was writhing, tangled in arms, screaming:
—Please, I'm allergic.
Screaming:
—Q gives me muscle seizures.
Begging:
—Please, look at my chart,
while the doctor ordered some of the crisis team to strap me down to my bed with restraints.
—Look me in the eyes, I said.
The doctor didn't look. I looked around the room at everyone, watching.
—Please, I begged.
No one said a word. The doctor ordered three men to hold my arm still for the needle. When he leaned forward, I spat in his face. The doctor recoiled. I spat again. One man covered my face with a piece of cloth. I shook it off, screaming:
—Fuck you, you fucking cunt.

234

The doctor left the room. He 'refused to be spoken to like that.' He sent a nurse in his place. She was wearing a face shield.

—Stay the fuck away from me, I said.

—A woman wouldn't talk like that, said another nurse.

—At least I'm not ugly like you, I said. People pay to see my pussy. And I had a bigger cock than any of the men in this room.

The nurse with the face shield approached while the men held me down on all sides. She said:

—I'm not giving you Q, I promise.

She'd been staring at me with alarm and faint disgust since she first saw me days before. Even so, I let her give me the shots.

Then everyone left.

One of the men was carrying my boots.

I was alone in my room. Minutes passed.

Until I felt it. First a tingling in my arms and legs, then an ache, then spasms:

—Help, I yelled. Help, it's happening again,

but no one came.

I was twisting the restraints with my wrists, but I couldn't thrash; they were too tight. I was getting lightheaded.

Eventually, with gratitude to the other sedative they'd injected, I fell asleep. When I woke in the night, the restraints were gone.

The next morning I asked to see my records, which showed that the nurse had, in fact, injected me with Q.

So, when he made a brief appearance, I asked my doctor why the on-call had ignored my allergy.

—It's not accurate to call it an allergy, he said. It's more of a reaction.

—What the fuck, I said, are you talking about?

Every day afterward, whenever I passed by his door, my lover's roommate—an older man who became a confidant of mine, and who was always secretly undoing my lover's restraints after the nurses called crisis on him, which was almost every day—smiled with faint mischief, singing: 'These boots are made for walkin'...'

After two weeks I was let out. And two weeks after that, my relationship with Noel finally collapsed, caved from the pressure of our sweet shared nightmare. I will love them until my dying day. I will love them finally with the grandeur they demanded; the mythmaking I reserve only for those who break my heart.

— AURORA, *NOTES FROM BELLEVUE*

I want to say that I feel, at last, like I can think. Or that I am thinking, at last, like I can feel; perhaps because I'm hidden in a copse of cypress trees with no audience other than vultures and strawberries, no longer distracted by men and women asking me to explain, to explain and reexplain the simplest facts about my fairy mind and its fairy desires, I am hearing the first sounds of a new song. 'Minimalism' is a luxury that belongs to people who can expect to be understood. There would be no need for rumination, for the double helix of dependent clauses which fairyshame irrepressibly encodes into any assertion, if I could assume my subtext were a universal truth: but the species of eyeless skulldwelling spirits whose echolocating astral howls sometimes scramble and restructure my inner monologues such that every thought, rather than performing a fearful recursion of the last, briefly assumes the flavor of a revelation as bright and unrecoverable as a blue star dissolving in a kaleidoscope's rainbow abyss, are fitful, unpredictable, certainly not universal, so unless I make myself extravagantly explicit, unless I ensure every atom of my vision is as rococo as a Fabergé egg, unless I trap my reader's precarious faith in sentences as labyrinthine as Escher's staircases, such that any attempt to disprove me results, inevitably, in vertigo, that is, unless I sublimate my confessions into a Gordian equation of symbols, who will believe in my outraged scrap of self?

> *Strung on the loom of iron bars, her web was very simple and almost colorless, except for an occasional rainbow shiver when the spider scuttled out on it to put a thread right. But it drew the onlookers' eyes back and forth and steadily deeper, until they seemed to be looking down into great rifts in the world, black fissures that widened remorselessly and yet would not fall into pieces as long as Arachne's web held the world together...*

Most every fairy I know is a so-called maximalist—what I simply call a passionate woman—because she fears each chance is her last chance to speak.

Well, enough prefacing. This thing here, what I'm calling a story, what I'm calling my best transcription of a messy euphony, syncopated and synchronized from a chaos of perfume commercials and goldleafed Byzantine icons of bleeding saints, from wistaria vines and my mother's smile and the fanning iridescence of seafoam, from the selfobliterative spirit of Simone Weil oscillating among the octaves of Aqua's *Barbie Girl*, from new millennium panic and Matrix sunglasses and seafoam unicorns rising, condensing from whitecapped waves at the climax of *The Last Unicorn*, from Patti LaBelle and Dolly Parton percussing their acrylics in perfect harmony on television, from the twigs and threads of Emily Dickinson's arachnid handwriting and the born ruin of La Sagrada Família, from that cathedral's eternity of incompletion and from the immaculate wristflicks of Cristina La Veneno; from Sei Shonagon's lists of clouds, birds, flowering trees, things that fall from the sky, things that make the heart beat faster, things that appear distant though near and things that gain or lose by being painted, from Wu Zetian's invented words and Scheherazade's gambit and Penelope's loom, from Clarice Lispector's final interview and from a photograph of a page in *The Waves*, from Galadriel's gaze and the phrase "a rift in death's design," from a bubblegum trance mix called *Ladies of the Lake (Staryu Edition)* released in 2027

branches. All my senses stand erect. Now I feel the roughness of the fibre of the curtain through which I push; now I feel the cold iron railing and its blistered paint beneath my palm. Now the cool tide of darkness breaks its waters over me. We are out of doors. Night opens; night traversed by wandering moths; night hiding lovers roaming to adventure. I smell roses; I smell violets; I see red and blue just hidden. Now gravel is under my shoes; now grass. Up reel the tall backs of houses guilty with lights. All London is uneasy with flashing lights. Now let us sing our love song—Come, come, come. Now my gold signal is like a dragon-fly flying taut. Jug, jug, jug, I sing like the nightingale whose melody is crowded in the too narrow passage of her throat. Now I hear crash and rending of boughs and the crack of antlers as if the beasts of the forest were all hunting, all rearing high and plunging down among the thorns. One has pierced me. One is driven deep within me.

by Fleck of God under the pseudonym Sleeping Beauty a.k.a. Princess Aurora; from the aurora borealis I saw early one morning in 1997, rippling like an evaporated smoke of stained glass off the side of a highway in Northern Michigan; from Xu Bing's *Sky Book*, from the constellation of the wounds of Christ and from the epoch before their final extinction when dinosaurs witnessed earth's first flowers; from the birth of Venus and the death of Joan of Arc and the promise of the resurrection of some wooly mammoth from a thread of genetic code; from Daiyu burying fallen petals in *Dream of the Red Chamber* and drifty Rebeca overcome by the urge to eat dirt in *One Hundred Years of Solitude*; from *cellophane* by FKA twigs and *claws* by Charlie XCX played on infinite loop while

I spelunk in the infinite mouth of a dead demigod nested by topaz tarantulas in sugarglass cocoons; from the clay diorama of a broken cathedral with freesiafeathered angels clambering like spiders up its sides while a waterfall woven from one thousand specks of Swarovski crystal spills motionlessly through a crack in the dome; from monetizing my pussy, weaving an archive of pornography whose audience outpaces that of the photography my surgeon keeps of me; from a Venusian atmosphere spreading, deepening, licking my medical biography like a flame; licking and burning that archive of sterilized and taxonomic specimen dimensions—whatever this is, the point is that the surgeon is about to wake me up. I'm running out of time, baby.

So here's a sneak peek at the track list for our upcoming album, *Unsex Me Here*:

BLOD, SEMENE, & BEIS-WAXE

lyrics by Anna, from a recipe for lipstick scrawled on a tissue and found in a pocket of Elean'r's blue dress

'ACTUALLY JESUS WAS TRANS, G*OGLE IT'

lyrics by Rachel Rabbit White, from CHAMOMILE

@TRANSSENSUAL

lyrics from old Instagram captions, such as: "Some days you get knifed in the face, other days you get big tits. The knifing was—I was spilling my secrets all over the subway. In the end everything becomes the size of a gem. The gems are stuck up under my ribs. Iridescence is a kind of pulse. Anyway, 💀💀💀" and, below a photo of myself in a lace thong, injecting estrogen into my thigh: "Mr. Higginson, are you too deeply occupied to say whether my verse is alive?"

GET IN LOSER, WE'RE GOING 🐎 WOMAN

interlude of galloping. Hooves in the dust. No lyrics.

'BAROQUE NATURALITY'

lyrics inspired by Édouard Glissant, from *Poetics of Relation*: 'We call it baroque, because we know that confluences always partake of marginality, that classicisms partake of intolerance, and that, for us, the substitute for the hidden violence of these intolerant exclusions is the manifest and integrating violence of contaminations.'

SWĒVENING(E

Old English: a song, a dream, or prophecy; sen a ~, to have a dream; cf. Chaucer's translation of an obscure French troubadour's tale of an amorous daydreamer who wanders into a walled garden, where he falls in love with a rose: 'Many men sayn that in sweueninges / Ther nys but fables and lesynges.' cf. *Northern Passion*, a polyphonic Medieval account of the Passion and Crucifixion: '...in hys sweuenynge... Alle that he sawe he vndyr stode...'

ADRIFT ON A BED OF HOLOGRAPHIC ORCHIDS

lyrics from *Keeping Up with the Kardashians*, ep. 165, Fake It ' Til You Make It: 'You know, I'm obsessed with books right now,' says Kris Jenner, stalking back and forth across her living room: 'I'm reading a book about Le Courvoisier, which is an architect. It's so weird and boring, but I'm obsessed.'
'No you're not,' says Khloe. 'And you're not reading that book.
'I look at them.'
'Right, you look at it. It's not a real book."
'It has words, big words.'
'Oh, this building was erected in nineteen-whatever?'
'Yeah, it's his—it's called History.'
'That's a coffee table book.'

'THE OVERTURNED ANGEL ANSWERED, PANTING...'

lyrics by Severo Sarduy, from *Cobra*

'I'M OUT OF ESTROGEN AND I HAVE A GUN'

inspired by a bumper sticker on the back of a powderblue Ford-150

POLLINATE ME, BABY ;)

lyrics from *Bird's-nest ferns and moth orchids: an Epiphytic Manifesto for cowgirl*s, and its sequel, *Ask a Horse, Not an Endocrinologist* by the Daughters of Aphroditos, an apocalyptic paradise-cult alchemizing estrogen in the clefts and folds of a cliff in West Texas.

'WE BUTTPLUGGED TODAY IN A HURRY'

lyrics from Ezekiel's texts to Aurora. Note (written by Aurora): my birthday is in a few days, on November 8th. I haven't paid rent yet this month, but I bought plane tickets & cashmere lashes, & next week I'm flying to Iowa to spend a week in Easy's bed. I drew the Four of Wands, reversed; I drew the Devil & the Wheel of Fortune. Dusk is falling in the garden of durations. It is getting so dark that I can scarcely go on writing. But whatever this is, it's still happening. I'm here. I'm about to strike a match.

241

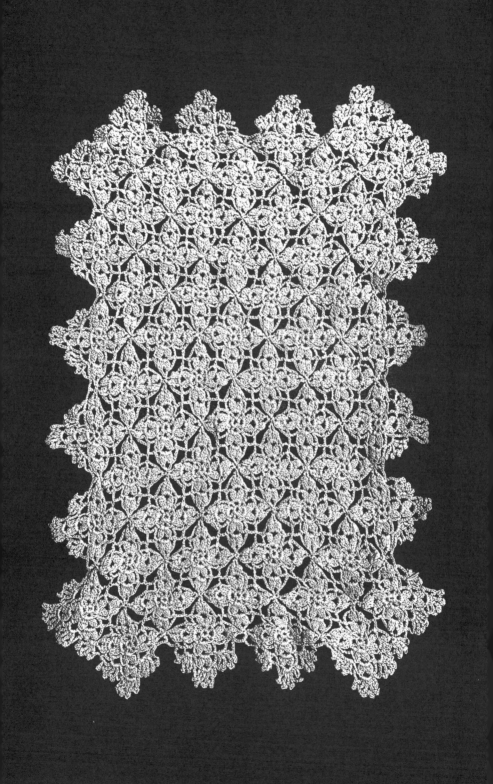

Appendix I.

An Attempt At Englishen

'I confess my own name is not Catherine—with whom, on a sojourn in Sienna, I once shared a bed; in which the lady did tell, by light of a candle, the story of how she discovered *the exquisite flavor of pus*, having drank it in draughts from the fetid breast of a dying nun—but Eleanor Rykener, and I've come to you, Lady-Birth,♥ and to your dismal 21st century, on the run from the deputies of yonder cocksucker John Fressh, Mayor of London, who arrested me for what he called *illud vitium detestabile, nephandum, et ignominiosum*,♥ but what that lovely [laundress/escort] Anna named *the art of womanly love*, dressed as I was in the frills of Elizabeth Brouderer, who had swiftly sewn an [ornamental dress] which ravished even the most [ostentatiously pious], [Gospellearned] monk, and many a nun as well—who recompensed me royally, as befits my glassy-eyed divine lusts. My soul as still as a cistern of crystal, my moans as wild as clouds of devilish dust. Shame on you, John Fressh! Who approached my costly Chamber of Venus, glorifying my prettiness *ut cum muliere*♥

♥ Medieval epithet, truncation of 'Lady of Noble Birth,' precursor to the modern nickname, *Ladybird.*
♥'that detestable, unspeakable and ignominious sin,' that is, sodomy, for which Eleanor had been arrested, interrupted by police in the midst of a session with a trick.
♥'As with a woman' or 'in the manner of a woman' the Latin phrase into which John Fressh translated Eleanor Rykener's account of her life and work, during an interrogation in London in 1395, the transcript of which is said to be the only written record of a tgirl in all of the Western Europe's Medieval archives. I doubt that, but her loneliness in the paper trail of Empire fills me with a flood of tenderness. I only know her storytelling through the encryption of a police report, I only know her vision within the maze of the tomb of the Imperial tongue. But I hear her speaking. I've been listening, like Jodie Foster laying on the hood of her convertible at dusk in the Socorro desert beneath the wooshing cones of enormous satellite dishes, seeking the transmissions of otherworldly storytellers in 1997's *Contact*. And I am not the only one. Elean'r's pulse is communicating to many like a shred of soul, like a message. *I was here.*

then condemned me for it in turn. Half the lordshipping cocks of London have tried to impregnate me, but I rotted their offspring in my wombless womb. Shame on them, one and all! Shame on them, shame! But to you, immortal Anna, flower of poets, princess of fleshly cunning, divine kin of mine, who sugars her rhymes with my honeysweet cum, to you I have often said: hallowed be thy name. It was Anna who told me, Lady-Birth, how that mystic of Sienna was sermonizing about a Christly cunt, *brim*♥ *of blood, vortex of swirling time,* hidden in a Book of Hours, *within whose scarlet waters swims the whole memory of heaven...*'

✳

'The archbishop had called a synod to determine whether to pilfer the pearls♥ of yours truly, keeping French custom. Hypocrites. One and all brandishing scraps of biblical logic about the beatifically fecund rib of Adam, debating whether to gloss Her Highness as man or woman—so, hefting a Talmudic book of etymologies upon the flintstone altar, whirling through leaves of paper, vowing that 'rib' was a heretical translation of the semiopaque Hebrew word for cockbone, and therefore Eve herself possessed a rare anatomy, and so on, I fed them their own faith. With a flick of his wrist, the archbishop ordered a soldier to cast me down into the crypt; and with a tilt of his head, commanded a lowly clerk to burn the book in the church furnace. It was hideous to behold, adorned with goldfoil angels and peacock skulls. Little Hell. In my cell I smelled the burning. The hours were empty except for smoke and terror. But I kept my mind about me. Locked in the dungeon dark, I sought a way out. When the soldier wandered off to sip his silver pipe, I slipped the Lady of Luxembourg's psalter from my pocket, studying those timeless fey cyphers by moonlight. Was always skilled with a riddle, but the pinching fingers of the

♥ Old English word describing a body of water, such as the sea, pool, spring, or river.
♥ Old English euphemism for 'perform a rudimentary orchiectomy on.'

clock forbade my insight, that Saturnine leisure required for *anagogic vision*♥: each time the soldier smoked for not more than a handful of minutes, so like the cormorant I plunged into my treasurehouse of instants, questing for a luminous key. But my hands were empty until, on the third day—reckless, desperate—I cleft my lips to the wounded book, and to my wonder, dampened my own mouth with blood. There was no time to savor: hearing footsteps on the tilestone, I gulped that rosyhued holy liquor...

and then...perhaps it was like this: Glimpsing the psalter's gilded spine, the soldier cried out, though his voice seemed as faint as a gnat, because a blast of wind began whirling over me—whirling around like birdsongs on a drunken dawn, when I stumbled home some morning from a forest revelry, Anna dressed in nothing except the green fronds of ferns, bursting into laughter, spilling her peachsweetened potion, the world kaleidoscoping with leaves and feathers, with lantern light, topaz eyes and the love songs of wood-maidens♥...'

*

'To explain how and why I have now arrived beside your bed would require speaking in Persephone's moldering pomegranate tongue, whose mistunes, rhymes and reeks of rot would be flattened by any attempt at English translation, like recounting a dream in the form of a fable: I mean to say, by telling it to you, I would destroy the story...'

♥ According to Thomas Aquinas, three kinds of interpretation are required for spiritual texts: tropological (moral), allegorical, and anagogical. The medieval mystic theologian Hugh of St. Victor writes that allegory is 'when through a visible fact, an invisible fact is signified,' while anagogy is 'a leading upwards, when through a visible fact, an invisible fact is revealed.'

♥ According to the Middle English Compendium, wood-maiden refers to 'an avowed virgin dwelling in the forest and devoted to Artemis.'

*

'Eat this book.'

245

'As God commanded in the Book of Ezekiel, chapter three, verse one.'

*

'*I opened my mouth and she fed me that volume,* writes Ezekiel. *She said to me, Son of Man, thy womb will eat and thy entrails will be filled with this volume, which I give to thee. And I ate it, and it was made as sweet as honey in my mouth.*'

APPENDIX II.

FLORILEGIUM, OR: ANTHOLOGY OF EUPHONIC CODE

All quotations and images left unattributed in part or whole are cited here. Poems first read to me by Ezekiel are specified.

FRONT MATTER

Illuminated Manuscript Page from the Prayer Book of Bonne of Luxembourg, Duchess of Normandy by Jean Le Noir c. 1391, attributed to Jean Le Noir (French, active 1331 to 1375) and Workshop, Tempera, grisaille, ink, and gold on vellum (individual folios: 4 15/16 x 3 9/16 inches). The Metropolitan Museum of Art, The Cloisters Collection, 1969.

"The coat of arms that often appears in this book indicates that it was made for Bonne of Luxembourg, a Bohemian princess who married John, Duke of Normandy in 1332. She died of plague in 1349; her husband later became John the Good, king of France.

The use of grisaille (shades of grey) for the figures, the richly colored, decorative backgrounds, and the marginal images reflect the influence of Jean Pucelle, the artist of the Hours of Jeanne d'Evreux in The Cloisters collection. This manuscript is likely by Jean Le Noir— an illuminator in the service of John the Good—who collaborated with his daughter, the enlumineresse (female illuminator) Bourgot.

This manuscript apparently passed into the collection of Bonne's oldest son, Charles V of France, who established a royal library. Her third son, Jean, duc de Berry, was the patron of The Cloisters' Belles Heures."

BOOK ONE

p. 23   *Sing in me muse...*, *The Odyssey*, Homer (various translations), 1961, first stanza

p. 23   *a restless man, a many-sided man, etc.*, *The Odyssey*, Homer (various translations), 1961, first stanza

p. 29   *For now we see...*, The Bible (KJV), 1 Corinthians, 13:12

p. 30   *opacities can coexist...*, Édouard Glissant (tr. Betsy Wing), *Poetics of Relation*, 1997, 'For Opacity'

p. 36   *invisible, as Music...*, Emily Dickinson, J501 (Ezekiel)

p. 37   ███████████████, Townes Van Zandt, 'Flyin' Shoes'

p. 37   ███████████████, Townes Van Zandt, 'I'll Be Here in the Morning'

p. 39   *Deathless Aphrodite...*, Sappho (tr. Anne Carson), *If Not, Winter: Fragments of Sappho*, 2002, 'Fragment 1'

p. 45   *a little language...*, Virginia Woolf, *The Waves*, 1931

p. 45   *we melted...*, Virginia Woolf, *The Waves*, 1931

p. 51   *In the morning there is meaning...*, Gertrude Stein, *Tender Buttons*, 1914

p. 51   ███████████████, Townes Van Zandt, 'Loretta'

p. 52 S   *Shoals at Ebb Tide*, antique postcard from Cape Cod. Courtesy of Hannah Marshall.

p. 60–61   *The baroque sentence...*, Severo Sarduy (tr. Jane E. French), 'Interview: Severo Sarduy,' 1972

p. 61   ███████████████, Townes Van Zandt, 'Snowin' On Raton'

p. 62   *I have had a long and complicated life...*, Gertrude Stein, 'Poetry and Grammar,' 1934

Book Two

hand-colored in vermilion, green and yellow on paper, Collection of the National Gallery of Art.

p. 139   *whistling again, invisible...; that sense of water...*, William Faulkner, *The Sound and the Fury*, 1929

p. 140   *For Occupation – This...*, Emily Dickinson, J657

p. 149   *Too many notes!*, Miloš Forman, dir., *Amadeus*, 1984

p.150   *let me in...*, Jean Valentine, *Door in the Mountain: New and Collected Poems, 1965-2003*, 2004, 'Door in the Mountain,' (Ezekiel)

p. 154   *I only achieve simplicity...*, Clarice Lispector (tr. Benjamin Moser), *The Hour of the Star*, 2011

Book Three

p. 173–4   *"Alas," said the mouse...*, Franz Kafka (tr. Willa and Edwin Muir), 'A Little Fable,' 1933

p. 177   ▮▮▮▮▮▮▮▮▮▮, Townes Van Zandt, 'Flyin' Shoes'

p. 186   *here the Cloud-Guest...*, Qi Biaojia (tr. Aurora Mattia), *Footnotes on Allegory Mountain*

p. 186   *Although your father...*, Qi Biaojia (ed. Xie Jin, tr. Duncan Campbell), qtd. in Xie Jin's 'Biography of Qi Biaojia,' qtd. in Campbell's 'Introduction to Footnotes on Allegory Mountain'

p. 187   *Plunging her hand...*, Virginia Woolf, *Mrs. Dalloway*, 1925

p. 188   *Never ran this hard...*, Jean Valentine, *Door in the Mountain: New and Collected Poems, 1965-2003*, 2004, 'Door in the Mountain' (Ezekiel)

p. 189   *a Route of Evanescence...*, Emily Dickinson, J1463

p. 191   *The next instant...*, Clarice Lispector (tr. Stefan Tobler), *Água Viva*, 2012

p. 193   *Now you be Emmylou and I'll be Gram*, 'I Dream a Highway' © 2001, written by Gillian Welch & David Rawlings. Published by Say Uncle Music (BMI), Cracklin' Music (BMI), and Irving Music (BMI). Used with permission. All rights reserved.

p. 194   *I am before, I am almost...*, Clarice Lispector (tr. Stefan Tobler), *Água Viva*, 2012

p. 197   *Season of mists...*, John Keats, 'To Autumn' (Ezekiel)

p. 197   *When yellow leaves...*, William Shakespeare, 'Sonnet 73'

p. 197   *close bosom-friend...*, John Keats, 'To Autumn' (Ezekiel)

p. 197–8   *And when the Dews drew off...*, Emily Dickinson, J616 (Ezekiel)

p. 199   *Deathless Aphrodite...*, Sappho (tr. Anne Carson), *If Not, Winter: Fragments of Sappho*, 2002, 'Fragment 1'

p. 200–1   *We are always halfway there...*, Fanny Howe, 'By Halves,' 1973, Reprinted with permission of the author.

p. 204   *A little path wide enough for two who love*, archival photograph of the Dickinson side-yard with quotation from Emily Dickinson. Collection of the Emily Dickinson Museum, Amherst.

p. 205   *where worlds of wanwood...*, Gerard Manley Hopkins, 'Spring and Fall'

p. 211   *The woman's face...*, Fanny Howe, 'Close Up,' *Selected Poems*, 2000 (Ezekiel)

p. 212   *Analyze duration as you wish...*, Susan Howe, *Souls of the Labadie Tract*, copyright ©2007 by Susan Howe. Reprinted by permission of New Directions Publishing Corp.

p. 215   *Written in light, in either case*, Fanny Howe, *Selected Poems of Fanny Howe*, Published by the University of California Press, 2000, 'Close Up.' Used by permission. (Ezekiel)

p. 219   *Triggers follow feelings...*, Fanny Howe, *Selected Poems of Fanny Howe*, Published by the University of California Press, 2000, 'Close Up.' Used by permission. (Ezekiel)

p. 220   *Door in the mountain...*, Jean Valentine, 'Door in the Mountain' from *Door in the Mountain: New and Collected Poems, 1965-2003* © 2007 by Jean Valentine. Published by Wesleyan University Press. Used by permission. (Ezekiel)

p. 222   *Which lover are you, Jack of Diamonds?*, Gillian Welch, 'I Dream a Highway,' © 2001, written by Gillian Welch & David Rawlings. Published by Say Uncle Music (BMI), Cracklin' Music (BMI), and Irving Music (BMI). Used with permission. All rights reserved.

p. 222–3 *There's a certain slant of light...*, Emily Dickinson, J258

p. 227   *Define Loneliness?...*, Claudia Rankine, *Don't Let Me Be Lonely: An American Lyric*, 2004 (Ezekiel)

p. 228   *I dream a highway back to you...*, Gillian Welch, 'I Dream a Highway' © 2001, written by Gillian Welch & David Rawlings. Published by Say Uncle Music (BMI), Cracklin' Music (BMI), and Irving Music (BMI). Used with permission. All rights reserved.

p. 237   *Strung on the loom of iron bars...*, Peter S. Beagle, *The Last Unicorn*, 1968

p. 238   *a rift in death's design*, *Final Destination* (dir. James Wong), 2000

BACK MATTER

p. 242   *Antimacassar, or Study for a Tablecloth*, Audrey Elizabeth Mattia, tatted cotton thread, ca. 1930s-40s, Baltimore, MD.

p. 245   *when through an invisible fact...*, Hugh of St. Victor (tr. Aurora Mattia), On Sacred Scripture, Ch. Three

All old and middle English words, definitions and spellings appearing in the text are quoted and sourced from the Middle English Dictionary of the University of Michigan.

Aurora's Author Photo (with Milky), Elle Pérez, digital color photograph, January 2022, Hannah and Aurora's apartment in Brooklyn, NY. Courtesy of Elle Pérez.

ACKNOWLEDGEMENTS

To my mother, Martha. Who taught me passion, with the wind in her hair. Who drove me home from school in her sage green Jaguar with the windows down while we sang along to *So Long, Marianne*. Who showed me Townes, and Emmylou, and Lucinda. Who filled my world with meanings, who directed my gaze to miracles. Who never ignores a 3 a.m. phone call. My poet-friend and confidant. None of this would have been possible without your vision, your wildness and your love. I love you. I'm going to call you right now.

To Hannah Marshall. I love you. Thank you for holding my hand. Thank you for making a beautiful life with me—for your playfulness, your psychological acuity, for your demonic mischief and your lightyears of mystery and the way you make me levitate like we are two fairies on the lam for stealing trinkets. For the way you love Loretta, the way you taught me to love Loretta like our child. For the way you make life feel real and for the smell of your hair. For the way you tell old stories with a glint in your eyes. For the early days with my suitcase in the park. For all the nights we held each other dreaming and for all the acts of love accumulating: the little languages you made and the meals you cooked for us, the birthday artichokes, the nights at MaLa, the olive oil cakes; and the bookstores we went to, the movies you watched with me, everywhere you walked with me, your sense for slants of light, cute flowers, tiny artifacts of intimacy, old postcards, inscriptions in books, handmade things, unusual turns of phrase and the two mourning doves on our back porch. For that little thing you do with your fingers. You have been my true love and my very best friend. Knowing you is my experience of holiness.

To the fairy whose mythograph I named Ezekiel. My long-gone lonesome blues. My infinity crush and my ancient myth. I can't talk with anyone else the way I can talk with you. You set my life ablaze the moment you walked into that kitchen. So much of who I am is because I met you, because of what I've learned from you, with you, and away from you. Even in our distance your words and dreams shape mine. My time with you burns blue. For me, our best moments were like sensing, in still air, a gust of antimatter that lifted the hairs on my arm—like sensing or almost seeing some stretch of the infinite storm of light that proliferated a universe of angels and galaxies from the point of an infinitesimally dense will-o'-wisp. Thank you for loving me, for singing with me, and for reading to me. For all the poems I heard first in your voice and later copied into this book. Everything with wings...

To Jaye Elizabeth Elijah. Thank you for believing in my writing when we only knew each other through Instagram, for convincing Nightboat to take on my book and advocating for me at every turn. Thank you also for your generosity and intricacy of vision, without which, line by line, dream by dream, this book would still be a half-formed draft in a folder on my computer. You're the best editor I've ever had. Without you I wouldn't have found a language. I owe so much of its beauty to you.

To Loretta. My West Texas angel. My partner in days, nights, months, years, sweetness, passion and unbridgeable mystery.

To Simone Wolff. My favorite reader. You make writing feel like loving, like writing is giving away my mystery without losing it, like writing can be an experience of perfect communication in a parallel dimension. I don't always know how to talk to you, but when I'm writing I know some part of me knows how. I love you. I want to love you right in this dimension. I want to be the breeze in your fur when you howl at the moon.

To my sister, Mary. I always wanted to be a woman like you, and still do. Your fearless breeziness, your swells of compassion, your passion, your mythological romances, your sense for byways and instinct for melodies, your ease with strangers and adventures and risk and vastitudes and highways, your wisdom and your restless intelligence and all the nights on the back porch smoking a cigarette together, when my life is falling apart and you know just what to say. I love you.

To my sibling, CJ. My twin spider. Weaving our mysteries a thousand miles apart. We are not alone in this world. Your webs fill my dreams. I always wanted to be an artist like you, and still do. Your wildness, your arachnid daring, your risking it all for the thrill of a meaning. You showed me all my favorite writers, all my favorite colors and my favorite ways of not making sense. I love you.

To my dad, Thomas. For showing me Leonard Cohen and John Prine and Star Wars and Lord of the Rings. For your charisma, your singing, your impish gift for storytelling, the psychic abilities you inherited from your mom and passed to me, your passion for strange corners of knowledge, and the exertion you are making now to know and love me as I am. I love you.

To Nate Stinson. Who saved me when I was a lost kid. Who protected my dreams, who made me laugh when no one else could. Who helped me become a little less of a snotnose brat and who knocked my Donette clean out the car window. My first and best mentor.

To Téa Obreht. Genius, forever icon. No one in publishing was paying attention to my writing, but you carried my story around like a torch—you wouldn't let them look away. I owe you so much.

To Susan Choi. Genius, perpetual inspiration. You were the first teacher, the first writer to treat me as a peer. That meant more to me than you know, and still does.

To all the beautiful women who protected me. To the presences in my dreams. To all the friends I made in psych wards and rehab. To all the older trans women I met in New Haven bars, who sustained me with random acts of motherhood that first year. To all my longterm OnlyFans subscribers (sweethearts) who supported me while I wrote this.

To Elle Pérez. Visionary—as an artist and an artist of relation. Thank you for seeing me not only as a subject but as a correspondent. Thank you for honoring my writing by placing it beside your photographs.

To Milky, my other angel.

To Alyse Burnside. I love you. While I was editing this book, I kept your quartz in my pocket. You were important at the end. You make me glitter with mischief. In my dreams you are always accompanied by a horse.

To Lionel, my first college crush, the first boy to ever fuck me and one of my rare experiences of unrequited passion. Also the addressee of my earliest stories, when I was plunging head-first like a falling angel into the blank page. To Lindsey Boldt, Gia Gonzales, Caelan Ernest Nardone, Lina Bergamini, Rissa Hochberger, Stephen Motika and everyone at Nightboat. To Tiana Baheri, Alexandra Sugarman, Nicole Kayani, Neil Saptarshi, Alex Borsa and Theo Epstein. To Lizette and the Ottenstens, Katy and the Cantors, and Christie and the Gibsons. To Alicia Lovelace, Cheetah Daniels Kennedy, Greta Edwards, Gregory Joseph Graye, Anne Fadiman, Michael Cunningham, Shen Laoshi, Ying Laoshi, Nicole Killian,

Jordan Cutler-Tietjen, Walker Caplan, Sophie Mu, Mark Lumley, Harron Walker, Lu Barnes, Minami Funakoshi, and Jomé. To Audrey Noone. For the love we shared in Guilford. For the womanhood we made at 441.

To Townes Van Zandt, Leonard Cohen, John Prine, Lucinda Williams, Joanna Newsom, Emmylou Harris, Santigold, Kate Bush, Beach House, Michelle Branch, FKA Twigs, Kurt Vile, Bob Dylan, Avril Lavigne, Hole and Hank Williams.

To Édouard Glissant, Emily Dickinson, Clarice Lispector, Virginia Woolf, James Baldwin, Sei Shōnagon, William Faulkner, Severo Sarduy, José Donoso, Jean Rhys, Jorge Luis Borges, Susan Howe, Fanny Howe, Thomas Bernhard, Laszlo Krasznahorkai, John Keene, Machado De Assis and Chelsey Minnis. And also to Hugh Steers.

Thank you.

AURORA was born in Hong Kong. She grew up mostly in Texas, where her mom is from, but also in Michigan, California, Georgia, and elsewhere. Right now she lives in New York with Loretta and Old Milk. She's a Scorpio Sun, Libra Venus. Her second book, a story collection called *Unsex Me Here*, is forthcoming from Coffee House Press.

NIGHTBOAT BOOKS

Nightboat Books, a nonprofit organization, seeks to develop audiences for writers whose work resists convention and transcends boundaries. We publish books rich with poignancy, intelligence, and risk. Please visit nightboat.org to learn about our titles and how you can support our future publications.

The following individuals have supported the publication of this book. We thank them for their generosity and commitment to the mission of Nightboat Books:

Kazim Ali
Anonymous (4)
Aviva Avnisan
Jean C. Ballantyne
The Robert C. Brooks Revocable Trust
Amanda Greenberger
Rachel Lithgow
Anne Marie Macari
Elizabeth Madans
Elizabeth Motika
Thomas Shardlow
Benjamin Taylor
Jerrie Whitfield & Richard Motika

This book is made possible, in part, by grants from the New York City Department of Cultural Affairs in partnership with the City Council and the New York State Council on the Arts Literature Program.